Myth in the Mountain

Mountain

Claire Buss

Other works by Claire Buss:

The Roshaven Books
The Rose Thief
The Silk Thief
The Bone Thief
Myth in the Mountain

The Interspecies Poker Tournament – The Roshaven Case Files No. 27
Ye Olde Magick Shoppe

The Gaia Collection
The Gaia Effect
The Gaia Project
The Gaia Solution
The Gaia Collection (Books 1-3)

Poetry
Little Book of Verse, Book 1 in the Little Book Series
Little Book of Spring, Book 2 in the Little Book Series
Little Book of Summer, Book 3 in the Little Book Series
Spooky Little Book, Book 4 in the Little Book Series
Little Book of Love, Book 5 in the Little Book Series
Little Book of Autumn, Book 6 in the Little Book Series
Little Book of Winter, Book 7 in the Little Book Series
Little Book of Christmas, Book 8 in the Little Book Series

Short Story Collections
Tales from Suburbia
Tales from the Seaside
The Blue Serpent & other tales
Flashing Here & There

Anthologies

Underground Scratchings, *Tales from the Underground* anthology

Patient Data, *The Quantum Soul* anthology

A Badger Christmas Carol, The Sparkly Badgers' Christmas Anthology

Haunted, The Sparkly Badgers' Halloween Anthology

The Last Pirate, *Tales from the Pirate's Cove* anthology

Chapter 1

Winter had barely begun. It shouldn't even be snowing and yet determined snow fell in swirling patterns, buffeting this way and that thanks to a cheeky gust that was amusing itself. Jenni hunched down further in her blue coat. It wasn't as warm as the red one. It wasn't as long either. Nor did it smell right. She to admit it, but she had rushed acquiring this coat, swayed by its cobalt tones, and not thinking clearly upon the ramifications of new outerwear. Jenni came with coat. They were a package and this non-red one just wasn't holding up to its end of the deal. Especially with this unexpectedly harsh weather. If it carried on like this, the entire city of Roshaven would grind to a snowy halt.

A particularly snowflake-packed eddy swooshed into Jenni, making her splutter at eating unwanted weather. She tried to magic the flakes away from her vicinity, but her power sputtered before refusing to do what she wanted. Unfortunately, that was standard practice these days, so she went for a stern talking to instead.

'Ere, cut that out. I'll 'ave words wiv yor mum.' Jenni wasn't entirely sure that the wind elemental was female, but she knew them, in passing, and if this mischievous little gust didn't stop blowing around... well, words would be said. Not that you could talk to the elementals if they didn't want to listen to you. But at least Jenni could still shout in the wind.

The snowflakes stilled as the gust blustered off somewhere else, and gravity took over their slow

1

descent. The streets of Roshaven fell into a hush and the tired lamps did their best to glow. It was neither cheery nor warm.

The Black Narrows loomed, and Jenni's shoulders slumped even further. She knew if she patrolled down the Narrows, she'd find someone doing something they weren't supposed to, and for the first time ever, she couldn't be bothered to check it out. Patrolling the Black Narrows was meant to be an easy job. A quick collar for the office and a tick on the chart Joe had put up, recording everyone's arrests. There was a prize hamper for the winner come Yule Eve.

Jenni tried to muster up some enthusiasm. She was two points behind Sparks. The crafty little firebug had been using his extensive network of friends and relations to ferret out crimes and misdemeanours. They would both be behind Willow if she activated her plant network, but the tree nymph was taking the high road and wanted to prove her Catcher skills to their boss without resorting to her wiles.

Thinking about their boss, Ned Spinks, drove Jenni further into her own personal gloom. Their changing relationship was something else she had no control over, along with all this weather and her unreliable magic. Things between them had shifted. To be fair, they'd been evolving slowly but surely for a while. And yet, to Jenni, it had seemed as if they hadn't quite changed–not yet, and that they were always teetering on the verge of change, so it felt like she still had time to adjust. But then, when she hadn't been looking, suddenly everything was different.

Okay, so Ned had found out his dad wasn't who he thought–which was a good thing as his previous dad was the ex-Chief of T.A.R.T.S and no one wanted to be officially associated with the official association of Thieves, Arsonists, Raconteurs, Tarts, and Solicitors. Then he'd married Rose and whilst Jenni had nothing against her empress, she missed living with her boss. True, he'd kept his little narrow house on Wide Street so he could escape the imperial palace from time to time and true again, Jenni was still living there, but it wasn't the same. After Jenni had met her own father, been hoodwinked by him, and lured into illegal magic skimming, she had become temporary persona non grata with her mother and now her father was one of the most wanted criminals in Efrana. The whole thing gave her an all-over icky feeling.

Jenni kicked some loose pebbles into the opening of the Black Narrows and heard several things scuttling.

'Yeah, you'd better 'ide,' she muttered before wheeling away from the crime encrusted alleyway and heading instead for the tiny pub on Castle Avenue. None of the other Catchers went there because the ceilings were too low. It was a fae pub, the only one in Roshaven, and whilst non-fae were of course welcome, they would find it rather difficult to get inside the smaller than average door and stand up in the smaller than average interior.

Jenni pushed open the door to The Pegasus and breathed in the heady fumes of spiced scumble. There were a few cries of greeting - she was after all the daughter of Momma K, queen of the fae, no matter if Jenni was on speaking terms with her at the moment or not - but on the whole patrons of The Pegasus left her alone. Here she could just be Jenni.

'Momma K is looking for you, so she is.'

'Snails!' Jenni flopped down onto a barstool and ignored the comment from the leprechaun behind the bar. Instead, she raised a finger and watched as the barman poured her a cup of spiced scumble.

'I'd not be ignoring her if I were you. Are you not going to spell a reply?'

Jenni slurped her drink and scowled over the cup's rim. She didn't know if her magic would behave enough to do that.

'Who says I'm ignoring 'er? Mebbe I'm just ignoring you.' She scanned the bar top. 'Where's the nuts?'

'Where's the nuts she says. For sure, that's the biggest of your problems, so it is.' The bartender leaned closer to Jenni. 'The message has gone out high and low. Tis luck if I'm the first to tell you, but I won't be the one getting the rap for you not replying.' He picked up a small golden handbell from a shelf behind the bar and rang it. Delicate chimes rang out.

'Fanks for that.' Jenni's mood soured further. Momma K would now know that Jenni had been told she was looking for her and the longer she left it, the more annoyed Momma K would be. She downed the scumble and reached into her pocket for a coin to pay for her drink.

'No, no, this one's on the house,' grinned the leprechaun, picking up a cloth and wiping sparkly clean glasses that hadn't been used. 'What are you going to do about the Jacks, then?'

'Wot?'

'The Jack Frosts. They're here in the city, so they are. Causing mischief and getting up to all sorts of trickery.'

Jenni snorted. Bit rich for a leprechaun to be complaining about a fellow fae getting up to mischief. The barkeep raised an eyebrow at her, so she muttered her thanks and hopped down from the bar stool. She really didn't feel like heading back out into the falling snowflakes and she really didn't want to go talk with her mum, but it looked like she didn't have much of a choice. At least she could pass on the enquiry and ask Momma K what she was doing about the Jacks.

As she came out of The Pegasus, she was surprised to see Ned trying to come in. He was hunched over and walking sideways in an attempt to fit himself through the doorway. On seeing her, he unfolded and backed out.

'Ah, Jenni, good. I was hoping I'd find you here. Momma K is…'

'Yeah, yeah, I know. She's looking for me. S'awright. I'm on me way.'

'No, that's not what I was going to say. Well, it is, but she's not just looking for you. She wants both of us,' said Ned.

At first Jenni felt better. That meant she probably wasn't in trouble for anything. Then she felt worried. If Momma K was calling them both, it most likely meant Roshaven was in danger.

'You 'eard anyfink about Jacks?'

'Jack? I don't think so. Is it a person of interest we need to be aware of?'

'No, not Jack, Jacks. They're Jack Frosts. Spiky little fae wot cause mischief when it gets proper cold. Don't usually see 'em in the big city but apparently they is 'ere getting up to stuffs. I dunno. It's just wot the leprechaun said.'

'Okay, well, we can add it to the Eyes Open board when we get to the office. Tell the others. What sort of thing are we talking about?'

Jenni huffed. She wasn't sure. She'd never seen a Jack before. They were country fae, and she was firmly a city gal.

'C'mon then, we'd better crack on. We can always ask 'er wot to look out for.' Jenni led the way through the thick, silent flakes of snow that continued to fall down relentlessly onto the cobbled streets and tiled roofs of the city.

It wasn't far to the fae grove. It was more or less in the centre of Roshaven, but Jenni was surprised to see how much snow was obstructing the entrance. She didn't think *that* many flakes had fallen since it had started snowing. It was almost as if they had been specifically attracted to this spot. They had to scoop out several handfuls before Jenni could make the connection and whisk herself and Ned through to the fae realm. It didn't help that she had to really concentrate in order to make the connection. Usually it was dead straight forward, second nature. It was a bit of a surprise that she'd had to focus as much as she had.

She was even more surprised when they arrived. The entire realm was encased in deep winter. There was a thick blanket of snow on the ground, on all the plants and trees, and falling heavily from the sky in far greater quantities than it was in Roshaven proper. Large icicles hung prettily from bare branches and jangled musically as cold puffs of wind danced around. Frost sparkled on every surface and both Ned's breath and her own puffed out in front of their faces like a dragon. Tiny blue dots zoomed about, tinkling.

'Thems is Jacks,' said Jenni, pointing the dots out to Ned. 'Ere, is Slinky awright wiv all this?' Momentarily distracted from the winter wonderland, she was concerned about the golden sea dragon that had recently adopted the Thief-Catchers.

'He's fine. Still sleeping in the bathtub. Joe keeps

topping it up with warm water, but Willow thinks he might need to head into hibernation if this winter keeps up. She thinks we ought to take him back to the ocean, where the warmer currents are.'

Jenni shrugged. She would be sad to see the little tyke go. He was fun to have around–scaring patrons of The Noose, great company fishing on the River Whine and a solidness upon her feet when she was stuck in the office doing paperwork. But Willow was probably right, it wasn't fair keeping Slinky away from his natural habitat. He was a sea dragon, after all.

'What do you think Momma K wants?' asked Ned.

Jenni shrugged again.

'You okay? You're very quiet.'

Jenni sighed heavily. She really didn't want to talk about how many things had changed at that particular moment. It would be a difficult conversation at the best of times, and right now wasn't the best time. 'Let's get this over wiv, yeah?'

As they stepped through into Momma K's inner sanctum, it was like entering a sauna. Beads of sweat soon sprang out on Jenni's forehead and she was glad she hadn't given in and wrapped up for the cold. Ned, on the other hand, was scrambling to get out of his hat, scarf, gloves and coat. It appeared as though he had two jumpers on underneath the coat as well. He stood still for a moment, one jumper half peeled off as he looked sceptically at the pile of winter clothes on the floor.

'S'alright, you can leave it 'ere. No one will touch it. S'all too big anyways.'

Jenni solved Ned's conundrum on how many layers to remove and he dumped both jumpers on the pile. He still had a fine-looking purple waistcoat on and a shirt that didn't seem to have any holes in it for once.

'New freads?'

'Eh?' Ned looked down. 'Oh, yeah. A present from Rose. She thought I ought to appear a little more professional, but they're just not as warm as my usual ones.'

It was hard to tell if the pink flush on the backs of his ears was caused by the heat or his embarrassment.

'Looks awright.'

And whilst it did look alright, it was yet another difference. Every aspect of Jenni's life seemed to have lots of differences these days.

'Why is it so hot here?' asked Ned, fanning his face with his hand.

'I spect Momma K's gotta bee in 'er bonnet bout the cold snap we're 'aving. You know wot she's like. Probably funnelling power to make it 'otter in 'ere by making it colder out there or summink.'

They were both glowing warmly by the time they arrived at Momma K's toadstool. The Fae Queen was being fanned and had an iced beverage in hand. She looked as cool as a cucumber. Ned stood as close to one of the large palm-leaf fans as he dared.

'Well, we're 'ere. Wot do you want?' Jenni was too hot to be polite.

'Daughta. Catcha. Is good ya come. Dis winter, it no right. Sometink is bringing it down de mountain.' She cocked her head to one side and regarded Jenni. 'Stop fighting it and de magic will flow.'

Jenni sniffed in response.

'We don't live near a mountain,' she said, deciding to ignore the magic advice. 'And ain't it the beginning of winter? S'meant to be cold, innit?'

'Me point exactly.' Momma K scowled at her daughter's avoidance. 'We doh and it is. It should no be dis cold! And you should no be trying so hard.'

Jenni tutted softly under her breath.

'Winter is the time for scarves and chilly weather.' Ned quailed a little under Momma K's withering stare. 'Admittedly, it is colder than we'd expect for this time of year, but it's not that unusual. Right?'

Momma K snapped her fingers and the tropical ambience they'd all been wilting under vanished. The fae realm grew dark, and great clouds of breath appeared before them all as they breathed out into the cold. Ned started shivering as snowflakes began rapidly falling. Giant icicles grew before their eyes and convoluted frost patterns materialised on the plants. Tinkly laughter echoed as the tiny blue Jacks swarmed.

'W w w what's going on?' Ned asked, his teeth chattering as he rubbed his arms frantically to try to keep warm, stamping his feet to stop them from turning into blocks of ice.

'Dis is wat me realm be like if me no warm it up. It no natural. Someone else's magic daring to change tings. Me no want it. You de catchas. Go catch dis winter bringa. Sort it out.' She sniffed and clapped her hands imperiously, bringing back the stifling heat. The Jacks squeaked and fled.

'Where did they go?' Ned cast about, trying to see the teeny creatures.

'De Jacks? Nasty little tricksters. Coming out foh de cold and de ice. Me doh approve but me doh have de energy ta control dem. Not when de weather is making dem so strong.' Momma K shuddered and pulled her wings in tightly. 'Dis frost... it no good foh wings. If dey freeze den...' Another shudder rippled through the queen, echoed by the rest of the fae huddled around.

'So the Jacks are here to stay, then?' Ned waited for

Momma K to confirm with a nod. 'And what sort of thing can we look forward to from them?'

Momma K sucked her teeth and flicked her fingers.

'Dey no big big trouble maker. Dey jus meddlesome. Freeze everyting, make pretty pattern dat will mesmerise. Cause slips and falls. Imagine if ice had meany taughts. Dat a Jack.'

While her mum was speaking, Jenni noticed Ned closing his eyes in distress, his human body not used to dealing with such massive changes in the environment so quickly. She was, of course, aware of the abrupt change, but her fae physiology was more robust than Neds and to her it was a fleeting discomfort.

'You awright, Boss? Mebbe sit down for a minute, yeah?'

Ned slumped to a handy log and took some deep breaths. He looked a little woozy around the edges.

'You didn't 'ave to do that, did you?' Jenni scowled up at her mum. 'Wot do you need us for? Can't you just go out there and find whoeva it is?'

Momma K inspected her fingernails.

'It too cold. Me wings, dey fragile. Me need ta stay and protect.' She glared at her daughter. 'You no got wings. You a catcha–go catch.' And she daintily unfurled her delicate appendages, gliding up off her toadstool. 'Be quick, it costing me ta keep dis heat up,' she said before heading away from Ned and Jenni, the ultimate dismissal.

Jenni sucked her teeth at her mother's retreating back before turning to check on Ned.

'Ow you feeling now, Boss?'

'Yeah. Um, I'm alright.' He stood up on relatively unshaky legs. 'Does Momma K really think someone is causing the cold snap? She knows winter is an annual

10

constant, right? And what was all that about your magic?'

'Nuffink to worry about,' Jenni said, trying not to care. Just because her magic was a bit stop start at the moment didn't mean it was anything for anyone else to be concerned about. 'Bout the winter stuff... I guess she finks there's summink weird going on. Bright side, at least we know wot the Jacks look like now.'

Jenni stomped to the entrance of the fae realm and waited while Ned put back on all his layers. 'All set?' she asked when he was finally redressed. Ned nodded, and she returned them to the streets of Roshaven, a swirl of tiny blue dots in their wake, giggling.

Chapter 2

Back at the narrow house on Wide Street, Ned filled the kettle up with water and set it on the hob to boil. He glanced at the dirty dishes in the sink and fished two relatively clean cups from the cupboard.

'Have you got milk, Jenni?'

'Yeah, fink so. Giv it a whiff, just to be sure.'

Ned cautiously checked the milk. It was still usable, but it definitely wasn't fresh. He rattled the biscuit tin. Empty. He slid the bread bin open. Empty. The milk had been on the windowsill and there wasn't much evidence of food anywhere else. Except for some empty Gariboldi pizza boxes.

'Are you looking after yourself?' he asked, trying not to sound too concerned. He didn't want Jenni to get defensive.

'Wot's it to you?' Jenni stomped out of the kitchen to go stoke the fire.

So much for that plan.

The kettle screamed in readiness and Ned's clumsy attempts at a sprite welfare check were put on hold as he made the tea. He took both cups through to the sitting room and let them brew on the table, easing himself into one of the two battered yet comfy armchairs.

'You've got to look after yourself, Jenni. Eating well, getting plenty of rest. All that stuff.' He glanced around at the room and noted the thick dust in places. 'Perhaps a housemate would help?'

'No fanks. It were bad enuff living 'ere wiv you wivout figuring out 'ow to live 'ere wiv someone else.'

That stung a little.

'What's that supposed to mean?'

'Dunno.'

Ned suppressed a sigh and fished out the tea bags, flinging them into the fireplace. That at least was in use, the fire burning merrily and easing some warmth into the room. Something was eating at Jenni, but he knew it was her way to be prickly at first before finally relenting and telling him what was wrong. They'd been friends long enough to understand each other's quirks.

'I'm just worried about you, that's all. I don't live here anymore, but I don't want you to be lonely.' He slurped some tea. 'The offer is still open, to come and live at the Palace. We'd love to have you.'

'Yeah. I don't fink it's really me, Boss. I'm awright, 'onest.' Jenni slurped her tea. 'I, er... it's... you know. Gets a bit quiet and that. I'll have a fink about it. Mebbe getting an 'ousemate ain't such a bad idea.'

She wasn't looking at him, but Ned felt a little relief. He didn't like the thought of Jenni living by herself, especially after everything that had happened with the Sea Witch.

'Great. Happy to help. If you like.'

'Cool. If you like.'

There was a moment of silence as the fire in the hearth did its best to spread more heat around the room whilst the driving winter outside countered by pouring coldness in through all the nooks and crannies.

'Is Momma K serious about this being some kind of magical winter?' asked Ned.

'I guess. It's brass monkeys out there, Boss. S'not zactly normal.'

'No, it's never usually this cold this early on. Any suspects?'

'We could ask the elementals, I suppose. See wot they reckon. If Momma K's asking us, we can rule out our fae. Wot about Kendra and that? 'Ave the Druids said anyfink?'

'Not that I've heard. Other than cancelling all rituals until the weather improves. Chaps were mentioned. That announcement was sent out yesterday.'

They both cogitated on the problems of performing sky-clad rituals in temperatures below freezing while enjoying their rapidly cooling beverages.

'Probably worth seeing if they've got any ideas, though,' said Ned, giving up on his lukewarm tea.

'And we can get Willow to ask 'er plant vine. Find out wots wot.'

'If any of it is still working. I think last night's frost might have had a bit of a devastating effect.' Ned rubbed his chin. 'We should check with all our resources, including Pearl. The mermaids might have some intel.'

Pearl was one of Ned's special recruits. As a mermaid, she couldn't partake in any land-based investigations, but she was very handy in the water.

'We got a bit of old-fashioned canvassing to do then, Boss. Go out and shake it all about, see wot falls out, innit?'

'Something like that, Jenni. Something like that.' Ned heaved himself out of his old armchair. 'We've got a team meeting tomorrow so we can divide and conquer. See what we can discover and get a plan together. If this winter is indeed nefarious, the Thief-Catchers will sort it out.' He pulled on his coat and associated accoutrements he had left by the front door. 'I'm heading back to the Palace. Let me know if anything urgent crops up, otherwise I'll see you tomorrow. And get something decent to eat, yeah?' He wanted to ask about her magic, but that would be an incredibly touchy subject and, after getting his head bitten off commenting on the state of the house, he decided to save that conversation for another day.

'Yep,' Jenni nodded, but didn't get up and walk him out. Ned could tell she was preoccupied with something. He lingered a moment in case she decided to share her thoughts, but when nothing was forthcoming, he left her sitting by the fire watching the flames dance.

Chapter 3

Ned felt like he was back on the street chasing undesirables in the Black Narrows, his boots clattering loudly in the palace corridors as he ran. He startled two maids gossiping by the indoor shrubbery and leapt over an unattended bucket in doing so. Internally, he grinned at the leap.

He was late, but he was late for a good reason. On his way to the palace from Jenni, a couple of public incidents occurred requiring Catcher assistance. Terry from the Allotment had got his wheelbarrow stuck in a snowdrift and it had taken rather more manhandling than Terry expected to get it unstuck. Several carrots were sacrificed in the kerfuffle, but with the help of a few spectators, carefully encouraged to do their civic duty by Ned, a few broken carrots on the floor wasn't so bad. Terry from the Allotment provided odd veg to the Druids who made soup with it and then made that soup available to all. You didn't even have to dance naked. It was one of Sister Eustacia's projects. She was a druid-adjacent nun, and the project was whole-heartedly supported by Rose.

Then, after the carrots, a couple of teenagers were messing about with icicles and daring each other to lick a rather large icicle that was hanging off a part of a statue of the old emperor that Ned had been informed was grossly over sculpted. Now, some might think the placement of the icicle was anatomically amusing, but the fact of the matter was, statues came under civic pride, which was related to the Catchers, so Ned had to intervene. He was too late for one of the poor lads. His tongue was well and truly stuck to the ice thanks to some Jacks' mischievousness, but Mrs Whitlock lived nearby and was doing some furious curtain swishing. She wouldn't come out of her house – the snow didn't lend itself to capes – but she was very good at providing a warm jug of water together with many and varied instructions on how to loosen the appendage from the, ah, appendage.

So it really wasn't his fault at all. As he reached the empress's study, he skidded to a halt, checking to make sure his boots hadn't left marks on the floor. It was all good. Smoothing down the front of his shirt, he patted his hair, confident that he didn't look like he'd been running.

'Nice slide,' commented Rose, Ned's wife and Empress of Roshaven, as he entered the study. Ned's lips twitched in a smile as he dropped her a cheeky wink and addressed the other person in the room, Griffin Bartholomew the Third, Duke of Kinglass and Proprietor of WGI Emporium, also recently revealed to be Ned's biological father.

'Griff – you have news? He's in Fidelia, like we thought?' Ned hadn't quite got his head around calling him 'Dad' just yet. Before the big parental revelation, they had been good friends, and then Griff faked his death, which had been a tremendous blow to Ned. There was definitely a lot to unpack over an ale at some point.

The 'he' Ned was asking about was Norm. With no recorded surname, he was Jenni's fugitive father, wanted for his involvement with the Sea Witch and confirmed magical skimming crimes. He'd escaped when Jenni and Ned had fought for control of fae magic against the might of the Sea Witch and her evil power.

Griff seemed to be looking for the right words as he smoothed his neat moustache with two fingers.

'I have heard... things. Worth checking into, eh? Finding out what's what. It'll be good to visit the city anyway and re-establish important connections. Make sure business is running smoothly.'

Ned was fairly confident Griff was referring to his semi-smuggling emporium that somehow wavered on the verges of legality whilst being simultaneously dodgy.

'You could come with me, eh? Check out the old city.' Griff raised eyebrows at Ned.

'No, no, I think not. There is too much work here. Official duties.' Ned cast a desperate glance at Rose, hoping she would back him up.

'I can't afford to lose my Chief Thief-Catcher at the moment, Griff. But please do travel to Fidelia with my blessing to see if you can discover Norm's whereabouts. We need to bring him to justice for what happened with the Sea Witch.'

Ned gave her a grateful nod. He was still not ready to face his parents in Fidelia after his brother's death. Half-brother. Or face his mother after the revelation that his father was, in fact, not. He didn't even know if they knew he knew about Griff. It all felt very messy and elsewhere, so for now, it could remain that way.

'Do you really think Norm is there?' he asked Griff, trying to shift the conversation focus.

'Honestly? I don't know, but if nothing else, we might get some leads on where he's gone, eh?' Griff turned to Rose. 'Are you sure you want to pursue him? It could get... expensive.'

Ned frowned. What was Griff implying?

'The law is the law, Griffin. If we allow one escaped prisoner to get away with their crimes, it gives the impression that Roshaven rule counts for nothing. And he didn't just break our laws, he broke magical ones. Momma K has offered to set a bounty on him, but I have convinced her to allow us to recapture him. For now. Her patience is...' Rose frowned, clearly seeking an appropriate word. 'Unreliable.'

Ned squirmed internally. As Chief Thief-Catcher, he longed to hunt down Norm personally. But as the Chief and now Imperial Consort, he was expected to delegate. Anyway, he could trust Griff. They'd been good friends for years. True, their relationship had wobbled when Griff faked his death, but they were finding new ground.

'Speaking of Momma K, she summoned me and Jenni to complain about the winter. Says it's too cold and unnatural and we *Catchas* need to catch whoever's making it cold.' Ned half-smiled, expecting Rose and Griff to be similarly amused by the absurdity of the request, and was surprised at their serious faces. 'Should we be worried?' He glanced out the window. Snow was still falling. 'Will you be all right to travel in this, Griff?'

'It does seem that our snow is somewhat of an anomaly.' Griff stroked his goatee. 'My sources in Fidelia say there's been a little frost at first light, but none of the white stuff. A mild start to the winter, by all accounts. But we may want to start salting the main roads at least, before they become impassable. And see about having some ice breakers in the harbour, because if the ships can't get into dock, then we can't trade.'

Trade was the lifeblood of Roshaven. It was one of the busier ports in Efrana thanks to its ideal location as a refuel stop for longer voyages, which in turn encouraged brisk trade in both staples and exotic items.

'Why would we have snow before them? It's usually the other way around, isn't it?' Ned looked to Rose for clarification, who nodded.

'As per Momma K's request, my dear husband, that is a job for you to uncover. I'm sure it's a freak weather pattern and snow will be falling elsewhere in Efrana, but I need you to investigate. Just in case.' Rose's brow creased in worry and despite her light tone, Ned could see she was seriously considering the possibility of a nefarious winter. 'I've tasked the street cleaners to shovel the show from the major thoroughfares to the best of their ability, but if it keeps snowing like this, I don't think they'll be able to keep up.'

'I will see if I can uncover anything about this winter on my travels as well,' said Griff.

'Have you told Jenni about the new lead?' Rose asked Ned. It was, after all, her father they were trying to apprehend.

'Er, no. I thought it might be better to wait until we had something to go on. After what happened last time…'

Everyone fell silent. Rumours of Norm hiding out in Narborough had set Jenni off on a wild escapade to catch him and bring him back. She'd been half feral about it and it had been all Ned could do to stop her from terrorising the inhabitants of Narborough with stink bombs and other foul tricks when she realised he wasn't there anymore and that the inhabitants had lied about him leaving, to help cover his tracks. Norm was a touchy subject. He was also as slippery as an eel and somehow able to get people to help him. There was a certain charm about him. Momma K had certainly fallen for something once upon a time.

'Right, probably a good idea not to tell her, then,' said Rose.

'Not to tell who wot?' Jenni entered the study and

was observing them all with suspicion.

'Jenni! What are you doing here?' Ned tried not to appear like he was hiding anything. He could feel the heat from the backs of his ears as they turned red, but luckily, they were facing Rose and not Jenni. He hadn't expected her to follow him to the palace.

Jenni squinted at him suspiciously. She always knew when Ned was lying.

'You said to come get youse if there were anyfink urgent and I wos 'eading out to get a pizza but then seed that Gariboldi's wos shut – summink to do wiv the weather. So I fawt to meself, I'll pop in the office, see wots wot. Might be a bit of summink 'anging around, you know. Only I didn't zactly pop on account of... well, snowference.' She grinned a little at her made up word.

Ned nodded. He had thought all the snow might be interfering with Jenni's magic. If she was pulling it from nature and nature was covered in snow, then it stands to reason it would be more difficult. Another voice in his head suggested that snow itself was natural, wasn't it? But he shushed that one for now and tried to focus on what else Jenni had said. Something about leftovers. He knew firsthand that it was completely possible to live off HQ leftovers for at least two days, more if you were less fussy.

'Anyways, Joe nobbled me when I got in and wos all stressing bout snowcapades and Jacks, so I never even got nuffink.' At Ned's blank look, Jenni expanded. 'There wos no leftovers. I fink Slinky 'ad 'em.'

'That's unfortunate, but, um, what are snowcapades?' asked Ned, pleased Jenni wasn't asking questions about the conversation she walked into.

'You know, snow-related reports. S'not zactly

urgent, but we got 'alf a dozen or so. Fawt you'd wanna know.' She pulled her tatty notebook out of the pocket of her coat and flipped through it. 'Jeff, wot works at the bakery told Aggie 'e can't get into work cos e's snowed in and lost 'is keys in a drift wot is outside 'is 'ouse that 'e can't get out of. Seems a bit suspect to me, but 'e does live at the bottom of the 'ill so mebbe the snow 'as gavvered or summink.' She turned the page. 'There's bin a fire over in High Trees Mall cos Bill and his lot wos trying to keep warm and one of the kids set fire to the rug. The put-out people 'ave sorted it, but we gotta file the report.' The way she said we clearly indicated someone other than Jenni would be doing that paperwork. She turned another page.

'I had a few of those as well,' said Ned. 'On my way here, actually. Funny story but…'

Griff cleared his throat, interrupting Ned and forestalling Jenni. 'Apologies all, but I must away. Trade deals don't make themselves.' Griff bowed low to Rose. 'My Empress.' He clapped a hand on Ned's shoulders. 'See you soon, son.' He had a wink for Jenni, and then he was gone.

'Wot was all that about?' asked Jenni, sounding a little peevish at being interrupted and a lot more interested in what they had been talking about before she arrived.

Ned decided not to share his own snowcapades and cast about mentally frantically before inspiration hit. He leant down to her and lowered his voice.

'He's going to Fidelia to see a man about… beetles. We're planning a birthday surprise for a certain someone.'

Ned held his breath as he waited for Jenni to take the bait. Her favourite dessert was beetle cheesecake. They had time to do the actual organising. It wasn't Jenni's birthday for another few lunar cycles. He risked a glance at Rose, hoping she'd heard, boarded and was driving the party bandwagon. He breathed out as she gave him a discreet thumbs up.

Jenni's entire expression relaxed, and she grinned.

'E knows to get the proper black ones, right? With the super shiny carapace. Them's makes the best cheesecake. Corse you can make it wiv ovvers but thems the best.'

'Super shiny.' Ned nodded, relieved that Jenni had swallowed the white lie and chuffed that Rose was on board. He hoped that meant she would sort the logistics which he could of course check on later. He turned his attention back to Jenni. 'Is there anything life-threatening in the reports? Anything that can't wait until tomorrow?'

'Nah. Just people panicking about the snow and the Jacks and that. Cos they ain't used to it. Nuffink that can't really wait till laters.'

'Okay, well, we can add these to the team meeting tomorrow. Get Joe to come up with some snow protocols.' Ned knew Joe would be more than happy to deal with the paperwork. The lad did enjoy organising. Jenni's stomach growled threateningly. 'Do you want to stay for dinner?'

Jenni beamed.

'Fanks, Boss.'

Chapter 4

The next morning Jenni stepped out into a deceptively bright, sharp cold. A knife-edged wind whistled around her head. The frigid air burnt Jenni's nose, causing her eyes to water. She was glad of her tufty ears and the scarf she'd found in Ned's wardrobe, which she wound snugly around her neck and chin.

The Jacks had been out to play. Ice lay in random patches across the path and her feet skittered across the cobbles. Large icicles hung from window ledges while pretty icy patterns adorned windows both inside and out.

A plume of white air puffed in front of Jenni's face as she huffed along. She spent a bit of time blowing fake smoke rings and was enjoying having dragon breath until she mis-stepped and went skidding across a nasty patch of black ice. She almost lost her footing, but having a sprite tail helped to centre her. The stiff body of a dead urban fox, half-concealed under a pile of snow, wiped the amusement from her face and reminded Jenni of the treacherous side of winter weather. How many other animals were suffering?

During the night, the city's street cleaners had done a good job of shovelling snow to the sides of the paths where it lay in crumbled heaps, speckled with dirt but how many other frozen birds, cats, foxes – heck even rats, were concealed within? Thinking she should suggest that something be done about the animal corpses, Jenni also decided it might be wiser to crunch through the packed snow rather than risk skating across more icy cobbles.

Concentrating on her footing took all her attention and the scrunch munch noise of her footsteps was inordinately pleasing. There was a slight resonance in each footstep. Like something in the snow was calling her, but before she could figure out what it might be, she found herself at The Noose, Thief-Catcher headquarters. Looking suspiciously at the white stuff, Jenni knocked her feet against the doorframe to remove any snow and she stomped on inside. Reg the innkeeper stood in his customary place behind the bar. He was wreathed in smoke.

'Everyfink awright, Reg?'

The man nodded while Slinky, the sea dragon, snaked out from behind him and spoke in Jenni's head.

I was just warming some scumble for the goodman of the house. A small thanks for letting me eat the leftovers.

A long, forked tongue slithered out, testing the air to make sure there weren't any more scraps that had been missed. Whilst The Noose was not known for its menu, the uneaten food that couldn't be reheated the next day would sustain a Thief-Catcher in times of desperation.

'See you later, Reg,' called Jenni, heading upstairs.

The man wagged a finger in response, turning to reveal a large steaming vat of what Jenni supposed was the hot scumble. She might investigate that after the meeting.

Slinky accompanied Jenni, slinking between her legs as she walked. Her stomach grumbled, and she was just debating whether to risk the icy paths and head back out to pick up breakfast when she smelt cinnamon.

Pushing open the office door, she saw Joe and Willow, the other Thief-Catchers, had already arrived. Joe was laden with several sweet-smelling packages.

'Wot you got there?' Jenni wasted no time with pleasantries. She was hungry.

'Morning Jenni. I picked up a few bits from Aggie's on the way. It's last night's surplus on account of Aggie having fewer customers than usual because of the weather, but if Slinky gives them the once over, they'll freshen right up.'

'Good thinking.' Jenni beamed at the lad and gestured for Slinky to do the business. She would've done it magically herself, of course, but seeing as Slinky was there, all set and ready, he might as well sort it. At least, she thought she would've been able to do it herself. After a couple of goes.

They were all tucked in when the door banged open and Ned appeared in an oversized, hairy coat.

'Wot you meant to be? You look like one of them big 'airy fings wot people say live in the mountains,' snorted Jenni, trying not to lose too much cinnamon goodness whilst laughing her head off.

'It's new,' replied Ned glumly, removing the hairy article and hanging it on the back of his chair, revealing smart, also new, trousers. 'Any going spare?' he asked.

Jenni raised her eyebrows at the snazzy legwear, but Ned was avoiding her gaze. Joe handed over a paper bag of pastry goodness and turned his attention to Jenni.

'What are you on about – big hairy thing?' he asked.

'Ah, it's a fae-tale. A creature wot lives in the mountains and keeps it snowy. A miff really. No-one's ever seed one, so if they is real, they must be dead shy and super 'ard to find.'

There wa a contemplative silence as the Thief-Catcher team tucked back into breakfast, each lost in their own personal swirl of thoughts.

'No Sparks?' Ned asked finally.

Jenni watched with a smirk as he absently wiped his sticky fingers on his new trousers.

'He sent a message. Flight is too risky, what with all the flakes and that. He's staying down at the docks. Must be investigating something big,' said Joe, glancing in pride at his arrest chart on the wall. 'I have no doubt he'll get to the bottom of it.'

In Jenni's opinion, the lad suffered from bouncy optimism.

'We will have to cover the snowcapades and the Jacks. I've had a few more incidents.' Joe cleared his throat and pulled his own notebook out. In contrast to Jenni's, it was pristine. 'Aggie passed on a few messages from concerned citizens. Mr Fennywick said he had to dig a tunnel from his house to the street on account of the snow and he wants compensation for shovelling. Broke his shovel.' Joe looked up and lowered his voice conspiratorially. 'Aggie says it was an old shovel and for us not to worry too much. She also said it was unlikely that he dug an entire tunnel. She thinks the snow fell off his wonky roof into a gigantic pile outside his door and he was maximising his experience for the sake of the audience. Aggie gave him an extra iced bun.'

Joe turned the page, then pointed to Jenni whilst addressing Ned directly. 'Did Jenni tell you about Bill? And the fire?'

Jenni watched in amusement as Ned nodded and tried to get a word in, but he wasn't fast enough. It wasn't surprising that most of the reports mentioned Aggie. She was Roshaven's baker and one of the most popular vendors in Roshaven. Especially around closing time when she gave away her surplus.

'Well, Aggie says Bill is just pulling a fast one and not to mind him at all. She'll dock his wages until he can be bothered to come to work.' Joe sat back in his chair, looking extremely pleased with himself. 'I've done the put-out people paperwork. It's on your desk.'

Since Joe had taken over the filing of reports and associated paperwork, Ned's desk was no longer supported by towering columns of paper. It meant that the desk was twice as precarious as it had been, and Jenni knew it remained at the top of Ned's must-do-something-about-it list that he kept remembering about and then instantly forgetting.

'Good work on the snowcapades so far. We'll keep on top of those, but we've got a new case to investigate. Momma K wants us to find out why it's winter,' said Ned.

'Well, that's easy – because it's winter.' Joe beamed and then his brain caught up to what his mouth said and he flushed. 'I mean, it's the winter season, so…'

'Momma K says it's unseasonably cold and there is too much winter.' Ned glanced at Jenni. 'When we went to the Fae Grove, it was very frosty. The whole place is being taken over by extreme winter, which suggests there could be a magical element beneath the weather we've been experiencing. Momma K is trying to keep it warm there but says it's costing her. And let's be honest, it's not a normal winter out there, is it?'

'Surprised you could tell under that walking carpet,' muttered Jenni, peering into the food bags on the off chance that anything had been missed.

'Jenni! It was a gift, to keep me warm.'

'Well, it don't suit you, if you ask me.' Not happy that even Ned's clothing was changing, Jenni looked to the other Catchers to back her up, but they took the opportunity to look anywhere else.

I can see the appeal. It tickles. Slinky had wound

himself across the top of Ned's coat as it hung on the back of a chair.

'You are right, with it being an unusually harsh winter, I mean. My network has been badly affected by frost. There haven't been any new shoots recently and flow is sluggish. If this weather doesn't break soon, I fear we may lose plants.' Willow's voice trembled, and she leaned gratefully into a concerned hug from Joe.

'Does The Vine have any ideas why there is so much winter?' asked Ned.

The Vine was Willow's plant network that branched out all over Roshaven and was useful for passing simple messages and looking for things. As a tree-nymph herself, it had been Willow's natural inclination to add The Vine to the Thief-Catchers infrastructure, especially as running the network was second nature, she was already rooted in.

'I can try to find out, but it'll be awhile before we get an answer,' she replied. 'Much of the network is in protective hibernation.'

'I didn't know plants did that,' remarked Jenni.

'Oh yes, it's a protective move from adverse weather conditions. No new shoots, or growth or flowers etc. Slow down the internal flow and conserve energy, ready for the Spring burst. It's a very exciting time, usually.'

Jenni watched as tiny flowers bloomed on Willow's bark in response to her excitement at Spring. But they quickly shrivelled and fell, it was too cold for them. Jenni noticed her breath was frosting in the office.

'Plants ain't the only fing we gotta worry about. I saw a frozed fox on the way in and I reckon there's probably more animals wot ain't pets suffering in all this weather. We gotta make sure the city cleaners are picking up the corpses, but mebbe we can organise a warm space for the strays to go or summink. I mean, it ain't their faults they ain't got nowhere to go, is it?'

There was a murmured agreement and Joe added it to his To Do board that was meant to be an indicator for everyone on what needed to be done, but usually ended up being Joe's personal task list.

'We got some 'eat going on or wot?' She peered around for Slinky, but the sea dragon was nowhere to be seen. It had even abandoned Ned's furry coat.

It was up to her. Taking a deep breath, Jenni began concentrating on the fireplace, forcing out magical feelers to see where she could gain some extra energy from. These days it took immense focus and intent for her to draw on the natural energies around her and when people were watching, it was like being a spriteling again before she had developed her powers. But there was something out there. Something sparkling just at the edges of her consciousness that whispered power at her. It matched the resonance she'd felt crunching in the snow.

Joe bustled over with a shovel of coal, tipping it noisily into the grate, breaking Jenni's concentration. He had already done something with wood shavings and crumpled paper to coax the pitiful embers in the grate into doing something more flammable.

'Er, I was gonna do summink wiv that,' protested Jenni, more upset at not being able to explore the odd power than not being able to make the fire.

Slinky appeared and curled itself up as close as dragonly possible to the hearth. Jenni hunkered down beside the sea dragon and scratched behind one of its ears.

'It ain't warm enuff for youse, is it?'

I have to admit, this winter is not for the faint-

hearted, but young Joseph is doing a grand job of keeping me warm. Besides, it would be a long trip to find warm currents at this time of year.

'Ain't you gotta stay in the sea, though? On account of being a *sea* dragon and that.'

Much like you and your grove, Jenni, I can exist within and without. I am of the sea, so as long as I return to the sea eventually, all will be will. But I have much time left before I need to return. Be at ease. I am content.

Slinky let out a low rumble that the Catchers had likened to a cat purring, so Jenni let the sea dragon be.

'Willow, can you try to get something out of The Vine, please? Shake a few bushes, that sort of thing – ask them to report anything unusual.' He amended his statement. 'Anything more unusual than this harsh winter.'

The tree nymph nodded her agreement and Jenni tickled Slinky behind his ears as Ned turned his attention to Joe.

'I've got two jobs for you, lad. First, set up some snow protocols based on the snowcapades that we've had in so far and how they were resolved. Create a file. With a separate one on Jacks. Momma K says she can't deal with them, but if they start getting out of hand, we'll need to try something.'

Jenni knew Joe would be happy with that, and the huge smile on his face was confirmation.

'Good. Okay, second, I want you to get some – ahem - information about the mountain to the north.'

Ned was a city man, born and bred, and looked a little embarrassed about the fact that he didn't know anything about the mountain nearby. Nearby was a general term. It would take at least a week, possibly two, to travel out to the foot of the mountain. Like most of the inhabitants of Roshaven, Jenni knew there was a mountain there. But it formed a somewhat decorative aspect of the horizon rather than a place you could go visit. She even knew it was snowy, but that was the extent of her mountain knowledge. She had never travelled that far north, never had the need.

'We need to figure out if that's where our snow has come from, somehow,' said Ned. 'I mean, as far as I know, snow can't move on its own, but Momma K seemed adamant about it coming down from the mountain. We'll need to know if it's inhabited – by non-magical and fae folk – are they usually snowy all the time and have any other towns and villages in their wake been experiencing the same deep winter as us. Start with Neeps. She has maps and things. I'm sure she'll be happy to lend them. Plus, she'll have the scoop on similar wintry conditions elsewhere, if they exist. If she gets difficult, tell her she can have the exclusive.'

Mariah Neeps was the owner, editor and publisher of *The Daily Blag*, Roshaven's newspaper. Jenni knew her father had been a history enthusiast, so she had inherited the best maps collection and archive outside the Imperial Palace. She was also Joe's ex-girlfriend, a fact that Ned allowed himself to conveniently forget, but something Jenni was sure Willow would not.

'Won't the Palace Library have maps, Boss?' asked Joe, glancing sideways at Willow, making Jenni smirk again. 'I don't mind popping in. We could ask the Librarian about any fae myths.'

Ever since Ned had told the Catchers about meeting Esme, the Palace Librarian, and telling them about the amazing library, everyone had wanted to visit. Ned had confided in Jenni that he wasn't sure Esme would approve of casual visitors en masse. And after what Ned had told her about Esme, Jenni was certain the librarian wouldn't allow maps to be physically removed from the library. If they had maps. Which, to be fair, they probably did.

'Let's start with Neeps and if we don't have any luck, then we can approach the Librarian,' said Ned. 'I'm not sure Esme will approve of myth hunting.'

Nevertheless, Joe beamed and looked excited at the prospect.

'Jenni, I want you to head over to the docks.' Ned finally turned his attention to her. 'Can you check on Sparks and get him to ask his friends and relations if they've seen or heard anything? I know winter isn't a great time of year for them, but there might still be a few antennae out there receiving.'

'Wot you gonna do?' It seemed to Jenni there weren't many jobs left.

'I'm going to speak to Queen Anne and then pop in and have a chat with Kendra.' Jenni noticed Ned's ears growing red as he realised it was unusual for him and Jenni to split up and he tried to make up for it. 'If we split up, we'll cover more ground quicker – a good thing, especially in this weather. You can meet me at the Dead Pier if you like, and we can speak to Pearl together.'

'Awright,' said Jenni sulkily, knowing it made sense but not liking it. 'If that's wot you wanna do. Who's gonna talk to the elementals?'

'Ah, yes. I thought...' But Jenni interrupted Ned.

'Cos I can do it easy enough. They don't always talk back though, that's the fing.'

'Um...' Ned scrubbed a hand through his hair. 'Rose volunteered to talk to them this morning. When we were having breakfast.'

Jenni sniffed and began picking at her fingernails, feeling a bit miffed at being practically replaced.

'It's just she has a bit of a unique relationship with them, and they've helped her in the past, so when she suggested the idea, it seemed like a good plan. You know, strength in numbers and that,' explained Ned.

Jenni shrugged. She was annoyed at how much it bothered her, but she wasn't about to bring it up now.

'You good?' asked Ned.

'Yep.'

'Fine. I'll meet you at the pier after lunch. Willow, Joe – we'll come back to the office after we've spoken to Pearl, so we'll debrief then.'

'Okay, Boss.'

Ned stood up and rubbed his hands together, relieved to be doing something and also clearly trying to get a bit of heat into them. Jenni managed a brief smile as Ned decided against putting his hairy coat back on and instead pulling a spare, long, waterproofed coat off the hook near his desk. It might not be as warm, but it smelled right and looked more like Ned.

They left The Noose together, Jenni stepping cautiously into the snow, testing her footing. Ned frowned at her, wondering what she was up to.

'You alright there, Jenni?'

Jenni flinched, as if she'd forgotten Ned was even there.

'Yeah, yeah corse. Just er… checking the snow.'

She didn't elaborate. She had no idea what was in it yet.

'Um, okay then. Well, good luck, Jenni. See you at the pier.' Ned was waiting to see if she wanted to tell him why she was acting so weird with the snow, but she didn't have a proper theory. Yet.

'Awright. Laters, Boss.' She stomped away towards the docks and Sparks.

Chapter 5

Ned watched Jenni walking away. Well, snow stumbling away. The blue coat she wore looked odd. He was so used to the red. Maybe that was why she was so crotchety and acting weird – because of the coats. He resolved to do something about that. A person should be able to wear a coat of their choice. One that matched them. It was almost as important as the right boots.

A sneaky chill blew through Ned's own coat as he stuffed his hands into the pockets and headed off towards Queen Anne's court. He hoped it would be warm inside. His knee was pinging with all this intense cold.

The Beggar Court nestled alongside Residential Row, just beyond the market stalls. Oddly, there were no residential properties despite the name, just like Market Street was not the actual spot where the market set up and sold its wares. Ned couldn't help but feel nervous. The last time he'd been here, he'd spoken to the new Queen who hadn't told him what had happened to her predecessor and hadn't seemed keen to renew the standard agreement between the Catchers and the beggars. It would be interesting to see how this meeting went.

The Beggar Courtyard was eerily empty. There were no lookouts, no hopeful begging bowls, and no piles of rags. The Jacks had run riot, creating massive swirly ice patterns all over the cobbles. Ned knew where the secret entrance was from previous visits, so he knocked and waited. He could hear rustling, but it was several minutes before the door opened and the nose of the current beggar queen poked out through a minuscule gap.

'What do you want?'

'To talk about the weather.'

'Hmpf.'

The door shut and there were further rustles before it swung fully open.

'You may enter.'

Ned ventured forth into an empty room. Queen Anne was sitting on the edge of her throne, under several layers of fur wraps.

'It's excessively chilly,' she remarked in her own frosty tone.

'And icy. Plus all the snow,' replied Ned, rubbing his hands together to warm them. There was a long pause.

'Dark evenings and dark mornings,' said Queen Anne eventually, unwilling to move the conversation on but not wanting to be impolite.

'Winter is best spent indoors, wrapped up, roaring fires and the like.' Ned glanced at the fireplace. It was empty save for some grey ash. In fact, the entire room had the feel of an icebox. 'Is everything... alright?'

'Pickings are slim. Many of my subjects have gone home for the winter.' The queen pulled her patchy fur wraps closer. 'That or returned to their maker.'

Ned blinked. He hadn't realised beggary was an employment option. Then he registered what else she had said. People were dying.

'We have fewer eyes available at this time. If that's what you're after.'

'Er, no. I really did come to talk about the weather,' said Ned. 'But you have my sincere condolences on the losses to your court. Please, let me know if you need anything.' He paused, but Queen Anne didn't reply. 'Do you have any theories on why Roshaven is gripped in such a winter?'

'Nothing besides you being the prime suspect.'

Ned was stunned.

'Me? What did I do?'

'At the moment, I don't know. But it's always something with you Catchers.'

Ned breathed a little easier.

'First you let a murderer run rampant through the fae – I lost some dear friends before you apprehended that shifter. Then there was the business with the loss of love, followed by those goons from Fidelia terrorising the streets when your brother was in town. You had the Spice Ghosts destroy prime beggar spots on the wharf, and now, now, my people are dying.' She glared at him and huffed out of her nostrils. 'It has become a dangerous occupation being a beggar in this city.'

Ned opened his mouth to reply, but nothing came out. Technically, she was correct. Those things had happened and whilst he had fulfilled his duty as a Catcher, had he done enough to support the beggars during these difficult times?

'Please, Queen Anne, is there anything I can do now? To help improve the situation?' he asked again, softer this time, with as much respect as he could muster. He wanted her to accept the offer of help and not be too proud to refuse it.

Queen Anne's face softened marginally, and she pulled at her fur wraps again.

'I will agree to reinstating the contract between the network and the Catchers provided you make a monthly donation to the BWO fund.'

BWO? It took Ned a second to figure out the

acronym. Beggar Wives and Orphans.

'Of course. I'll see that it's done. And send Joe round with the paperwork.'

The queen's face softened into almost a smile. Joe was popular with the network.

'I'm afraid I don't know what's causing the winter. I mean, obviously, its winter, so there's that. But the rest is abnormal.' Queen Anne narrowed her eyes. 'Have you interrogated Momma K yet? Magic is clearly involved.'

Ned hesitated. He didn't want to tell her that Momma K had asked them to investigate the alarming winter in the first place. And despite his own misgivings, there was no actual proof yet that magic was the culprit.

'We are making every effort to discover the source of the problem.'

Queen Anne sniffed and held out a very ordinary brown, wooden begging bowl. Ned patted his pockets before finding two gold marks. He put them both in, making a mental note to send over a sack of coal.

'Thank you. I'll see myself out.'

A flash of surprise crossed the beggar queen's face as she glanced into the bowl and she threw Ned a genuine smile that revealed how vulnerable she was.

Barely older than Joe, thought Ned as he nodded his goodbye. Maybe two sacks of coal and some tea, sugar and biscuits. Just the spare ones they had lying around.

As Ned headed across Roshaven towards the Druid Grove, he wondered if the others were having more luck. Trudging through the icy terrain was freezing his feet despite the fact he was wearing his Gunningtons, the best boots on the market. The wind had picked up and was driving the snow into furious flurries, making it hard for Ned to see the streets in front of him. An enormous shadow passed by his right shoulder, causing him to flinch. He stopped and looked but couldn't detect anything other than the Jack dots zinging. Just snow falling in thicker and thicker eddies. He hunched his shoulders and hoped the druids had something warming on offer.

Chapter 6

Joe crunched along to the office of *The Daily Blag,* enjoying the sound his feet created in the fresh snow. It had been snowing enough now for him to avoid the darker patches that hid wicked black ice beneath them. He'd only fallen over six times, but knowing his luck before long, he'd end up with a broken arm.

At least he hadn't repeated the same mistake that he made this morning on the way to work. The snow had looked so beautiful and pristine that walking into the smooth white drifts had been so much fun. Until he completely misjudged the depth of one and sunk down to his waist. Luckily he'd been just outside Aggies and she'd heard his calls for help. It had taken a bit of doing and involved several other customers' help, but they'd managed to haul him out. Slinky had dried his soggy legs off when he'd finally made it to the office, and Willow had presented him with some new winter wear to keep out the chill.

The scarf Willow had knitted him was so snuggly, he didn't mind the vicious wind trying to blow through him, although it stung his eyes and made them water. By the time he got to the door of the newspaper office, his eyes felt very sore.

'What's happened? Who died?'

'What?' asked Joe in confusion.

'You look like you've been crying,' explained Mariah Neeps, editor and publisher of *The Daily Blag*, her pen poised, ready to take down the details.

'Oh, no. It's just the cold weather, made my eyes run

41

is all.'

'Hmm, I suppose I could use that,' muttered Neeps, scribbling something down on her pad. 'Seeing as I've got you here, can I ask a few questions?' She didn't wait for Joe to reply. 'What are the Thief-Catchers doing about the rise in snow-related accidents? Has there been a city-wide curfew to protect the more vulnerable residents? How many limbs have been broken on black ice so far? Do the Druids have enough resources to cope with the increase in treating injuries caused by winter? Is there any truth to the rumour that we've run out of salt and you're literally taking your limb safety into your own hands if you step out the door? What about the rampaging animals? Any comment?'

She arched an eyebrow at him, tapping her foot, waiting for him to respond.

'Um.' Joe's Adam's apple bobbed rapidly in his throat as his brain tried to catch up with all the questions. 'Off the record...' he began. He had been learning about how to talk to Neeps after he'd let slip some rather embarrassing revelations about the lunchtime pastimes of the Thief-Catchers that the reporter had spun to make it seem like the Catchers never did anything.

'We have set up a command centre for snowcapades and are dealing with each case in a professional and sensitive manner. The Chief Thief-Catcher is meeting with the Druids as we speak.' He was about to say something about the curfew – a palace matter – the salt – a Jimmy Fingers matter – and the animals – a matter he had no idea about – when he remembered what Ned had told him about speaking to Neeps. *If you don't know, don't say anything. No comment is a powerful shield.* 'As for your other questions, no comment at this time.'

Neeps gave a small nod and made some notes on her

pad, before smiling widely at him. Joe felt like he might have just passed a test, one that he hadn't revised for, but one that seemed to have gone well.

'What can I do for you?' asked Neeps.

'Ah, I'm here on official Catcher business. I'm looking for information on the mountain.'

Neeps smirked.

'You might want to be a little more specific than that. There are a couple of hundred mountains in Efrana, you know.'

'Gosh, really? That is interesting, but I need to find out more about the mountain over there,' said Joe, pointing towards the front of the newspaper premises. His brow furrowed as he thought about it some more. Then his arm swung to the left. 'Is that the right direction?'

'Depends, which landmass are you after?' Neeps asked in an amused voice.

'North. I need to know about that mountain to the north. Please. The one that sits behind us, on the horizon.'

'Ah, you mean Mount Firn. I'm not surprised you know nothing about it. Most city folk don't go that much further than the woods.' She shot Joe a shrewd look. 'But you're not from here originally, are you?'

'No, I'm not, but I travelled in from the east. No mountaineering.' He shuffled foot to foot, keen to change the subject. 'So, do you have any files on, er, Mount Firn?'

'Is that where you think the winter is coming from? Besides it being winter, I mean.' Neeps cocked her head sideways, regarding him.

'I cannot divulge any information at this time. Investigations are...'

'Yes, yes, ongoing. Got it,' interrupted Neeps. She stuffed her pen and pad into the large pocket of her cardigan. 'Come on, let's go have a poke around in Dad's archive. I'm not sure I have anything useful, though.'

Joe followed her through the main office of the paper and into the back room where the magical printing press churned out *The Daily Blag,* looking with interest at the machinery. Neeps bent down to wiggle a rusting key into an old lock and used her shoulder to force the door open. The smell of musty documents hit them both in the face.

'I, er, don't come in here often,' explained Neeps as she rubbed the old-fashioned light globe on the wall. It took a while, but eventually began emitting a sickly yellow glow that illuminated the small room. 'Here, prop the door open with that. Let a bit more light in.' She handed Joe an enormous book, and he duly wedged the door open.

The room had shelving that ran all the way around and extended from ceiling to floor. Every shelf full of rolls of parchment or dusty boxes. There were letters carved into the shelving. Neeps followed them three quarters of the way around.

'Here we are. M. If Dad had any information on Mount Firn, it would be here somewhere. Come and help me look.'

There were two boxes, some scrolls and a file on the shelves near the M. The boxes proved to be accounts on a highly active mole family, the contact details of several mediums and the thick file was labelled mermaids.

Joe turned to the scrolls and began to unroll one, getting excited when he saw they were maps. Elation didn't last for long as they turned out to be maps of

Roshaven, Fidelia and one of the towns that lay further west. Nothing on Mount Firn.

'Sorry. I thought he might have had something,' said Neeps as they put back the material and left the mildewy archive, returning to the main office. 'Is that the official angle, then? Extra winter coming down from the mountain? Something bringing it down, perhaps?'

Joe flushed. 'I'm not at liberty to discuss any ongoing…'

'Investigation. Yes, yes, I know.' Neeps smiled. 'I might have something for you, though. Had a few strange reports of a large shadow being seen around town. No-one's managed to see what's causing the shadow, which is odd. And then there's this. What do you make of this?' Neeps was holding up a picture of a giant footprint in the snow that she'd taken out of her other cardigan pocket. They were perfect reporter pockets. Capacious and waterproofed.

Joe leaned in to get a better look at the image.

'It's a prank, right? No-one has feet that big. Not even the trolls. It's got to be, what… fifteen inches?' He peered at the foot again. 'Maybe twenty? Trolls don't have feet that big, do they?'

'Not that I'm aware of. They tend to be squat rather than tall. And you're right – the footprint measures fifteen inches.' Neeps nodded at the photo. 'Keep it, I have copies.'

Joe nodded his thanks and carefully folded the image so that it fit into his pocket.

'Have you come across the Jacks yet?' asked Neeps. The notepad was out again.

'Er… yes. Mischievous fae that like the cold.' Joe gulped at being put on the spot.

'That's right, short for Jack Frosts. I checked Dad's

archives for an article. They're fae pranksters, a kind of vermin really. You don't often get them in the city, but we don't usually get such heavy snowfall. They're more common in the countryside. Little blue flecks, they look like. Fond of icing up paths and freezing doorways, that sort of thing.'

'Yes, of course. Well, I'm sure Momma K will keep them under control.'

'Quote you on that, can I?' Neeps smirked again and her eyes gleamed as she latched onto a potential story.

Joe flushed at his rookie error. You never spoke for Momma K. Ever.

'No, no. That's not what I said. I just meant...' Joe floundered for a way to take back what he'd said. 'I mean, she's got us looking into what's causing the winter. She doesn't know, that's why we're on the case.'

'Really?' Neeps had her pen and pad out again and was scribbling furiously. 'Would you care to elaborate?'

Joe's heart sank. So much for not involving Momma K.

'No comment,' he croaked before clearing his throat. 'Thanks for your help.'

'You'll keep me in the loop, yeah?' called Neeps after him.

'We'll give you the exclusive, promise!' Joe called back. He couldn't get into trouble for saying that. It wasn't like there were any other newspapers in town. He hurried to Thief-Catcher HQ to see what the others made of the giant footprint. He was so focused on getting there, he didn't notice the ground abruptly change and he ended up tumbling down.

'What the...?' Joe looked down. He appeared to be inside a large impression. One that looked remarkably like a giant foot. He scrambled out of it and scanned around, but there weren't any more nearby. He brushed the snow off his clothing. *Must be some kind of prank,* he thought, but he walked more cautiously back to The Noose, eyes peeled for further tracks.

When Joe got back to the office, he was bursting to tell someone what he'd seen, but when he walked through the door, Willow collapsed on him in a weepy tangle of leafy hair.

'What's happened? It's not… it's not the plant vine, is it? Frostbite?'

'Oh, Joe! It's the Holly and the Ivy. They should know better, the pair of them are fully grown but the Ivy has got the hump about Holly's prickly crown. I was on The Vine – it's quiet, there are a lot of plants in hibernation – but then I got an urgent warning about deer.'

'Deer?' Joe was trying to keep up, but he was struggling. 'There aren't any deer in Roshaven, are there?'

'Exactly!' Willow had extracted herself from his embrace, but her tendril hair was standing out around her head like agitated snakes. 'Apparently, the Ivy enticed deer into their part of the woods in order to take Holly's crown, but they lost interest after getting a nose full of prickly leaves so they rambled on – as deer do – and began eating random foliage. But because of the weather, pickings are slim. The deer have to range much further than normal to find something to eat and now they've strayed into town, eating their way through gardens and vegetable patches that they can dig through the snow to access and the network is in a panic. We're hanging on by a thread as it is – we can't afford to lose swathes of foliage to hungry deer. And while the Holly and the Ivy are fighting, the deer aren't going to want to return to the forest. It's becoming a hostile environment.'

'Er…' Joe swallowed what he was going to say. He didn't think Willow would appreciate *don't deer usually eat plants?* at this point. 'How so?'

'It's a berry bath. There are squished cases everywhere. The Holly bleeds red, you understand. I mean Ivy has berries too – they're an important food source too, but this sounds like… carnage.'

'I can imagine,' replied Joe, thinking now might be a good time to go make some tea.

'Made worse by the snow, of course. Awful, just awful.'

'So what does the Ivy have to say for itself?' called Joe as he filled the kettle. He watched as Willow brightened at his use of capitalisation.

'It turns out that the Ivy has always been jealous of the Holly's red berries and white flowers. I mean, I don't know why. The Ivy has its own blooms. Different kinds too. Some are like tiny bulbs of yellow stalks, whilst others are deep purple stars or white trumpets.'

Joe eased a hot cup of tea into Willow's hands.

'Perhaps all this cold weather got under Ivy's skin. I'm sure it didn't mean it.'

'Maybe, but now we've got deer on the loose to worry about. Ivy should understand that it doesn't grow prickles. Never has, never will.' Willow seemed unaware that prickles were bursting in and out of her skin in an agitated manner.

'We'll round up the deer, don't worry. They might disappear on their own accord once they discover what's out there.' Joe took a swallow of his own tea while he waited for Willow to filter what he'd said.

'Why? What's out there? What nonsense did Neeps

fill your head with?' Willow asked tartly, and there was a distinctly zesty aroma in the room.

Whilst she and Joe were in the early stages of their relationship, she was all too aware that Neeps had also been a semi-romantic relation of Joe's, when he first came to Roshaven.

Joe tried to ignore Willow's tone, although the citrusy element in the air was making breathing a little sharp.

'Could you turn it down a bit please?' he wheezed.

Full of apologies, Willow pulled in her emotions. The prickles stopped erupting. The lemony tang disappeared and her tendril-like hair finally fell back down over her shoulders.

'She didn't have much to say, really. No specific mountain information, but I know its name. It's called Mount Firn. Shame she didn't have anything else, but she's had various reports of a shadow and then,' he paused for effect. It had no response except for a quizzical look on Willow's face. 'A giant footprint! What if it's that fae myth monster Jenni was talking about earlier?'

Willow's bark rippled with amusement.

'You can't be serious? A monster? Roaming around Roshaven? Don't be ridiculous.'

'I don't know if there is one or not, but I did fall into a giant footstep.' Joe puffed out his chest a little at having survived such undefined danger.

'Where? Can you show me?'

'Yep. I was coming to report it, but we could go back and take some measurements, possibly make a cast.'

Joe was bouncing up and down in so much excitement that he made Willow smile.

'Go on then. Get the stuff ready. And don't forget your scarf!'

Chapter 7

As Ned approached the Druid Grove, he was relieved to see the gates were open. It had been a slog getting through the snow that kept sticking to his boots as he tried to avoid the slippery ice patches, but thanks to the street cleaners, the major thoroughfares were mostly passable and parts of the city were still working. To be fair, the gates had never been closed in his memory, but with all the cold weather going on, it felt like anything could happen.

Entering the inner courtyard, Ned noticed rock salt scattered across the cobbles forcing a path through the icy patches to the buildings within. On the left, amidst the piles of snow, he saw an igloo. At least, he thought it was an igloo. Rose had shown him some pictures at breakfast about different snow related activities and had been excited about putting long sticks on the bottom of her feet and going snowing or icing or something. Ned was sure one picture had been a building like this. He stepped closer to get a good look.

'Coo-ee!' It was Sister Eustacia. She was wearing a woolly nun's headpiece and a large padded coat with a pair of bright red mittens holding two steaming mugs. 'You were spotted heading up to the Grove, and I figured you could do with one of these. Hot chocolate with honey.'

Ned liked Sister Eustacia. She was a bubbly personality with a vast religious knowledge of many faiths. For some unknown reason, she'd settled in Roshaven and attached herself to the Druid Grove. They didn't seem to mind that she was a nun and not a druid, and if anything, the druidic services to Roshaven ran more efficiently than they ever had before. He took the mug gratefully and slurped. It was almost too hot to drink, but it warmed him all the way down.

'Igloo?' he asked, the word popping into his head.

'Yes! I spent a couple of weeks with the indigenous clans of Snieg when I was on my spiritual travels and they lived in the things. Never had the opportunity to build my own before, something to pass the time while we wait for winter to finish its elaborate show. Keeps you warm building your own igloo.'

They both slurped contentedly.

'Did you know, the Sniegish have fifty words for snow? Fifty!' Sister Eustacia shook her head at the marvel of it all. 'I wonder if we'll develop any of our own this year. It's rather excessive, isn't it?' She gestured expansively at the weather.

'I could think of a few words myself,' murmured Ned.

'How are you getting on with the Jacks? Little buggers, but there's not much you can do about them, really. I'd recommend not swatting them. Brother Douglas, one of the Blue Monks, had a run in after accidentally doing that.' Sister Eustacia took another swig of hot chocolate, shivering at the memory.

'Well, I know about them. The Jacks, that is. I will tell Joe about the swatting. He'll pass it along.' Ned decided not to ask about Brother Douglas. It didn't sound like a tale with a happy ending.

'Great idea. Fun little things, but best to leave them to get on with it and praise their icy patterns. Never hurts to be on their good side.'

Ned nodded. 'Is Kendra about?'

'Yes, she's in the main hall dealing with mistletoe. Did you hear about the fight?'

'What fight?'

'The Holly and the Ivy. It's all over The Vine – we keep our ears to the ground, so to speak. One of the druids is half dryad. Comes in handy when we need to replenish supplies. And the deer, oh, terrible problem with the deer. They've got the whole vine in uproar.'

'Deer? We have deer in Roshaven?' Ned was surprised. He'd never even seen one before.

'Oh yes, causing a horrendous ruckus.' Sister Eustacia looked him up and down. 'Shouldn't you be a bit more… on top of this sort of thing? After all, it's a disturbance of the peace which comes under your beat, doesn't it?'

'I've been investigating other leads,' replied Ned stiffly. 'Willow is my plant expert. I'm sure she's already handling the problem admirably.'

'I do hope so. The infirmary is busier than ever. There's been a rise in walk-ins since the bad weather began. We're almost running out of space, so many broken bones to set. At this rate, we'll have a bandage shortage. Then, of course, there's the frozen pipes. If it's happening to us, you can bet your honeycakes it's happening to others in Roshaven. And what happens when water pipes freeze?'

Ned knew the answer to this one.

'There's no water.'

'Exactly. And water is one of the pillars of life. Can't survive without it. You finished?' Sister Eustacia pointed at Ned's cup and he handed it over.

The enjoyment he had in drinking the hot chocolate had already disappeared and an icy knot of worry had taken up residence in his stomach.

'I'll see you later,' he called to the nun as headed inside to speak to the High Priestess.

'Cheerio!'

The main hall usually had rows of tables and benches where the druids would gather to study, eat, and hang out. But today, most of the surfaces were covered in masses of mistletoe. The High Priestess, Kendra, was standing behind one table, consulting a list and chewing on the end of a pencil.

'Problem?' asked Ned.

'Hmm. Oh, hi Ned. Did you hear?'

'The Holly and the Ivy are fighting.' Ned tried to pretend he knew what the hell was going on.

'Yes and for some reason, the mistletoe has gone crazy, and masses of the stuff are growing all over the city,' Kendra replied.

'I hadn't noticed.'

'Well, my druids have been out collecting as much as they could. It's more in the outer areas of the city now and it's attracting a lot of wildlife from the forest.'

'The deer,' said Ned, feeling like he had a good grip on the situation.

'No. Deer don't eat mistletoe.' Kendra frowned at him. 'We've had a surge of squirrels and some rather ardent porcupines. Apparently it's like catnip to them.'

'Porcupines?' Ned didn't think he'd seen any of those before, either.

'Yes, their quills are extremely painful and they will shoot them at you if you scare them, so make sure you tell your Catchers to keep people away. My druids will continue to remove the mistletoe, but the Thief-Catchers need to step in with the human element. Perhaps Willow could mediate and sort out the argument between the Holly and the Ivy so they can get back to keeping the winter plants in order.'

'Yes, of course. The Catchers should be able to resolve the conflict with the Holly and the Ivy but what about the deer? And the other animals?' asked Ned, hoping the Druids had a plan to solve that issue as well.

'That is your problem, I'm afraid. And I'd be quick about it if I were you. Some of my acolytes said they saw a group of young men stalking the streets, armed with bows and arrows. If you can get the Holly and the Ivy to stop fighting, I'm sure the animals will return to the woods.'

'Great.' Ned's mood sank, then brightened. Jimmy Fingers would be the perfect person to help him sort out that kind of problem. He knew the younglings of Roshaven could be a handful, determined to flaunt their perceived superiority and unfounded authority, but they would listen to Ned if he had Fingers on his side. The lads thought Fingers was cool because, although not exactly a conman, if you needed something, Fingers was your man, especially as he was now the Lower Circle and officially in charge of imports and exports.

'What are you going to do with all this?' Ned asked, changing the subject.

'Oh, mistletoe is an excellent medicinal plant. We'll use it to make tinctures, poultices, infusions and the like. It helps with seizures, arthritis and headaches. In fact, it makes a great oil that you massage into your joints, take away some of the stiffness. I can send you some at the palace if you want?'

Ned resisted the urge to rub his knee, which had been complaining a little about the intensely cold weather.

'That would be very kind of you, thanks. I actually came here to ask if you had any theories on why this winter is so... wintery.' The backs of Ned's ears reddened at his poor choice of words. He really needed to come with a better description.

Kendra tucked a strand of hair behind her ear, then inspected her fingernails.

'Look, we haven't been able to do our usual rituals – at least not as regularly as we would like – and that is worrying. I can't lie. Have we angered the gods? Let's face it, it doesn't take much. Has the weather turned worse because we can't do our rituals, which in turn means the weather gets worse so we have even less opportunity to perform our rituals. A vicious cycle.' She began biting a fingernail. 'I am worried.'

'Do you have any...' Ned searched for the right phrase. 'Wintery-based rites you can do more of? Anything that might help redress things?'

'We have our Winter Solstice coming up, where we honour the power of darkness and the mother with winter symbolising our time in the womb. But... that is more about the shortness of the days and the celebration of those days becoming longer again. It's not specifically about snow or ice or freezing cold.' Kendra shrugged a little. 'Do you really believe this weather is our fault?'

'Honestly, no, but you do have to wonder if Mother Nature is punishing us for something.' Ned felt silly saying that, but you never knew. 'Not that I'm looking for blame, please don't think that. I'm just trying to figure out what's going on. How I can fix it.'

'Nature never punishes, she seeks balance in all things.' Kendra gazed out of the window at the falling snow flurries. 'We look for patterns, of course, but all I can tell you is that something is bringing this winter upon us. It's definitely magical, but not, I think, fae?'

Ned knew Kendra was half fae but had left her magical roots behind when she became a druid, so if she was feeling something, it must be powerful.

'You're right – it's not fae. Momma K has tasked us to find out who or what is at the bottom of this. Although Jenni reckons it might be a mythical creature nobody has ever heard of,' Ned chuckled. 'At least, I can rule out…'

Kendra grinned at Ned's discomfort as he looked up in dismay, realising he'd spoken aloud.

'Yes, you can rule out the druids. We didn't call this winter down upon Roshaven. And we will redouble our efforts to complete more rituals. We have seen an increase in frost-related injuries, at least all this…' she rustled the piles of vegetation on the table, 'can help with the treatments.' She smiled with such warmth that Ned couldn't help but smile back, relieved he hadn't offended her. 'But we'll continue to read the signs and I'll let you know if anything new occurs. And maybe you should investigate Jenni's myth. She could be on to something.'

'Thanks, Kendra. I'll be in touch.' Ned lifted a hand in farewell and set off out of the main hall and back through the courtyard. Sister Eustacia was nowhere to be seen, but Ned could hear yodelling coming from the igloo. He grinned and headed for the Dead Pier where he was to meet Jenni.

Chapter 8

Jenni popped into The Pegasus for a hot chocolate and a bite before heading over to the docks. All she needed to do was find Sparks, have a chat, and then she would already be close to the Dead Pier for talking with the mermaids. And in this weather, she didn't want to hang about in the freezing cold any longer than she had to even though she was beginning to have her suspicions about the snow. There was something in there beside frozen water.

Ned was visiting Queen Anne and Kendra, so she definitely had time for second breakfast and a couple of games of darts before she headed out again. Perhaps she would come up with some snow theories. Was it accumulating magic because it was blanketing everything and the power had nowhere else to go? And she was just being sensitive to it because she drew her magic from natural sources? Could be, could be. Jenni's attention was taken by the doorstep bacon sandwich with brown sauce delivered to her table and for a while, all her focus was directed on demolishing that.

Sparks had told Joe he was at WGI Emporium, which was one of the biggest storage warehouses at the docks and owned by Griff. Jenni wasn't sure what 'leads' Sparks thought he had on the excessive winter, but her toes felt like they were frozen solid so at this point she would take any theory he'd come up with.

Plus, she'd seen what Ned probably hadn't fully realised – the immense strain Momma K was under keeping her kingdom warm. Put that together with the difficulty she was having in accessing her power and this winter needed to end. Polishing off her sandwich, she reluctantly headed back outside.

As she neared the WGI Emporium signage, she became aware of tiny cries for help. Casting around, she noticed an exhausted honey bee laying somewhat bedraggled atop a pile of fresh snow.

'Oh pleazzzze help. I'm zzzzzo clozzzze. If you could juzzzzt lift me to the door?'

Jenni thought it was a bloody good job she spoke bee and carefully helped the insect into the palm of her hand before heading into the warehouse.

'Quickly, quickly! Shut the door!' a voice yelled at Jenni as she entered the storage facility. 'You'll let the Jacks in!'

'Awright, awright. Keep yor socks on.' Jenni looked around to find out who was shouting at her. A little old woman of indeterminate size due to the many layers of clothing she wore was scowling up at her. Even to Jenni, who stood the height of an average ten-year-old child, this woman was tiny.

'Sup,' greeted Jenni. 'Found this one outside. Can you 'elp?'

The old woman held the perfect bee sized box in her hands, complete with some beads of nectar so the insect could refresh and refuel.

'Easy, easy. Gently, gently. There we go.' She eased the bee from Jenni's palm to the box, where it gratefully slurped at the nectar.

'Sparks about?' Jenni asked once the bee was settled.

'He's overseeing.'

'Overseeing wot?'

'The big sleep.' The tiny woman looked Jenni up

and down. 'You are not a bug. Why are you here?'

'Gotta talk to Sparks, innit,' replied Jenni cheerfully as she went in search of the firefly.

She pushed open a pair of double doors and entered a cavernous room. The lighting was dim, and it smelt a little musty. There were hundreds and hundreds of tubs tied together in a hexagonal pattern — like a giant wooden honeycomb. It was eerily quiet.

'Sparks – you in 'ere?' she whispered.

A speck of light began bobbing towards her from the other end of the space, revealing itself to be Sparks.

'Awright, Sparky. Wot's going on 'ere?' asked Jenni.

It took a while for Sparks to finishing flashing his bum and by the time he got to the end of what he was telling her, he had to sit down on her outstretched palm. Jenni looked around again in wonder.

'So all this is a bug 'otel? A place for all the insects to come and go to sleep for a bit while the winter is on. S'brilliant. Yor probably saving 'undreds of lives 'ere Sparko.'

Sparks sputtered feebly.

'It weren't yor idea – it was Fingers? Huh. And 'e got Griff to agree?'

Jenni inspected Sparks more closely.

'You ain't looking too good, mate. Wot can I do?'

But the firefly was too exhausted to reply.

'I'll get him settled in.'

The diminutive woman had caught up with Jenni and gently took Sparks off her hand.

'Don't worry, we'll take good care of him and all the bugs.' She smiled at Jenni encouragingly. 'Without them, we'd be in a sorry state. This winter will lift eventually and Spring will arrive. We need insects to

60

help pollinate the plants and encourage the nature's rebirth. That's why this place is so important.'

'Good, good. I hear you. Trusting you to look after 'im. E's a crucial member of the Catchers. Vital.' Jenni blinked. 'Musta got a bit of dust in me eye.' She rubbed them. 'I'll come an visit, mate.' Lifting a hand in farewell, Jenni pushed back through the doors.

Jimmy Fingers. That bloke had an odd relationship with bugs. He was the only non fae person Jenni knew who could speak their language, and now this, a full-blown hotel for the entire insect population. Saving lives. *Bloody sod deserved a medal.* And the old biddy doing the day to day. Champions, the pair of them. Especially as they'd obviously finagled the use of a part of Griff's warehouse for this new establishment, most likely without payment, although talk of favours had probably occurred. Jenni's smile soon disappeared as she realised the lead Sparks had was clearly about this bug haven and nothing to do with the actual cause of the winter. If she told Joe, he'd have to update the crime board and Jenni would be back in the lead. Maybe she'd leave it as is for now.

Unbidden, the ancient myth she had half remembered that morning whispered at the back of Jenni's mind. *Meh-Teh.* That was its name. She shivered, and not just because it was bloody freezing. At least she didn't have to go far to meet Ned. The Dead Pier was only round the corner. Hopefully, he would have more news.

Chapter 9

Jenni huffed at him as Ned arrived.

'You took yor time.'

'Sorry. I had a very interesting chat with Queen Anne. Did you know…' But Jenni wasn't listening.

'Sparks is fine. He's all snugged in at the Bug 'Otel wot Fingers sorted out. All the bugs is. They got this little caretaker lady wot is keeping an eye out on everyfink and I spoke to 'er bout minding Sparks specially and 'ow important 'e is and that. So that's that.'

She didn't wait for a response and went ahead, sticking her hand in the water to summon Pearl, their mermaid ambassador.

'Oof, it's brass monkeys in there,' she complained, wiping her hand on her coat.

'That's good news. About Sparks, I mean.'

Jenni nodded but didn't speak. Wisely, Ned held his tongue, not wanting to irritate her further.

They waited. Breath pillowing out before them. It felt colder on the Dead Pier. The wind had a piercing edge that found all your nooks and crannies, chilling them with a ferocity that made Ned's ears sing. The skull heads that festooned its length certainly seemed to be chattering in agreement. The Jacks had been at work here too. The wooden deck was slippery underfoot and swirling feathers of frost decorated each board, especially towards the edges. There was a great deal of rippling below the waterline and a pink bobble hat rose out of the water, followed by Pearl's distinctive golden tresses. She was wearing a rather fetching cerise cardigan.

'Why..? How..?' Ned scratched his head.

'S'good spell that. Where'd you get it?' asked Jenni, wondering if she could manage something like that at the moment.

Pearl tried to toss her locks back, but the effect was marred by the bobble hat.

'Had it ages. Just not had a chance to test it out. It's bloody freezing.' She turned her attention to Ned. 'What are you doing about this weather?'

'We were actually hoping you might have some ideas… as part of our investigation, we're talking to everyone. Gathering facts. Assessing.' Ned rocked back and forth on his heels, then pinwheeled his arms rapidly as his boots failed him and slipped. Recovering his balance, he gestured carefully. 'That sort of thing.'

'So you don't know, then?'

Ned spread his hands.

'It is winter,' he replied.

'I'm aware of that,' snapped Pearl. 'But this… this is way more than that.'

'Ow's it looking down there? You awright for food and stuff?' asked Jenni.

'Migration has been huge. A lot of shoal activity to warmer waters – even by those who don't like to travel. It's had a massive impact on the food chain. You can forget putting fresh fish on the menu. They've nearly all gone. Left these waters. Which causes issues for the creatures they eat and the ones that eat them. It's a delicate balance in the ocean. Tiny changes have a colossal effect and this is not a tiny change.' Pearl took a steadying breath. 'I mean, the sedentary lot are staying put. They've dug in, found shelter, protected themselves as best they can. But the problem is, the colder the water gets, the more it sinks down to the bottom. It's getting pretty dense down here. And there have been reports of floes.'

'Floes?' asked Ned.

'Fields of floating sea ice. Fine when they're floating but when they start aggregating. I mean, a girl's got to surface, you know?'

Ned and Jenni nodded. Whilst their mermaid experience had been brief and terrifying, they remembered how great it felt to surface.

'It's not us, if that's what you've come to ask. Absolutely nothing to do with us.' Pearl's teeth sharpened and her fingers echoed claws.

'No worries, we believe you. It ain't us eivver.' Jenni eyed Ned sideways. 'Least it ain't fae.'

'What's happening then? I mean, we're managing, but if it gets any thicker down here, swimming is going to be tough and frosttail is not pretty, let me tell you.'

'As I said, we're eliminating, er...' Ned faltered.

'Lines of enquiry,' finished Jenni, sharing a smile with her boss.

'Look, would it be alright to shovel snow into the harbour?' asked Ned. 'We're going to have to get rid of it somehow and it'll melt when it reaches the water, right?'

The razor-sharp teeth and claws were back with a vengeance. Pearl snarled.

'Absolutely not! All that snow would be packed full of contaminants – bacteria, faeces, salt, oil and pollutants from all your contraptions, people and animals. Plus, adding tons of snow into our already cold waters will lower the temperature even further. You could end up killing hundreds of creatures, destroying habitats and any accord you have with the mermaids would be instantly void.'

'Right, yes, of course. I wasn't thinking. I can assure you, we will not dump snow into the ocean.'

Ned was trying to sound sincere and reassuring, but Jenni could see that inwardly he was panicking and she thought she knew why. Surely the snow would naturally melt into the sea, anyway?

'Um, we'll keep in touch, Pearl, and let you know what we find out, but it may be worth taking a migration of your own. Should things continue.' Ned tried to give her a comforting smile but was concerned to see her teeth and nails had not retracted.

'Migrate? Migrate? Do you have any idea what would happen if we lost our territory?' Pearl's eyes were turning shark black, and she looked ready to slaughter the pair of them. 'We're not some random fins living here, you know. We fought hard for this prime real estate. We can't just migrate. Who knows who would move in and try to take over?'

'Okay, I get it. I'm sorry. Don't migrate.' Ned spoke quickly. 'I didn't mean to upset you. We're honoured that you chose Roshaven to stake your claim. No one is going to try to take your territory away from you.'

Pearl visibly relaxed. Talons and fangs retracted and her eyes returned to normal. She smiled placidly at him, waved and splashed down underwater.

Ned and Jenni both moved smartly back to avoid ice cold droplets.

'You was lucky then. Fawt she was gonna go for you. Never clever to annoy a mermaid, Boss.'

'That wasn't my intention. We have no idea how long this winter is going to last and even if it does come to an end, how long it will take to thaw. What if it's everlasting? We need to have a Plan B for everyone. That includes mermaids who might not survive much more of this severe winter.' Ned hunched his shoulders and began walking back down the pier to dry land. 'I didn't realise them living here was a territory thing. I haven't got that far in my mermaid relations history.' Ned did his best to learn as much as possible about the different denizens in Roshaven in his spare time. It was just a shame that he had so little spare time.

'I fawt we didn't 'ave a Plan A.'

Jenni sniffed in disapproval at his lack of knowledge, if only because it matched her own.

'Well… fact collecting is a solid start,' conceded Ned.

'Still fink it could be a Meh-Teh, Boss. That's wot the creature is called. The one wot likes the snow.'

'Yeah?' Ned still wasn't sure, but they were quickly ruling out everyone else. 'Do we really think a mythical creature we don't even know for sure exists is attacking us with winter? Why would it? What did we ever do to it?'

They were striding with feeling now, at least, Ned was. Jenni was at full gambol in order to keep up.

'E might not be attacking us. E might be visiting and not realise wot 'e's doing.'

Ned misjudged a patch of black ice and slid around the corner, arms and legs pinwheeling as he struggled to maintain his balance.

Jenni followed with much more glide and smirk.

'I just fink we should consider it.'

Ned put one hand out to steady himself on a nearby wall.

'If you're so convinced it's a Meh-Teh, why didn't you say something to Momma K?'

66

Jenni flicked an icicle with her finger.

'Cos we're eliminating lines of enquiry, innit.'

'Ok look, head back to HQ without me. I need to find out how Rose got on with the elementals and go to the library. Then we can regroup and see where we are.'

'Are you gonna ask about Meh-Teh's?'

'If it comes up.'

'K.' Jenni hovered, looking like she wanted to say more, but nothing was forthcoming.

'Right. See you in a bit.' Ned turned and made his way gingerly down the street towards the palace.

'It could be a Meh-Teh,' grumbled Jenni as she ice-stomped back to HQ.

Chapter 10

Rose pulled on her gloves in deep contemplation. Whenever she'd spoken to the elementals before, they'd approached her. She wasn't entirely sure how to catch their attention, so with that in mind; she had gathered some things.

A blue bowl of water. A white candle. A smooth, naturally polished stone and a feather. She hoped they were all representational enough. They were in a blanket she could put outside on the snow. Squaring her shoulders, she opened the study door that led into the imperial gardens.

The cold took her breath away and pricked her eyes with tears. Her booted feet crunched in the snow as she walked out to lay down her altar of sorts. Rose had barely placed the candle down when it lit of its own accord. The feather began dancing. The rock rolled back and forth whilst droplets of water rained upside down out of the bowl.

'Thank you for coming.'

It's not us. The disembodied voice sounded warm and gravelly, solid and reassuring and yet a little stiff.

'I'm sorry?' Rose was fairly certain that was the element Earth who had spoken.

We did not bring this winter to you. We would not upset the balance so.

-unless you annoyed us- This voice has a definite sloshy quality. Water.

Well, yes, unless that.

~or ignored us~ This one crackled. Fire.

Rose grinned, unable to contain her excitement at getting to hear the elementals. Earth, Water and Fire anyway. Sure, they were just voices, but still. Not everyone could make the same claim.

Okay, that too.

-or claimed our brilliance as your own-

You done?

There was a definite tone followed by a slosh and flame flicker.

As I was saying, the extremes of winter are not us. But they need to be addressed. My brethren are frozen solid. We cannot breathe.

-My brethren are frozen solid. We cannot move-

~My brethren are cold. We have no warmth~

A bitterly cold wind whipped at Rose aggressively, finding a way through every chink in her clothing and chilling her to the bone. Clearly Air didn't speak but it too was freezing cold.

-you have a visitor-

Yes. He is here in Roshaven, and he needs your help.

'We'd be happy to help. They just need to come forward and speak to us. Or send a message.'

~pretty sure the weather is a message~

Rose blushed.

'Of course, I meant…'

We know.

-he's shy-

But he will speak to you. Look for him in quiet.

-and only a few of you, you don't want to scare him-

'Can you at least tell me what I'm looking for?'

The sprite knows.

'Wait, Jenni knows? I thought it wasn't fae?'

But the elementals had gone.

Whilst she had been prepared for half answers and

truth couched in trickery, Rose hadn't thought they would know what the problem was and just not told somebody.

'Maybe they told Jenni,' mused Rose, but that didn't explain why Jenni hadn't told everyone else.

Flexing her fingers against the bitter cold, Rose brought in her altar along with more snow than she meant to. Knocking her shoes on the door frame, she began making plans for what to do next when Ned strolled in.

'Oh, I was just going to find you.' Rose smiled at him.

Ned slowed his pace, gauging the room, wariness settling across his shoulders.

'According to the elementals, Jenni already knows what's bringing the winter,' said Rose.

'Really? Huh. Are you sure?' Ned was being cautious. Rose was likely to shoot down the mythical creature theory with no evidence.

'They wouldn't lie to me.'

'Elementals?'

Rose flushed.

'Okay, so yes, elementals are mischievous, but they're suffering in this weather too. I genuinely believe it's not them. And if they say Jenni knows, then we ought to talk to her. What if she doesn't know she knows?'

Ned scratched his head.

'Well… as a matter of fact, she mentioned something,' he said. 'About a winter fae myth. But she said she didn't know much about it. Called it a Meh-Teh. Do you think that's what the Elementals mean?'

'At the very least, we can look into it. It's not like we have any other leads, do we?' Rose arched an eyebrow at him.

'Not really,' admitted Ned. 'We've ruled out who it isn't. And Queen Anne is struggling. I'm going to send over some tea and biscuits with Joe, but I thought Ma Bowl could set up a regular food basket or something.'

'Of course. Just get one of the Highs to organise it,' Rose reminded him gently. Ned was still acclimatising to having a household chain of command and kept upsetting the staff by wandering into the kitchen to make himself a sandwich.

Ned quickly ran through his meeting with the mermaids and the Druids, updating Rose on the upswell of critters and the Holly and Ivy spat.

'I'm worried we're going to have a real fresh water supply issue soon,' he said. 'Everything is freezing. Joe had a report of frozen pipes and everyone on the corner of High Trees Mall where it meets Sixpence Lane had no water until they warmed the pipes up with some insulation. That might not work indefinitely though, especially if it gets colder. Some good news, Fingers has set up a Bug Hotel for all the insects finding the harsh weather too much. Sparks is there and apparently there's a caretaker specifically looking after hibernating bug needs.'

Rose smiled at the good news and repressed a sigh as the rest of Ned's list just reiterated the situation she was already fully aware of and desperately worried about. Staff had even been heard to mutter about taking their summer holidays six months in advance if the weather didn't break soon. Which would leave the palace massively shorthanded when all hands were needed on deck to keep things moving. Winter was all well and good, but not when it came brutally early and ten times worse than normal. Snow wasn't unheard of in

Roshaven, but they'd never had pile ups like this before. They weren't properly equipped to deal with it and so people were leaning towards panic, which would help no one. If there was a mass exodus, would any of them come back again? Rose realised she hadn't been listening to Ned, and he was looking at her expectantly.

'Hmm?'

'I said, after I've asked a High to sort out the donation to Queen Anne, I'm going to go ask Esme if she's got any ideas. Perhaps we've had a winter like this before.'

Rose nodded.

'And you could also ask her about winter fae myths. The elementals were pretty convinced that Jenni knew who it was and that we must approach *him* gently. So there's clearly a being of some kind involved. When you exhaust all other possibilities, what seems impossible is the only possibility. Winter should be just beginning, not turning us into an artic tundra.'

Ned gave her a quick hug.

'Okay. I'll see what I can find out, but I'll be heading back to HQ afterwards. The others have been making their own enquiries and I want to make sure we really have explored all possibilities.'

'Don't forget we have a status report council meeting first thing tomorrow. The Lower Circle is assessing our supplies and how much we've lost to frost. But I need action points, Ned. Not just facts.' She was addressing him as his empress now.

Ned nodded, snapping to attention, but the cheeky kiss he gave her was all for his wife.

Chapter 11

'Do you know what happens to books when they get cold?'

Ned shook his head mutely. From the moment he'd entered the Imperial Palace Library, Esme had swooped down on him and been berating him about the current temperature both outside and within the building.

'Would you like to go into a sub-zero room with no clothes on? Of course you wouldn't. What's harmful for the person is harmful for the book.' The librarian sniffed.

Ned was relieved he had not been expected to answer that question.

'And don't get me started on the potential damage caused by taking one of my cold books to a warmer environment to read it.' She took a sharp inhale through angrily pinched nostrils. 'Moisture!'

'Absolutely. That's why we're trying to uncover the reason for this much winter. All this snow will have to melt, eventually.' Doubt grew in Ned's mind as to how much damp proofing Roshaven had and whether it would be able to cope with large amounts of meltwater. He put that problem on the back burner for now. 'Do you have any books on... excessive winter? Have we historically experienced anything like this before?'

Ned watched Esme with hopeful eyes.

'Don't be ridiculous. I have volumes on ordinary winter, but this is straight out of a fae tale.' She sniffed in disapproval. 'We do not live in a fae tale, Mr Spinks.'

But Ned knew that they did live in a magical city

with a healthy fae community, a place where strange things happened, fae tale or not, so he bravely chose to push the issue.

'Can you show me where the winter-related fae tales are, then, please?' He wilted slightly under her fierce gaze but held his ground. There could be something useful in there.

Esme pursed her lips but said nothing as she did her weird inner librarian focus trick. A slip of paper appeared and floated down to the desk. Esme did not grab it like she usually did and present it to Ned. Nor did she give him directions on where to go. Instead, she sniffed loudly and glided to the other end of her desk, giving him the cold shoulder.

Ned shivered. It really did feel chillier than normal in the library and not just because of Esme's reaction to his question.

He picked the note up and read the information. 99 Z. So that must be at the far end of the library. Shouldn't be too much of a problem to find, thought Ned as he set off through the stacks.

After walking for almost ten minutes, Ned glanced again at the surrounding shelves. According to them, he was in Q. It was eerily quiet, and the light was a little dimmer. Shaking his head to dispel his imagination, Ned pushed on. A further ten minutes and he arrived in Z. His breath plumed out in front of him. It was definitely chillier here, and it was much, much darker than the library entrance. Ned wondered for a moment whether magic was forbidden in here. But he needed to be able to see the book titles, and he thought Esme would be more upset with him if he lit a match than if he spelled a small light.

Usually, casting magic was hard work for Ned. His

gift only ever seemed to work when his wife, Rose, Empress of Roshaven, was in mortal danger. Or when he needed to save Jenni or one of his team. Basically, whenever it was someone other than himself. But Jenni had been working with him on building up his casting, although they hadn't found much time lately for practising. He'd been so busy. They had expanded the range of pre-created spells stored in his spellcasters belt. Obviously there were limits to these things, but Ned did have a magical light orb available, so he accessed that spell and, with a little effort, was able to activate it. It would run off his innate magical ability - so as long as he didn't pass out, he'd have the light.

Ned wished he hadn't thought about passing out. The shadows loomed larger and the dark corners seemed to be edging closer to him. The shelf nearest to him had a number one carved into it, so all he had to do was continue on to find the number ninety-nine. That was all. Nothing to be afraid of. Only books here.

Wishing he'd brought Jenni with him, Ned carried on walking. His small light bobbed along by his shoulder, casting a small yet merry glow as the shadows continued to lengthen around them and Ned's breath fogged out further in front of him.

The shelf of fae tales was bathed in its own magical light. At least that's what Ned decided to call it. Each book was glowing faintly and in different colours. As he walked past them, they brightened, only to grow dim as he didn't choose them. He felt guilty for not looking at each one and his curiosity began itching wildly. Surely it wouldn't hurt to have a look through a few while he was here? Then he remembered what Jenni had told him about the lure of magical items. If you can't see its brain, then don't trust it. Ned was fairly certain she meant, if it wasn't a walking, talking person, don't trust it. But you never quite knew with Jenni. Luckily books didn't think for themselves. Right? Ned shook himself. He was letting the ambiance get to him. He knew better than that.

Thankfully it wasn't difficult to find the book he was looking for. There was a seasons shelf. Four books in total, each one creating a mini atmosphere that related to its time of year. Summer was pulsing a glorious heat that was especially warming in the current climate. There was the smell of barbecues and the tang of sea salt in the air. Ned fancied he could feel sand between his toes. He had to look down to make sure he wasn't standing on a beach. Looking away broke the spell.

A cursory glance at green things shooting and the strong perfume of flowers confirmed Spring whilst the rustle of crunchy leaves, and whiff of gunpowder made Autumn easy to spot. Winter was obvious, too. The book was solid ice. Ned figured that if he was looking for a fae tale about a magical winter that included a mythical monster that brought snow, then a book of ice would be just the thing.

However, he knew he couldn't just go and grab the ice. Joe had reported a snowcapade about one of Aggie's lads, who had made the rookie error of touching some icicles with his bare hand yesterday. After everyone had finished laughing at the poor lad stuck to the ice, it had taken a while to unstick him, carefully with warm water, and he'd had a nasty ice burn on his palm. Pulling on his woolly gloves, Ned gingerly reached out for the book.

Wishing he'd brought a bag, Ned held the ice book in his hands. It was heavy, but the actual book itself seemed to be a regular paper one. It just happened to be encased in thick ice. There was no way he was getting into it without some tools or heat. Although, mused Ned, heat would melt the ice, which would make it water and water and books didn't mix. Maybe Esme would have some ideas.

Ned turned to head back to the beginning of the library and tried to ignore the dark shapes that flitted in the shadows. Nothing to do with him. He'd found the book he was looking for. As he reached the stacks that had better lighting, he dismissed his little orb light.

It felt much quicker returning to the reception area. It also helped that it grew lighter and marginally warmer, although Esme was right. It was distinctly chilly within the library.

'Esme,' began Ned, then he noticed the sign on the desk.

Gone to lunch. Damages must be paid for.

Ned glanced guiltily around. He had no plans to damage the book but getting it out of its ice case might prove to be tricky. There was nothing saying he couldn't take the book with him, but he thought he'd better leave a message just in case. He didn't want a fine.

Turning over Esme's note, Ned grabbed a nearby handy pencil and wrote hastily, *Borrowing frozen book, will return as soon as. NS.*

He couldn't tell her the name of the book. The ice was too thick and distorting the cover. He was fairly certain she'd know who NS was. Either way, the cold was beginning to permeate his gloves, making his hands ache, and he still had to carry the book back to HQ, so he set off, confident he wasn't breaking any library rules. At least none that he'd been told about.

Chapter 12

Ned was seriously considering moving to warmer climes by the time he arrived at HQ. It was so cold, his goosebumps had goosebumps. Stamping his feet on entering The Noose to try to encourage some feeling back into them, he nodded at barman Reg who was engrossed in a pile of off-white material that was heaped upon his bar.

Ned hoped HQ would be warmer than the bar, but he didn't hold out much hope. Heat rises true, but it seemed to rise right out of the roof of The Noose, bypassing the headquarters office. At least Slinky would be there, a fishy smelling hot water bottle that could talk, happy to drape himself around shoulders upon request.

A babble of excited chatter flowed out of the office as Ned opened the door.

'What's going on?' he asked, smiling to see the Catchers excited about something that wasn't related to snow.

'S'Fred, e's got fermals.'

Ned hesitated. Usually he could translate Jenni easily but in this instance he wasn't sure if *fermals* were catching or not. Fortunately, Fred was quick to explain.

'Hello, Mr Spinks, Sir. Me Mam sent me over owing to the weather and the importance of keeping warm whilst on the beat. She said thieves won't stop thieving just because it's icy so she wanted to make sure you had every tool at your disposable. She's been knitting for days. Had to guess sizes due to not actually being here to measure you, but she wanted you to know that she's always been a good measure of a man. There's one for everyone. Except for Sparks, of course, on account of his wings, but she did send over a box of ends that will make a very snug bed for those of the bug persuasion.' Fred scratched his head. 'Although if you had enough of them, I expect they would make a snug bed for the persuasion of anyone, really.'

Ned tried to cling on to something in Fred's chatter.

'One of what for everyone?'

'I tole you, fermals.' Jenni held up a pair of very woolly trousers. The same off-white colour as the material Reg had been fascinated with.

'Oh, thermals.' The book in Ned's hands took that moment to remind him he was still holding essentially a freezing cold block of ice that was numbing most of his fingers whilst also providing sharp and tingly pins and needles. 'Just let me...' Ned looked around for a suitable place to put the book and decided to simply place it on his chair for now. It didn't look like it was going to melt anytime soon.

Fred held out a pair of woolly trousers to Ned, beaming with pride.

'I, uh, I'm very grateful for the thought, Fred. Very grateful. Not sure if they're regulation though – that colour is, er, noticeable.'

'Not if you was in the snow though, Boss.' Jenni smirked.

'Oh no, Miss Jenni. They're not for wearing on the outside. Oh no, no, no. You wear these on the inside. Like this.' Fred lifted the bottom of his trousers to reveal a woolly clad leg beneath.

'Ah. Excellent.' Ned was relieved and intrigued. Provided the wool wasn't too itchy, this would be perfect for snow patrol. 'Do pass my regards on to Mrs

Jones. She is a credit to the city. Very thoughtful.'

Fred's chest swelled alarmingly and his eyes glistened.

'Sir.' He managed to croak, it all becoming too much for him.

'Yes, well. Quite. If there's nothing else, we have a meeting. Catcher business, you understand.'

'I was just telling the others, Mr Spinks, Sir, my tried and tested methods of keeping blood flow moving when on cold patrol. You see, it's important to keep wiggling your toes. That's something that not everyone knows, you know. The toes. I was talking to our Malcolm about it and he said he didn't know it was the toes that were key. Once the toes go to sleep, that's it you're done for. Good boots go a long way, but I know you know all about those, Mr Spinks, Sir.' Fred looked longingly at Ned's Gunningtons.

Ned flexed his feet. They were good boots.

'Thank you for that, Fred. Toe wiggling. I'll make sure it gets around.'

'Oh, that's not all, Mr Spinks, Sir. Oh no, no, no. There's also ankle circles and calf raises. Best done on a doorstep, but it's a good idea to hold on to a doorframe in case. You remember what happened to Mrs Butcher's nephew's best friend's mum? Terrible business that. Terrible.' There was a short pause as Fred's gaze grew highly introspective. 'Hip swivels are next, followed by arm windmills. Very important those. Encourage blood to go all round, in and out. It is possible to do neck side to sides but I advise against circles as that encourages helmets to fall off.' Fred blushed. Everyone knew he had a great deal of experience with helmets falling off.

'Keep moving, gotcha. Thank you for bringing it to our attention, Fred. We appreciate it.'

Fred bobbed his head and twisted the bag, holding yet more woolly thermals in his hands.

'Er, before I go, Mr Spinks, Sir. Would it be possible, that is... can I... is it alright for me to, um...' Fred's voice dropped to a loud whisper. 'See the dragon?'

'Slinky!' called Ned and watched as Fred reverently sank to his knees to stroke the sea dragon, who purred in contentment, eyes lidded.

Glancing at the ice book, Ned saw that its enchantment still hadn't worn off, but a damp patch was growing in the middle of his chair. He had no idea why it was taking so long to defrost. Clearly, just being out of the library wasn't enough. Maybe there was a password that went with it that Esme should have given him. Or perhaps the colder and more snowbound it was outside, the more the book froze. He would have to keep an eye on it. It was still thickly encased in ice, but he didn't want a soggy chair and you never know, it might spontaneously start defrosting so Ned fetched a small bucket from the bathroom and balanced the book atop the opening, the theory being that the water would mostly melt into the bucket. One drop landed. It was going to take a while.

'Okay, thank you Fred. We've got important Catcher business to see to. Pass our regards on to your mum,' Ned said, smiling encouragingly and nodding towards the door as the young palace guard gave Slinky one last fuss.

The sea dragon wound himself around Ned's legs, just like a happy cat.

'Um, Slinky?' Ned spoke down to the dragon, who rippled his way up a leg and perched on his shoulder.

Yes, Ned?

'When I was talking to Pearl, we sort of touched on the topic of migration and, well, if they decide to leave for warmer waters, I think they'll take you with them. If you need to go, I mean.'

Ned was surprised how upset he felt at the thought of losing the little fella, but he had to consider what were his best interests, and a sea dragon might not survive a bitter winter.

Ah, that's very kind of you. And of the mermaids. I assure you I am adequately warm and quite happy with my surroundings for now. I will need to return to the ocean, but not yet.

The dragon tickled Ned's neck as he slinked around and travelled back down to the floor, retreating to the boiler cupboard where it was toasty warm.

'He's a clever young man, that Fred,' remarked Willow, making Ned blink in surprise.

'Clever?'

'Before you got here, he was telling us about his seed bank idea. Gathering seeds from all the plants in Roshaven and putting them in a safe place so that if any of the plants don't survive this winter, we can regrow from seed. It's a brilliant idea and I reckon I know of the perfect place we can store them. There's a WGI Emporium warehouse that has some spare space available to hire. It's looked after by a little old lady...'

Jenni interrupted.

'Yeah, I knows all about that place. Fingers 'as set up a bug 'otel and Sparks is there, all checked in and the like, but e's sparko now – 'e ain't gonna be back while this winter is 'ere. 'E ain't gonna get no more catches for now. Fingers done it to save all the bugs on account of it being way too cold for 'em all to survive. Bloody 'ero 'e is.'

Ned opened his mouth to speak but was interrupted by the office door banging open and Joe staggering in, trying to manhandle the door and hold on to an enormous piece of clay.

'Jenni! Get a load of this casting!' Joe was so excited he didn't register anyone else in the office. He reverently placed the clay on the floor. It had tons of tiny ice crystals around the edges. 'I couldn't get it out of my mind and we had the picture from Neeps, but this is so much cooler than a picture. Don't you think?'

'Wossat?' asked Jenni, her brain trying to take in the shape of the clay.

'It's a giant footprint! So awesome, right?'

'Why is there a giant foot in my office?' asked Ned, feeling like events were running away from him.

There was a clamour as Joe tried to tell Ned about how he fell into a massive footprint and Willow tried to explain that she'd gone with him to make the cast but had come back before Joe because it was too cold standing out there waiting for the clay to set and really Joe should've told her it was done and she would've come and helped him get it back to the office and then Jenni chimed in saying it could be a Meh-Teh footprint. But they kept talking at the same time, speaking over each other, apologising and immediately interrupting again.

'Hey!' yelled Ned, the backs of his ears flushing. He didn't like yelling. He knew who had brought the clay foot into the office, and now he wanted to know why it had been brought in. 'Joe, explain.'

'Well, Boss, I went to see Neeps, but she didn't have any maps or anything about the mountain. She did tell me it's called Mount Firn, but that's all she had. But she did give me this.' And he handed Ned a picture of the very large footprint. 'That's the footprint I tripped in on my way back to the office. I couldn't stop thinking about the thing and then Willow reminded me about the modelling clay we had left over from the mould making training course we did with Mrs Wicket so I figured, why not take a mould and go from there. I thought it might be useful evidence. I've only just arrived back at the office with it because it took me a while to manhandle it through The Noose. Obviously I didn't want to break it.' He patted the clay foot reverently. 'If you measure the thing, it's fifteen inches, give or take! That makes the owner about eight and a half feet. That's a big guy.'

'Are you saying something out there is making these footprints?' Ned was trying to get his head around the sheer size.

'Well, footprint. This was the only one I've seen. But it could be that mythical monster Jenni said about this morning, couldn't it?'

Ned frowned.

'One footprint on its own, in the middle of the snow?' Ned wanted to think about it for a bit. The elementals had told Rose that Jenni knew what had brought the snow to the city and a giant footprint might well belong to a mythical monster. He tried to marshal his thoughts. 'Excellent job with the casting. You clearly listened to Mrs Wicket's instructions and retained everything. Great work.'

Joe gave Ned a grin of appreciation.

'What do you think made it?' asked Joe.

Ned puffed out his cheeks. He wasn't sure, but a massive footprint was pretty hard to ignore.

'If we're confident this isn't a hoax of some kind, then the elementals said Jenni knew what was bringing the winter to Roshaven and…' Ned looked at Jenni. 'You were talking about a creature…'

'Yeah, but I ain't a fousand per cent or nuffink. S'just wot I fink it might be.'

Ned could tell Jenni was trying hard to not be too pleased at being right.

'And what is it again you think it might be?' he asked.

'A Meh-Teh.'

'A Meh-Teh?'

'Yeah, a Meh-Teh. S'like ten ana 'alf feet tall, all shaggy wiv tusks and claws and fangs and stuff.'

'I thought you said nobody had ever seen one before?' asked Joe, on the edge of his seat in barely concealed excitement.

'Yeah, well, there's always rumours, ain't there?'

'The evidence is starting to suggest that you might be right,' said Ned. 'No one else is owning up to being responsible for the weather. I admit, it's a little odd that nobody has reported seeing an eight and–'

'Ten,' interrupted Jenni. 'Cording to the legend.'

'Sorry, ten and a half foot monster roaming the streets and I'm surprised that we don't have more footprints reported. What else do we know about them?'

Ned eyed the ice book that was dripping ever so slowly into the bucket below. It was annoying that it hadn't defrosted enough to open it yet.

'Jenni?'

'Er… like I said afore, they're a miff. Nobodys seed one that I'm aware of, but I ain't never been to the mountain or nuffink. Momma K ain't seed one neiver. Which is probably why she never said it was one. Probably forgot they exist or summink. The cold getting to 'er.' She scratched her head as she thought about it.

'Um, I dunno really. They live in the mountain and they like snow. S'all I know. Sorry, Boss.'

Ned tried to hide his disappointment. Usually Jenni, or her mum, were the fount of all knowledge for unexplained things happening in Roshaven, especially when they had some kind of magical or mystical element. He turned his attention back to the clay foot.

'Um, what are you going to do with this now, Joe? It can't stay in the middle of the office floor.'

'I'll store it down the side of my filing cabinet, Boss. Shouldn't get in the way. I'd like to keep it, if that's alright.'

Ned rolled his eyes inwardly.

'Yes, okay, fine. As long as it's not in the way.'

Joe did his best to pull the clay foot towards his corner of the office but was having some difficulty. Willow took pity on him and generated some strong vines to wrap around the huge footprint and assist with the relocation. Ned decided to get back to the enquiries Catchers had made earlier that day, the problem of the existence of a Meh-Teh put to one side for now and asked his team for their reports.

After she'd given her update, Willow was trembling, losing several handfuls of leaves in the process. Ned leaned over to pat Willow's gnarly shoulder encouragingly.

'Don't worry. You and me will go talk to Holly and Ivy. Knock some sense into them.'

Some of Willow's tendril-like hair snaked over Ned's hand, binding it briefly as she flashed him a huge, green-toothed smile.

'Oh, thanks Boss. They'll listen to you.'

Privately, Ned didn't think they would do anything of the kind and the vegetation would, in fact, listen entirely to Willow, but he didn't say anything.

'And Joe, well done on finding out what the mountain is called, but we need a bit more information that just the name. Looks like we'll have to ask Esme after all. I suggest you meet me at the Palace first thing in the morning. I'll get you into the Library researching before I have my council meeting. Then we'll go do our bit, Willow.' Ned tried to ignore Joe bobbing up and down in excitement. Anyone would think the lad had never seen a book before.

'Also, Joe, can you organise some coal to be sent over to Queen Anne please and set up a monthly contribution to the BWO.' Ned paused to see if Joe knew what the initials stood for but he was looking up expectantly, having flipped open his pocketbook and scribbled down notes. 'Right. Well, send some tea and biscuits. I've asked Ma Bowl to send a regular food parcel. Queen Anne also finally agreed to sign our agreement, so if you can get that squared away today, that will be good.' Ned declined to add, *before she changes her mind.* Having access to the Beggar Network was a useful tool in the Thief-Catcher arsenal. 'Kendra's going to try to keep the winter rituals happening, but it'll probably be touch and go.'

Jenni was studying the foot picture intently.

'Wot did the elementals say, Boss?' she asked.

'Ah, well. They said you knew what was causing the winter. And to search for *him* carefully. But other than a weird footprint in the snow, we haven't got much to go on, have we? We don't know how to find this mythical creature.'

'What about the book, Boss?' Joe nodded towards the frozen tome.

'That is from the fae-tale section of the library. It's

Winter or at least covers wintery fae-tales. We might be able to discover how to find this Meh-Teh. But obviously we need to wait for the book to defrost some more before we can open it.'

'I'll watch the book, Boss. Let you know if anything happens. I was planning to stay here tonight anyway,' said Willow. The freezing temperatures had made her usual orchard abode a less than cosy place to spend the night, especially as the fruit trees had all gone into hibernation and the barks were slick with ice. Tree-nymphs could survive normal winters, but the excesses Roshaven was experiencing were too much for Willow to handle all night long.

'OK, good. And Joe – you'll sort that paperwork, right?' asked Ned, giving Joe a thumbs up at his nod.

Ned began wrapping himself up to face the cold walk home.

'I'll come wiv you, Boss,' said Jenni. Ned's old house on Wide Street was on the way to the Palace. They just had to walk down Palace Lane and it was the first street on the left, although the narrow, wonky house was at the far end.

With a final goodbye to the others, Ned and Jenni left HQ and began the treacherous journey home.

Chapter 13

'Bin finking about it.'

Jenni's declaration put Ned on the back foot as well as the ice. There were many things she could have been thinking about. He hedged his bets.

'And?'

'I'm definitely gonna do it.'

It wasn't the illuminating answer Ned had been hoping for. What exactly was it that Jenni was going to do?

'Er…' Ned groped for inspiration. 'What's the plan, then?'

'Gonna do wot you said, innit.'

Ned tried to reign in the confusion that was no doubt plastered all over his face and went with the classic save; smile and nod.

'Asked Neeps to run an ad for a 'ousemate so I can see wots wot.'

'Oh, right.' Ned grinned at her, genuinely chuffed to bits that she'd taken his advice for once.

'Yeah, I was chatting wiv Willow, and she was all like, it ain't good for a person to lives on their own and that. I said wot about you, yor all in the orchard on yor tod and she was like that's different. A tree nymph's gotta have space to stretch out 'er roots. Then she s'plained 'ow she's never really on 'er own cos of the network eggsetra.'

Ned knew this was Jenni's way of saying thank you, even though she just made out that Willow was the only person who had convinced her.

'Do you think you'll get much interest?' he asked.

'Dunno. I went to see Neeps afta we spoke to Pearl and that. Just tole 'er to say turn up at the 'ouse at two tomorrow and I'll 'ave a chat wiv 'em. Could be that no-one wants to live wiv me.' She twiddled with one of the buttons on her coat.

'Nonsense. I can't imagine a better housemate,' Ned smiled, pushing down a mini surge of homesickness at not living with Jenni anymore. 'I will, er, still have my room, right?'

'Yeah, course. It's yor 'ouse.'

Relieved, Ned nodded.

'Do you want any help – vetting the potential housemates I mean?'

'Nah, I got it. Ain't you got vegetation to sort out?'

Ned scowled. He really wasn't looking forward to dealing with the Holly and the Ivy. He wasn't sure they were willing to listen to him, even with Willow in tow, and from the sounds of things, their feud had been ongoing on for years. They arrived at the narrow house he used to call home. Ned had ended up walking with Jenni all the way. He waited while she fumbled the key with stiff fingers and got the door open.

'Right, I'd better get going, I suppose. Have a good evening,' he said.

'Sames to you.' Jenni gave a little wave and shut the door behind her.

Ned was glad he would still have his room there, he found that he didn't feel as put out as he thought he might at the idea of someone else living in his house. Jenni needed company. She was, after all, a sprite, and they usually lived in large groups in the fae realm. Jenni's insistence on independence from spritedom was unusual, but Ned had always considered it a unique quirk. There really wasn't anyone quite like Jenni. But living on her own hadn't done her any favours. Especially after all that business with her dad and the Sea Witch. Ned had been seriously worried about her for a while. A housemate would be good for her. And if nothing else, at least they would wash the dishes in the sink.

Chapter 14

The next morning saw a bleary-eyed Ned stamping his feet and rubbing his hands together as he waited for Joe to arrive. He hadn't slept well the night before. Rose tossing and turning hadn't helped. They were both worried about Roshaven. For one, it had been freezing cold and even using four bed warmers had done little to generate heat in the oversized imperial bedroom. The howling wind hadn't exactly helped to send him to sleep as it screamed round and round the palace windows, rattling all the casements and causing candles to flicker and blow out. Sounds he wasn't used to. And the piles of snow outside had shifted shape. Ned guessed that the wind was doing that. He knew for sure it was the Jacks that had left the pretty patterns etched across all the windows.

Joe appeared, slipping and sliding his way through the palace gates and across the courtyard. Ned should have thought about it and put some salt down. Just as he had the idea, two members of palace staff began scattering at will.

'Sorry Boss. Took me a little while to get through all the snow. Some huge drifts out there. I dropped off the paperwork to Queen Anne. Did a few welfare checks on the way, just in case. I don't want anyone to run into trouble and not be able to get any help.'

'Quite right, good thinking.' Ned made a mental note to ask Rose for some extra bodies to go out and check up on people, especially those unable to dig themselves out.

'Willow says the ice book is still encased. It's dripping into the bucket, but at a rate of one to two drops an hour. She didn't think she could see any significant melt. Slinky says the book is magically resisting the thaw and would be happy to add some flaming encouragement, but I told him to wait until you said. It being your book. That you took. From the Library.'

Ned felt his stomach squirm. He had forgotten to check in with Esme about the book. But that being said, he hadn't received any recriminatory notes either.

'I am so excited about seeing the Library. Do you think I'll be allowed to take a book out? Can I join? Or do you have to be a member of the imperial family to use the Imperial Library? Did you know that it's the second biggest Library in Efrana?'

'I wouldn't mention that to Esme if I were you,' said Ned as they ambled up the palace corridors towards the double doors that Joe was so excited to walk through. He put on his best smile before they walked through, ready to deal with the wrath of Esme.

'Fill this in.'

It was like she had been waiting for him to come back. Esme stood to one side of Ned, thrusting an index card and pen in his face. It read *Book of Ice, borrowed by* _____ *on* _____. *To be returned within 2 weeks.* Hastily, he scribbled in his name and yesterday's date. Esme snatched them from him as soon as he'd finished.

'Miss Esme, it is an honour.' Joe gave a very impressive formal bow to the stern librarian who, Ned was shocked to see, twitched a very small smile.

'You are welcome, young man. I trust you will abide by the laws of the Library and do your duty to uphold the sanctity of knowledge.'

'I do,' breathed Joe, still bent low.

'You never asked me to do those things,' remarked Ned. He was met with a derisive sniff. 'We've come to find out about the mountain.'

'There are over a million mountains in Efrana, with five major mountain ranges. You are going to have to be a touch more specific with your knowledge request.'

Joe leapt to Ned's rescue.

'We want to know more about the mountain to the North, behind Roshaven. Mount Firn. Any inhabitants, nearby towns or villages and whether it's snowy all the time.'

Ned nodded and watched as Esme went into her odd, vacant librarian trance.

'What's happening?' whispered Joe.

'She's finding the shelf we need. In a minute, a piece of paper will appear out of nowhere with the location details.'

Joe frowned, then gaped as the paper did indeed magically materialise. He reached out to catch it as it gently floated down.

'It says M17,' he said with more than a hint of awe.

'Excellent. Thank you, Esme,' said Ned but the librarian had already bustled off to her desk and whatever important shelving and classification lay waiting for her.

'Where do we go, Boss?'

'We head for M. The stacks are labelled alphabetically, so we'll need to travel just over half way through the Library. Just follow the letters.'

Ned strode off confidently, this being the third time he'd ventured within the mysterious structure. He wasn't sure if the Library actually had any magical powers, but it seemed to him highly unlikely that so many books collected in one place didn't exert some kind of powerful force.

'This is so exciting! I can't wait to tell Willow all about it.' Joe let out excited squeaks as they ventured further in, commenting randomly at stack junctions and reading aloud the odd book title that caught his eye. He was practically hopping foot to foot when they made it to M.

'Right, now we need to look for…'

'Seventeen. Found it, Boss!' Joe practically vibrated as he stood next to the right shelf. 'What do we do now? Take them all?'

'No, let's read the covers and find the ones most likely to help. Then there should be a little alcove nearby with a reading table and chairs. We can take the books there and start looking for the information we need.'

'Gotcha.'

M17 turned out to share its shelf with M18. Ned concluded that the number seventeen related to Mount Firn alone and that Joe's initial idea of taking all the books wasn't actually such a daft one. Between them, they carried the twenty odd books along the row for about five minutes before a merrily lit alcove appeared.

'This will do. Start looking and let me know if you find anything.' Ned eased himself into one of the chairs, pleased to discover that it was actually pretty comfortable, and pulled the first book towards him. *The fauna and flora of Mount Firn.*

The two of them sat in focused quiet as they perused the various books. Unfortunately, Joe was one of those readers. His whispered voice intermittently rose and fell within Ned's hearing as he read his way through the chapter headings and it was beginning to grate. Ned shifted and tried to concentrate. The book he had now seemed to be focusing on the types of rock the mountain was made of. Ned sighed. Rock was rock unless it was trollish and trying to eat you.

'Ah! Aha! I've found something. Here look.' Joe turned his book to Ned and pointed to the bottom paragraph, which read:

It is of the opinion of this author that the search for such mythical creatures as the Meh-Teh is a complete waste of time, funds and resources. Claims from the villagers who dwell at the foot of Mount Firn are utterly unsubstantiated. Merely a money-making scheme in an attempt to drive tourism to their poverty inclined domiciles. Blyz should be blacklisted as a pit of lies and deceit.

Ned turned the book over to find out who the author was.

'Hmm, old Wendlebury certainly didn't like Blyz, did he? Sounds like he didn't have much luck trying to find the Meh-Teh. Not sure how helpful this is, though.' He looked up at Joe to see the lad positively thrumming with excitement.

'It's proof that these villagers have seen the Meh-Teh. Or at least their ancestors have.' He clasped his hands together in a reverent gesture. 'We have to mount an expedition. Ha! Mount. We've got to go to Blyz, Boss. It's a lead.'

Ned scowled. To be fair to Joe, they had investigated other leads way more tenuous than this one, but... a respected mountaineer categorically debunking the myth wasn't exactly the positive information he had been hoping to find. Although he supposed the magical frozen book was more likely to have details on mythical creatures. A bell tolled to mark the hour and Ned shot up. He would be late to the council meeting if he didn't leave now.

'Joe, check out the books that mention Blyz and for gods' sake return the others to the shelf before you do that. Esme seems to like you. I'm sure she'll allow you to take them. If she causes you any trouble, pull the Thief-Catchers card. I'll meet you back at HQ after this council meeting. Tell Willow I'll pick her up to go to the woods.' Ned called out the last instructions as he hurried out of the stacks towards the library's exit. He really didn't want to be late.

Chapter 15

Rose pinched the bridge of her nose. How could frozen water cause so many problems?

'The issue is clearing the streets.'

'No, the real issue is where we're going to get enough salt from to melt the ice.'

'Pft, ice. You can't even see the ice. There's too much snow!'

She cleared her throat.

'Gentlemen.'

It was enough for the two Highs to stop staring daggers at one another. Rose wasted no time in getting right to the point. On taking up the imperial mantle, the first thing she'd abolished were the meetings to plan having a meeting to regroup and schedule a meeting. She preferred to just get things done.

'What we need are solutions. The Lower Circle is preparing a report on current supplies, what we are short on and how much we've lost to frost. Once we have that, we can figure out how to get what we're running out of. The snow continues to fall and is beginning to pile up alarmingly, so clearance is going to be a top priority. I propose that we close the school. I understand from Miss Tipps that they can't keep the building warm, and attendance is spotty at best due to the weather. Next, we need to assign volunteers to work with the Palace Guard shovelling main walkways and access to houses. This is particularly important for the old and vulnerable. Sister Eustacia has sent through her report of those individuals that may be struggling more than others. There has been a rise in snow-related injuries, so please make sure the Druids get everything they need.' Rose spoke as calmly as she could, doing her best to leave her rising panic out of her voice.

'When you say *volunteers*?' The High Right arched an eyebrow.

'I mean anyone fit enough to wield a shovel.'

'There will be complaints,' replied the High.

'Tell them they will be paid in coal.'

'Excuse me, your eminence, but even if you can get the people to help er... the people, where will the extra shovels and extra coal come from?' The High Left was holding a sheaf of paper that Rose knew held lists of supplies and costs. One list was considerably longer than the other.

'The dwarfs have generously offered to assist in our time of need.'

'Because?' The High Left looked quizzical.

Rose suppressed a sigh.

'I agreed to their suggestions that a memorial be raised in Tea Cake Alley,' she said.

Both the Highs blanched.

'But what about the trolls? They'll never agree to it.' The High Right's voice trembled.

'Actually, the trolls have agreed to join the snow shovelling teams and lend their brute strength so long as they also get a memorial in Tea Cake Alley.' Rose tried not to smile. 'I have agreed to one at either end of the street.'

The High Right relaxed, but the High Left raised a finger.

'The cost of two monuments could be...'

'They agreed to fund their own monuments and stay within size guidelines,' said Rose. She took pity on the

High's bewilderment at having got the trolls and dwarves to agree to help the city and do so out of their own pockets. 'Momma K oversaw negotiations via an extremely persuasive negotiator. She is staying firmly in her realm for now.'

Both High shoulders relaxed and knowing nods replaced their frowns.

Rose suppressed another sigh. There was no doubt that having Momma K on her side was useful, but sometimes she wished she didn't have to rely on the Fae Queen so heavily when it came to fae issues. A problem for some other time.

'Fingers has been in touch with Salzwytch who have large salt mines and struck a deal for an emergency ongoing delivery of salt.' Rose braced herself for a High retort.

'Why is he not at this council meeting?' asked the High Left with a scowl.

This was something of a sore point between the Highs and Jimmy Fingers, the Lower Circle. He was excellent at his job, just as Ned had promised Rose he would be, but he wasn't so keen on the rigidity of reporting to the Imperial Council claiming his odd working hours made it impossible for him to attend all the meetings. Rose hadn't pressed the issue when the level of dock crime had fallen dramatically and resisted the High's insistence at his attendance after she'd seen the improvements in trade in such a short time. Upon hearing about his creation of the bug hotel to save the insects of Roshaven, Fingers had climbed even further in her estimations. He also reported promptly, just not always in person.

'The Lower Circle assures me he will be in attendance at our next council meeting.'

'What about the cost of this extra salt? He hasn't cleared it with me and the Imperial accounts.' The High Left's nostrils flared. 'He can't just spend money willy-nilly.'

'I am confident that Fingers has struck us a good deal for the salt.' Rose knew for a fact that it was a great deal but didn't want to steal Jimmy's thunder when he made the report to the Highs. And he had promised that he would attend the next council meeting. Maybe she would have to have a word with Ned about it. She frowned. Where was he?

'We are left with what to do when the snow melts,' she continued.

'If the snow ever melts,' muttered the High Right, flushing when he realised the others had heard him.

'Well, there is that, too. As it continues to snow and pile up, and with the new teams working to clear paths – all of that accumulation needs to go somewhere. We can't just build snow tunnels for people to walk around in.'

Rose and the two Highs fell silent as they each considered what a snow tunnel might look like. Ned chose that moment to bang open the door and sheepishly join them. He tried not to knock over any water glasses or make too much noise, moving his chair in and out. He wasn't entirely successful.

'Apologies, I was in the Library looking for a lead. What did I miss?' he asked, deftly helping himself to a slice of Ma Bowl's lemon drizzle cake before it got cleared away. He decided to listen to the points on the agenda before he brought up the Meh-Teh and the potential expedition.

'We were just discussing what to do when the snow melts,' replied Rose. 'Snow tunnels were briefly mooted.'

'But it'll be too risky,' said the High Right. 'We have enough weather-related accidents as it is. We don't want to be digging people out of collapsed snow tunnels.'

'Can't we put the shovelled snow in the lake?' asked the High Left.

'Of course we can't!' retorted the Right. 'It's frozen solid.'

'The harbour then,' said the Left, clinging to his idea.

'Not possible.' Rose reached for a shortbread biscuit. 'When Ned spoke to the mermaids, they warned against throwing snow into the sea. It's not just frozen water anymore – it's full of dirt, rubbish, salt, sand and goodness knows what else. It will pollute the water and harm the animals that live there, not to mention the mermaids.'

'I thought they were leaving?' queried the High Left.

'No plans yet. And maintaining good relations with the mermaids is crucial for a harmonious harbour,' replied Ned.

The Highs nodded, and they all fell silent again.

'What if we made snow piles?' asked the High Right.

'Isn't that exactly what the shovellers will be doing?' The High Left cast a withering look at his fellow official.

Rose thought the pair of them were bickering more than usual but decided to put it down to the cold weather. Perhaps it was making their joints ache. Neither one was backwards about coming forwards, so if there was a serious problem, no doubt she would hear about it soon.

'No, I mean yes, they will be shovelling but, if we get them to make piles in particular places, we can form snow dumps near drains and encourage natural melt to occur where drainage is designed to take water away.' The High Right smirked back at his counterpart.

Rose smiled in agreement.

'That way, the extra water will go through the Sieve and the natural waterways won't get full of all the rubbish the mermaids were worrying about,' she added.

The Sieve was the filtration system implemented by Rose's grandfather around the city. It was made up of very fine nets that caught detritus from the city's sewers as water passed through on its way back to the ocean. Roshaven was very proud of its sewer system and looking after the nets was a solid source of employment. Water's always going to flow.

'What if the piles get too big?' asked Ned. 'We'll have to be very strategic about where we dump all this snow. We don't want to cause more of a problem than we've already got. And has anyone thought about how to deal with the damp? After the cold wet snow has gone. Black mould is a silent killer, you know.'

'Let's overlay a street map with the sewer grates and pick out some areas that will work for the snow piles. The market place will do for a start. No one is trading with all this bad weather and there's an excellent drainage system in the middle because of the animal trade.' Rose felt like they were getting there, slowly but surely. She would conquer this winter, one snowball at a time. 'We can also get some of the snow shovellers to take on melting duties. But let's make sure we give that to the most responsible people – we don't want everyone walking around with a fire torch.'

'Perhaps that sort of thing should be done out of

hours, so to speak. We don't want to encourage the local population to follow suit. I don't think the put-out wagon will be able to traverse the city all that well in this snow. Last thing we want is an out-of-control blaze.' Ned made a note on the paperwork in front of him. Rose always made sure she brought him an extra set, as he always forgot. 'I can think of a few responsible people among the Palace Guard.'

'Perhaps not Fred.' Rose flushed a little at mentioning names. As much as she liked the earnest palace guard, he was well known to be more accident prone than the average person.

'No, perhaps not.' The High Right smiled in agreement.

'And the dampness, well…' Rose had to think about that one. 'I guess we could ask Neeps to run a piece on how to air your home in *The Daily Blag*. I think most people know ventilation is key. If they keep all their doors and windows closed and have a fire going all the time, water is going to build up inside.'

Ned nodded along with the Highs. That explained why the palace windows were opened so regularly. He probably ought to do the same with HQ.

'What about the lake?' asked the High Left.

'What about it? It's frozen solid,' replied Ned, wondering why the High was bringing up the topic again.

'Quite. Has anyone thought to check on Nellie? And whether residents are being sensible at the temptation of frozen ice?'

'Hmm, good point. Willow and I are headed to the woods after this meeting, to speak with the Holly and the Ivy, get to the bottom of whatever that is. We can swing by the lake afterwards and carry out a welfare check.

She'll talk to Willow even if she won't talk to anyone else,' said Ned.

Nellie, known locally as Piss-Eyed Nellie, was a water sprite who lived in, and cleaned, the lake fed by the River Whine. She filtered the water through her facial orifices leading to the unfortunate nickname.

'There's not much we can do to stop people walking on the ice, but perhaps Jenni will have a few ideas. A keep-away spell or something.' Rose refused to suggest that Momma K could probably stop people from going on the ice. She already felt indebted to the Fae Queen for the shovels and coal agreement, plus the negotiations between the trolls and dwarves. Besides, according to Ned, Momma K was suffering herself from this wretched winter.

'How are you going to discover the reason behind this plant fight?' The High Left asked Ned. 'And what about all these animals? One of the maids was attacked by a creature shooting spines.'

'That's a porcupine, and it was just protecting itself,' replied Ned. 'We've got deer and squirrels too, but I'm sure once we've sorted out the Holly and the Ivy, they can be encouraged to return home. Something sparked the argument between the two plants. We'll find out what it was and offer some solutions. Maybe it all boils down to being exceptionally cold.'

'It's the middle of winter!' exploded the High Left. 'You can't very well expect sunshine and rainbows.'

'I know that!' snapped Ned, momentarily losing his cool. 'But Willow says The Vine is in danger of collapsing. The vegetation can't cope with this much winter so quickly and so heavily. Usually they ease into it, have time to go into safe hibernation and hunker down. This winter isn't exactly what we are used to.'

105

It had grown darker outside as heavy snow clouds gathered and the study took on a chilly edge. Not just to do with the weather.

'There's been a sighting. A footing actually.' Ned cleared his throat, trying to decide exactly how he was going to explain a Meh-Teh to the Highs.

'A footing? What's that?' The High Right's pen hovered over his paperwork.

'Um, we believe it could be the footprint of a... well, a Meh-Teh. Come down from Mount Firn most likely and brought the weather with it. Maybe.'

Ned's explanation was met with a chilly silence. Only part of that was down to the cool temperature within the room.

'A what?' spluttered the High Left.

The High Right had not yet made any notes.

'A Meh-Teh,' replied Rose. 'A somewhat mythical creature due to the limited number of sightings but my sources tell me it could be a potential source of this harsh weather we've been experiencing so worth investigating, don't you agree?'

There was a pause. The Highs didn't like to not agree with the Empress. She was the Empress. But this was also a myth. You can't just expect a man to accept something at face value. Especially when there was no proof in front of their noses. Begrudgingly, they both nodded.

'Excellent. Ned, you will pursue that line of enquiry. Now, is there any other business?' asked Rose.

'I suppose nothing can be done about the bothersome blue blobs?' asked a High.

It took Rose and Ned a moment, then realisation dawned on both their faces. She nodded for Ned to take this one.

'Jacks or Jack Frosts. They're harmless, really. Just ice fae drawn by the extremes of weather. The advice is to compliment their work and try not to swat them.'

Although the Highs muttered at that they confirmed there was no further business so Rose adjourned the council meeting, making a third mental note to encourage Fingers strongly to attend the next one and re-emphasise that his continual no show was being disrespectful to the empire. She gratefully let the Highs bustle out, both of them intent on sorting out the teams of volunteers needed to clear the snow. She got Ned to add another log to the study fire, grateful at the thoughtful supply stacked nearby that meant they didn't have to call for a member of staff. Her mind wandered to Griff, who had left on his fact-finding mission to Fidelia a few days ago, before the weather took a further turn for the worse. She hoped he would return soon. She valued his insight.

'You okay?' asked Ned, pulling his wife in for a hug. 'Thanks for the support re the MT.'

'Of course, but…' Rose bit her lip. 'What if it is a Meh-Teh? What can it possibly want in Roshaven?'

Ned shrugged. He didn't know either.

'Hopefully, it's some kind of prank footprint. Although why anyone would want to do that, I don't know.' She sighed, shoulders slumping a little. 'I'm just worried about this weather. I know we can get through it. But I want to make sure we haven't forgotten anything.' Rose looked up at him. 'Can you speak to Fingers? He really needs to make it to the next council meeting.' She pushed herself away from Ned to pace in front of the fireplace. 'I know he's good at his job. He's proved that. But he needs the backing of the Highs as well. He just needs to bend the knee a little.'

'I will speak to him. I want him to help me discourage the hunters.'

'Hunters?' Rose's eyebrows shot up in alarm.

'It's just a group of over eager lads trying to hunt the deer that have entered the city. It's all to do with the mistletoe. Remember, I did mention it.'

'Yes, yes. I remember now. Okay – well pass the message on and I'll see you later? Do you think Willow will be able to de thorn the Holly and Ivy situation?' asked Rose.

'Oh, I have complete confidence in her.'

Rose recognised that tone. He wasn't sure at all.

Chapter 16

Ned could tell Willow was agitated. Her leaves were trembling and blossoms were flash blooming.

'It'll be alright. They'll listen to you. You have the full weight of the Imperial crown behind you, plus Thief-Catcher jurisdiction. Rose wants you to handle this as her trusted and valued plant representative.' He tried to sound as reassuring as possible as they walked past the outskirts of Roshaven and into the woods. He was a little nervous about what they would be up against.

As they entered the treeline where the city faded and nature took over, Ned was relieved to see Willow relax at being in comfortable surroundings. Willow's bark rippled, and several blossoms rapidly appeared and disappeared. She started talking about the entities.

'Um, as you probably already know, the Holly and the Ivy originally began as a copse but have been growing together harmoniously in the woods on the outskirts of Roshaven for years, encouraging others to put down roots and branch out. They've been there for such a long time, they've developed sentient representation. A type of dryad if you like.'

Ned had never actually seen the Holly and the Ivy but most people were aware of their existence. Taking heart from her surroundings, Willow continued talking.

'The issue seems to be that the Holly is getting more attention, especially after the popularity of the song about them both.'

'It's a catchy little ditty, isn't it?' Ned had heard several renditions already as they grew closer to Yule

Eve.

'Yes, but Ivy says they should have corresponding verses talking about their flowers, berries and occasional poisonous touch. I think it's a case of anything one can do, the other can do better.'

'Seems reasonable enough. I'm sure the bards will write a verse in for them. Why has this musical tiff caused such a problem with the deer?'

Willow's skin hardened momentarily, looking like highly polished wood before relaxing again, whilst extra tendrils of her willow tree hair gathered around her, protecting her space.

'When the Holly and the Ivy aren't fighting, they keep an eye on the parasitic plants, like mistletoe, and make sure it doesn't take over too much. Unfortunately, things have got out of hand, the mistletoe has gone crazy and there's masses of the stuff growing all over the place. You might think that's not a big problem, just more greenery, but it's a real issue. The parasites choke the natural plants, taking their nutrients, blocking their access to sunlight and, worst-case scenario, begin to kill off species.' Willow took a shaky breath, thorns pulsing in and out of her bark.

'The massive amounts of growth is probably thanks to a magical boost as a result of the Holly and Ivy argument, but what if it doesn't stop? We could lose great swathes of diversity. And the knock on effect on the food chain doesn't bear thinking about. There are so many creatures, big and small, that rely on the variation of foliage in the woods. Take that away and what are those creatures going to do? Starve. They'll starve. Look at the deer. They don't eat mistletoe, so they will move to graze somewhere else, meaning the plants will have lost a crucial pollinator and fertiliser. If the whole woods are full of mistletoe, the deer will come into Roshaven search of food. Eating vegetable patches and thatched roofs. Angry people might decide to start hunting.'

Ned decided against telling Willow about the hunters. All of her leaves were fluttering in agitation, as it was. Ned wanted to pat her shoulder and tell her it was going to be alright, but her arms were so prickly there didn't seem to be a clear spot.

There was a rustle to the left. Then a rustle to the right. Willow stopped walking so abruptly, Ned almost crashed into her. They were standing in a small clearing.

'We're here,' she said quietly, motioning Ned to stop moving. They both stood still, barely breathing, ears twitching at the rustling noises coming from either side of them. A young doe trotted out of the bushes to Ned's left, making him jump and his heart leap into his mouth. It eyed the pair of them nervously before springing away, back into the safety of thicker woods. Ned felt something move on his shoulder and was beyond relieved to find it was several of Willow's tendrils that she'd obviously sent over to reassure him.

Two figures entered the clearing, one from each side. They came alone. The Holly was resplendent in dark waxy green with large, pointed spikes jutting out from their elbows and knees. Whilst humanoid-ish in shape, its limbs were very definitely concave in design, like a holly leaf. Bright red berries adorned their entire being and a delicate, yet thorny crown sat atop a head full of tiny holly leaves. The Ivy was a paler green with delicate cream veins traversing its skin. Hands, feet and head were shaped in the classic ivy leaf configuration and tiny clusters of matt black berries festooned the creature. Its head had all three types of species of flower – the tiny domed yellow umbels, purple stars and white trumpets – that fell in waves down its neck. The effect of both demi-dryads was stunning, especially their shiny black eyes that skewered Ned with a fierce intensity.

'Thank you for coming,' said Willow, a slight flutter in her foliage the only reaction to having the two demi-dryads focus their attention on her. 'We have come from the Empress to help you reach an agreement. It's time to cease this feud.'

'They started it,' hissed the Holly who in realising that Ivy out flowered them, had added tiny white blooms to their appearance.

'They continually overlook us,' retorted the Ivy.

'How can we help?' asked Willow.

The demi-dryads glanced at each other, then quickly looked away.

'I want my own crown. And my own set of verses,' demanded Ivy.

The Holly bristled.

'I thought you wanted my crown.' They prickled uncomfortably. 'And that you wanted your own song. I thought… I thought you wanted nothing to do with me anymore.' Their delicate blooms fell to the floor in a shower of petals.

'No! I never wanted your crown, just one of my own.' Ivy sent tentative tendrils over to Holly. 'I always want to be with you – we're the Holly and the Ivy. You can't separate us.'

With the tense atmosphere between the demi-dryads having relaxed, Ned braved a question.

'It seems like it was all a misunderstanding. Why didn't you talk to each other? If I may, things seem to have grown way out of proportion fast, but you've managed to resolve everything so quickly.'

'The snow…' Ivy looked around at the great swathes

that lay about. 'It's been so cold, making my sap sluggish. Affecting my reactions and thoughts.'

'Mine too! And frostbite has affected so many leaves. I've lost a lot of spread.' Holly extended a finger as if to touch the snow, but didn't quite manage it. 'There's an echo in the weather. A sort of menace.' They snatched their hand back. 'You sense it, don't you?''

Ned looked at Willow. He just felt cold and slightly soggy around the edges where the snow has made his clothes damp.

She closed her eyes, her tendril hair questing the air. It grew very still and quiet. The back of Ned's neck began to itch as if there were something dangerous behind him about to pounce. He couldn't resist and glanced back, making a crunching noise in the snow as his boots moved. There was nothing there. His movement, however, had broken the tension, and the woods felt woodsy again.

'I sensed... something. I understand why the mistletoe got out of control. You were both fighting the effects of the extreme winter. You couldn't keep up with it and the evergreen plant loves this kind of weather. It took advantage of you both. Will you be alright now?' asked Willow.

The Holly and Ivy looked at each other.

'If we work together and keep talking, we can hold this disturbance at bay, but... not forever,' replied Holly.

'You need to be careful in your hunt for the culprit. There is much at stake.' Ivy regarded Ned solemnly, and he knew they didn't mean only in the woods. He cleared his throat.

'We can take your request back to the Empress. I am confident a crown and a reworking of the song will swiftly be remedied.' Ned spoke in earnest. 'Can you tackle the mistletoe?'

'We will do everything in our power to reign in the parasite. With the two of us working together…' Holly shared a smile with Ivy.

'We'll get things back to normal in no time.' Ivy beamed back.

Both demi-dryads shuddered violently. The temperature in the clearing had dropped significantly.

'But you must promise to do something about this winter! It's too much. Plants will start dying if things don't go back to normal soon.' Holly pleaded with them.

Ned shot a look at Willow as she flushed dark green and a few thorns appeared along her arms.

'I know… it's not right. I don't…' She struggled to search for the right words.

'We are doing our best to get to the bottom of it. Because it's not a normal winter. It's all extra. It's not just cold, it's bloody freezing. And we don't have a sprinkle of snow, we've got an absolute whiteout.' Ned paused, trying to decide whether to share the fae myth theory or not. He decided against it. An unfounded theory about a mythical creature was likely to cause more angst at this stage.

'What about the woodland creatures that usually live here with us? Will you protect them from the opportunistic hunters that are roaming the streets?' asked the Ivy.

Willow gasped as Ned avoided looking at her.

'I am putting together a robust team of Thief-Catchers and volunteers more than capable of herding a few deer and apprehending illegal hunting weapons.' There was a challenging glint in Ivy's eye as they appraised Ned whilst he spoke. 'Jimmy Fingers will be assisting.' That did the trick. The corners of Ivy's mouth lifted slightly. Even here Fingers was well known and respected as a man who could get the goods, whatever the goods may be.

'If there's nothing else, we have some mistletoe to wrangle.' The Holly gave Willow and Ned a gracious nod, was joined by the Ivy and the two demi-dryads melted back into the forest.

'Do you reckon that will be the end of that now?' Ned asked Willow.

She fluttered her leaves.

'I think so. Ivy's probably got a touch of frostbite to be honest, but even they can't complain about the willingness of the Empress to fix the problem.'

'I'll get the High Right to source a suitable crown for both the Holly and the Ivy and get them both delivered to the woods at the same time. If we ask Holly respectfully to exchange crowns with the one from the palace, then they'll both have exactly the same. If they send a court bard along as well, they can amend the song. We'll promise to have the new version written up, publicly performed and copies distributed around the city. Not a bad deal to get the mistletoe issue resolved.' Ned waited for Willow to agree and was pleased as she nodded. 'Right, that's one problem sorted. Next, the River Whine. You okay to go straight there?' Ned was beginning to feel the pinch of the cold air in his feet and hands. He needed to get moving, get some blood flowing. A quick wiggle of his toes brought immense satisfaction. Maybe pick up some hot pasties from Aggies on the way through. They did, after all, have to traverse the city to make it to the river.

'I'm ok. But a pit stop at Aggie's would be good. She does a wonderful vegetable bake.'

Ned grinned. He loved it when a plan came together.

Chapter 17

The notice in the paper said *Room available, interviews at noon, bring cake.*

It was freezing as Fred stood on the pavement behind the baker's boy. He could also see Gladys Morphages's ears sticking out either side of her immaculate bun and his heart sunk a little. She was neat. And the baker's boy had brought a large selection. All he'd come with were a couple of rock cakes and that time he'd guarded the kelp hill when Mr Spinks had confronted Jenni and her black eyes. And the time he'd been transported to a field because of the magick shoppe that shouldn't have been there. And his mam's bunions. Not that he actually had those on him, but he was the one that fetched the special poultice from the druids, and it was Jenni who'd told him about that. Fred puffed out his chest, reconsidering his position. After all, not everyone could say they'd shared a cheese and pickle sandwich with Momma K's daughter, like that one time on a night shift when Jenni had been on patrol and Fred had been on break and she'd commented on what a good sandwich it was, and that was one Fred had made not his mum on account of her bunions.

'Next!'

Fred jumped. He'd been daydreaming about that time he'd had ice cream on the corner of Wide Street from that place with the little umbrellas. Made of paper and far too small to be of any use if it did actually rain, but fun to have sticking out of your drink. He hadn't realised both Gladys and the baker's boy had been dismissed. As far as Fred could tell, they'd never made it inside the property, although the large selection of goodies peeked out from the front door.

'Afternoon, Miss Jenni.' Fred saluted and then blushed.

'Wot you doing 'ere?'

'I saw your ad, and I thought to myself, Fred my boy, this is just the opportunity you need. Our Malcolm is getting married. Big surprise to all of us. I won't lie, because we always thought he was going to go with Big Vera down on Sweetheart Lane. Always see them together, done deal we all thought. But the other day, last week on Thursday I think it was, he comes in telling me mam that he was all engaged and the like to some slip of a thing from Treacle Lane.' Fred leaned in conspiratorially. 'We checked, no troll or dwarf blood, as far as we can tell. Turns out Big Vera was matchmaking the whole time. Didn't know she did that sort of thing, but apparently she's in demand. Gets results. Anyway, our mam is made up, but she also said, and quite right too, that a married couple needs their space so she's moving into my bedroom and I can either kip down in the kitchen or find my own place. I didn't fancy doing it on my own. Living, I mean. And then there was your ad, and it was like the heavens aligned. It's fate, Miss Jenni. I can feel it in my water. Me mam says to always mind your water.'

Jenni cocked her head to one side and was regarding Fred in an alarming fashion. He nervously smoothed his hair down. It was a little poufy around the edges because he hadn't had time to wash it after wearing his palace helmet all day yesterday.

'Ow do you feel bout washing up?'

'Um, never really thought about it one way or the

117

other, to be honest with you. I mean, I can see the value of it, nice clean cups and that. I would think the best time to do it is after a meal, save the pots from collecting. I usually cracks on with it when me mam tells me to get my chores done. She says it's important to do a little every day to stay on top of things. Great advice.'

'You wanna look around?'

'Yes, please, Miss Jenni. That would be grand.' Fred felt his hopes lift. He was getting the tour. That must be a good sign.

'Awright, come in. We got a sitting room in 'ere. This is my chair, that's Neds.' Jenni nodded towards the two clapped out armchairs set at a perfect equidistance from the fireplace and the table. 'You'll 'ave to get one sorted.'

'I should be able to manage that, Miss Jenni. I have a chair of my own that I can take being as it's mine and not our Malcolm's. I'm sure I can get some of the lads on my road to help me carry it over. They owe me for that time I looked the other way in pea-knuckle.'

She nodded and stomped through the doorway, leading him into the kitchen.

'Oh, what happened in here, Miss Jenni?'

'Wot do you mean?'

'Um…' Fred's gaze swivelled round, taking in the heaps of dirty dishes, laundry spilling over the floor and unidentified food scraps creating beautiful mouldy patterns. 'It's just… ah… well used. Clearly.'

Jenni's piercing stare made Fred acutely aware of sweat rolling down the back of his neck. She seemed to accept his comment and beckoned him to follow her up the stairs.

Ned's house was unusual. It was an end terrace, a filler building and as such had oddly shaped rooms, wonky ceilings and the general impression that it shouldn't really be there, but they had all this leftover timber and cement so they might as well do something with it. One could call it a disaster. Or one could call it a charming disaster.

'We got two rooms 'ere and then further up is Neds and the bathroom.' She pulled one door shut sharply. 'That's mine. This is yors.'

The room was clean and bare.

'Looks good. Who was here before?'

'Dunno. S'never been used long as I know. Fink it was just a spare for stuffs but we made sure all that wos moved. There's no furniture though.' She eyed him up and down. 'You got some?'

Fred gulped.

'I'll have to ask me mam. I don't know if I'll be able to take it with me when I go on account of our Malcolm and his new bride. They had terrible trouble getting the frame in, so she might say it's not worth the bother of getting it out again. Caused a lot of herniation that did. Uncle Steven never recovered. Never.'

'Well if you ain't we can sort you summink.'

Fred bobbed his head, then finally registered what Jenni just said.

'I got the room?'

Jenni shrugged.

'If youse want it.'

A large grin spread across Fred's face, and he clasped his hands together in excitement.

'Oh Miss Jenni, you don't know what this means. I thought for sure that Gladys Morphage would have got it on account of her tidy bun. Says a lot a tidy bun. Oh, this is grand. Grand it is. Me mam will be so pleased. She has a high opinion of you, Miss Jenni. A very high opinion. I can't wait to tell her. And to be living here, in Mr Spinks's house. Oh!' He did a little foot shuffle jig. 'The lads will be so jealous.'

'Awright then. We'll figure out the rent later. Just come up to HQ tomorrow and I'll sort you a key and that. You can move in whenever.' Jenni started walking back down the spiral stairwell. Fred hastened to follow.

'I appreciate it, Miss Jenni. Thank you for taking a chance on me. I won't let you down and I'll wash the dishes for you as soon as I move in. Very clean and tidy, I am, very clean and tidy. A credit to me mam, me mam always says.'

They arrived back at the front door. Jenni swept up the baked goods box and nudged Fred out, locking the door behind them.

'I gotta go. Got Catcher business so I'll see you tomorrow, yeah?'

Fred continued to thank Jenni profusely, even after she was well out of earshot and all he had for company were swirling snowflakes. It was with a very happy, snow-laden step that Fred went home to inform his family of the good news and organise the removal of his furniture and belongings. A process that turned out to be relatively pain free. People would eventually do anything Fred asked of them, usually because they had been lost in the swirls of conversation and weren't entirely sure what was going on.

Chapter 18

Pickings had been slim at Aggie's Bakery, so Ned had suggested they head back to The Noose, just in case Reg had something decent on the menu. However, upon perusal, it was especially undesirable, to say the least. As they were about to concede defeat and leave hungry, Jenni arrived with a box of cinnamon twists. Ned's mood improved drastically.

'Brilliant, thanks Jenni,' he said as he quickly helped himself when she offered the box. Cinnamon twists were very popular in the Catcher office. 'Can't stop, we're off to see Piss-Eyed Nellie. Unless you want to come?'

A vehement shake of her head made Ned grin. The lure of the pastries was stronger than the opportunity to wind up the river sprite. Jenni must be hungry.

He and Willow clattered down the rickety stairs and braced themselves for heading out again.

'Are you sure you're warm enough in this weather?' Ned asked, eyeing Willow's sage green tunic and single scarf with some scepticism.

'Yeah, I'm okay, I think. I'm releasing my internal heat – a bit like a personal hot water bottle. Plus, I have my natural antifreeze, which is still working, for now. I'm trying not to leaf as much as normal. Save some energy.' Her breath puffed out in front of them. 'Don't get me wrong, I'm still feeling the cold and I'm a little tired, but I have adaptations to keep the devastation of winter at bay. I should be okay, I think. Are you warm enough?'

Ned barked a laugh. He had two vests on, a shirt, a

thin jumper and a knitted, sleeveless vest as well as his coat, gloves, Willow's scarf that she'd given him, a hat - oh and Fred's thermal trousers underneath his work ones. They really were a marvel. Two pairs of socks made his feet very snug in his Gunnington boots, but at least he could still feel his toes.

'I'm managing, thanks.' He shared a smile with Willow before they both had to concentrate on keeping their footing across the icy cobbles.

They had to walk through Roshaven to get to the lake and before they even got to the lakeshore, they could hear the excited squeals of children. Upon arrival, Ned was momentarily dumbfounded at the sight before him.

It looked like every child in Roshaven was there. Sledging, skating, slipping and sliding all over the place.

'Is that safe?' asked Willow as she bent down to tap the surface.

The ice was so clear Ned could see the trapped grass beneath and the reeds stood at stiff attention, unable to bend in the wind.

Two enormous cracks echoed across the lake and the ice groaned. Ned searched frantically for the source of the noise but could see nothing specifically. The more pressing questions were how on earth were they going to get all these kids off the ice and where was Piss-Eyed Nellie?

A school bell rang loudly and Ned noticed the teachers from Roshaven Elementary stood on the other side of the river, their feet safely on the ground, not the frozen water.

As if by magic, the children stopped screaming like little banshees and began lining up in neat lines behind their teacher, ready to march off. Apparently, visiting the lake had been a field trip. Ned frowned. He was sure Rose had said the schools were closing because of the snow.

'They have got nowhere else to go,' remarked a deep voice.

Willow and Ned spun round to see Headmaster Thorn.

'The children. Whilst the school has been officially closed, these children don't have anywhere else to go and for a lot of them, there is no food or heat at home, so we opened winter school. Sister Eustacia marshalled the acolytes into building us a giant igloo in the playground and we have large vats of hot chocolate donated by Momma K.'

Ned blinked in surprise. He wasn't aware that Momma K had any philanthropic thoughts towards the youth of Roshaven.

'Excellent, well done. But er… are you sure the ice is safe? We don't want any accidents.'

The headmaster nodded towards the lake.

'We have been assured by Nellie herself.'

'And do you happen to know where Nellie is?' asked Ned, thinking it would save them some time to get the inside scoop.

'There's a small suckerhole just along the bank. You can't miss it.' The headmaster nodded to them both and strode purposefully back to his flock.

'Let's go find this sucker, shall we?' Ned led the way with Willow delicately picking her way behind him, letting out small sighs at the extent of the frozen vegetation.

Headmaster Thorn had been right. You couldn't miss the suckerhole. A large branch was sticking out of the solid ice, but somehow the weak winter sun had melted the immediate area around the branch and Piss-Eyed Nellie was lounging half in, half out of the opening. She was a good deal smaller than Ned remembered. He wondered whether that was permanent.

'Nellie, nice to see you.'

The river sprite turned her mournful head towards him, water trickling out of her eyes, nose, and mouth.

'Hello Willow, Ned. So glad of you to take the time to come and check on me. I knew you would eventually. Once you'd seen to the important things. I knew you wouldn't forget me. Not in this harsh weather.'

Ned suppressed an internal sigh. He'd forgotten how depressing it could be talking to Piss-Eyed Nellie.

'Yes, well, we wanted to make sure you were alright and not frozen stuck beneath the river.'

'And we do care about your welfare, just like we care about all the creatures within the River Whine,' added Willow.

'The plants are fine, if that's what you mean. I think many of them have gone into some kind of suspended animation, but nothing's growing. A dwindling food supply.' She sighed and a tiny chunk of ice fell out of her mouth into the suckerhole.

'Speaking of, the bugs have disappeared. Every single one of them. The ducks and geese migrated. The fish are hibernating. So it's pretty lonely here. Just me. On my own. In the river.'

There was a tinkle of laughter and a group of small, sparkly blue dots dashed past. A glitter of Jacks.

'Oh. And there's lots of those. Annoying little things. I've got flow obviously, being fed by a river, but it's definitely sluggish and we've had some mini ice bergs. Nothing like the ones they're experiencing in the ocean, I'm sure. But we hold our own here in the river.'

Water continuously poured out of Nellie's orifices, making it tricky to take her completely seriously.

'I bet the children cheer you up though, right?' asked Ned. 'Must be nice to hear their gleeful shouts and laughter.'

Piss-Eyed Nellie looked at Ned balefully.

'If you like that sort of thing, I suppose.' She streamed slightly more forcefully. 'I've also had to save a few people. There was a group of lads who stripped off and went snow bathing. At least that's what I think they called it. Said it would be invigorating to swim in the water beneath the snow. Little did they know the snow crystals had frozen, creating a layer of hard ice. There were some rather unfortunate skin-to-ice adhesions. I helped where I could.'

There was the smallest glimmer of amusement in Nellie's voice.

'I'm glad you're doing okay. You will let us know if you need anything, won't you?' Willow gently brushed the surface of the frozen river, careful not to stick her tendrils into the amorphous outline of Nellie, who undulated between humanoid and a great blob of water shapes.

'And keep the children safe. On the ice. Please. We really don't want any accidents.' Ned waited for Nellie to moan at him.

'Of course,' she sloshed stiffly. 'I would never let anything happen to the children. Headmaster Thorn always comes and has a chat before the children come onto the ice. I will keep him apprised on the safety levels. He's very nice. For a human.'

'Excellent. Thank you, Nellie. We appreciate it.'

'Before you go – what are you doing about this winter? I may not be able to maintain this hole indefinitely if it doesn't start to warm up soon. A full winter of this severity is likely to destroy my habitat.' There was a distinct timbre of worry in Nellie's words.

'We are investigating, I can assure you of that.' Ned glanced at the thick ice that covered the river. 'If it does, er, seal over – will you be alright, under all that? Should we come and move you to a safer location?'

'I will be fine. Much like my inhabitants, I can go into hibernation if needed. It's just not recommended for a long period of time. I may lose my cohesiveness.' She sloshed a little closer to them both. 'Do hurry and sort this out. For all our sakes.' Then she slunk back into the suckerhole.

Ned watched as she rippled away beneath the ice.

'Do you think that's a real danger?' he asked Willow as they tramped up the bank to the river path.

'What? Losing her cohesiveness? I expect so. I know Nellie likes to look on the bleak side of things, but she's right. Holding onto her form in such extreme conditions is going to be tough.' She patted Ned's arm. 'I will come back and check on her, make sure she's doing alright. And we'll sort this out winter. I know we will.'

They both shivered as the chilly wind blew, dusting them with snowflakes and stabbing them with its icy sharpness.

Chapter 19

Jimmy Fingers fell into step with Ned and Willow as they trudged back through the streets to what they hoped would be the relative warmth of the office. That was the funny thing about Fingers, thought Ned. He never seemed to be where you wanted him to be, but he could always find you.

'Figured I'd see you here,' said Fingers. 'How's Nellie?'

'She's okay. She has some movement left, but the lake is pretty solid. We're going to keep an eye on her,' replied Willow. 'Thank you for setting up the bug hotel. We are all relieved that Sparks has somewhere safe to go.'

'You're welcome. I was thinking about your vine. We could establish the same sort of setup for seeds, you know. I spoke with Griff, negotiated some excellent rates.'

'It's so funny you should mention that, because Fred was just saying that a seed bank would be a really good idea.' Willow was blooming with excitement. At least she was trying to, but the cold snap in the air was shrivelling the blooms as soon as they opened. Still, it made a pretty pattern on the icy ground.

'Let's meet up and figure out a plan. Someone will have to collect the seeds, bring them to the warehouse. I assume you could marshal some willing helpers?' asked Fingers with a cheeky wink.

Ned watched Willow blush ever so greenly.

'Oh yes, I can get something organised. Shall we sit

down tomorrow? And put the plan together?' she asked.

'Sounds good.' Fingers turned his attention to Ned. 'I hear you got animal control duty. Shame we can't put venison on the menu.'

'No, we can't. What we need to do is stop these idiots roaming the streets armed with bows and arrows.' Ned nodded at Fingers. 'You probably have a plan for that, I expect.' He followed that up with a grin. He got on well with the reformed criminal.

'Happy to give you a hand, mate,' offered Jimmy Fingers. 'I probably know most of the would-be hunters one way or another.'

'Appreciate it,' replied Ned, idly wondering if Fingers had organised the deer hunting in the first place. He was always one to capitalise on an unusual situation, but this was a bit much, even for Fingers. 'If you're meeting tomorrow morning to talk seeds with Willow, maybe plan to run the deer out of the city afterwards. With a few well-placed diversions, we should be able to steer them towards the woods. With the mistletoe now being removed from the forest, their food source will be reappearing there, so it stands to reason they'll return at some point. Not a lot for them to eat inside Roshaven anyway.'

'Eh, it's been my experience that animals don't always do what you think they will. I'll put the word out to my boys, tell them to discourage the hunting and anyone found deer stalking tomorrow will... what do you reckon? Have to volunteer on snow shovelling for a week? Seems a bit harsh to fine them when it's such slim pickings at the moment.'

Ned considered the suggestion. For Fingers to be saying the pickings were slim was serious. The man was in charge of everything coming in and out of Roshaven, so he would know. And Rose did want volunteers for the snow shovelling.

'Sounds good to me. But tell them to be at HQ mid-morning tomorrow to help with the herding. We might as well make use of their muscles. They can also help with the seed bank collection. Two birds and all that.'

Fingers nodded, but Willow looked quizzical.

'Do we need to save the birds as well? Can't they just fly away to somewhere warmer?' Her face was such a picture of consternation that Ned didn't have the heart to correct her.

'It's just an expression. We don't need to worry about the birds.' Ned flashed a quick glance at Fingers, who pursed his lips and shook his head. Definitely did not need to worry about the birds.

'Look, I'd better push off if I'm going to get the word out in time. Take care in this weather.' Fingers nodded farewell and sloped off down one of the side streets, back to his domain down at the docks.

'Don't forget the next council meeting. Rose needs you there!' called Ned after his rapidly retreating back.

Fingers waved a hand in the air. Ned figured that meant he'd heard him, but whether that would translate into actual attendance was anyone's guess.

'Come on, let's get into the warm. A cup of spiced scumble sounds like a great idea right about now.'

Willow nodded, her tendrils tinkling in the movement. They were starting to go frosty. Ned stamped his feet a couple of times to get the blood flowing and gestured for Willow to lead the way.

Chapter 20

It was an unusual-looking trio that knocked on the Thief-Catcher's door. Swathed in matching home-made bobble hats and large chunky scarfs, wearing backpacks and sturdy hiking boots and clasping thick, gnarly walking sticks. What was even more strange was who they wanted.

'Fred?' Jenni asked again, thoroughly confused.

'Yes, Miss. We were told by the guards at the palace to come here and ask for him,' replied one of the people standing in front of her. Jenni assumed they were people, but they were so wrapped up it was hard to tell.

'But 'e don't work 'ere. And we ain't seen 'im.'

Jenni's conscience flared up and tapped its foot at her. She had seen Fred earlier. She'd interviewed him for a housemate but in her defence, she had no idea where he'd gone after that. Well, that wasn't strictly true either. He had said he was going home to pack, but she wasn't about to tell these strangers all that.

'Whose are you anyways?' she asked.

The figure in the front puffed out their chest and stood a little straighter.

'We are M-TAC!'

Jenni looked at them blankly.

'M wot?'

The figure deflated.

'M-TAC, the Meh-Teh Appreciation Club? You have heard of the Meh-Teh?' He held out an ultramarine badge with the initials MTAC emblazoned in white on it. 'Badge?'

Jenni took the badge, grinned and swung the office door open wider.

'Come on in. I'm sure Fred'll be along at some point. Let's get you some 'ot tea.'

The three people ventured inside and slung their heavy-looking backpacks in a pile in the corner and began unwinding various layers of scarf while Jenni put the kettle on. She rattled the biscuit tin. It sounded half full so it would have to do. As the tea brewed in the pot, a finger tapped Jenni on the shoulder. She turned and was greeted with several flasks thrust at her.

'Do you think we could refill these while we're here, please? We've got our own leaves.' The leader of the group, now de-scarfed and de-hatted, was a middle-aged guy with the weathered skin of a person who spends most of their time outside.

'Knock yerself out. Teapot's brewing.'

They had a little dance as Jenni tried manoeuvring out of the tiny kitchen while the guy tried making a beeline for the kettle and stove at the same time.

The other two members of M-TAC were appreciating the fire and looking around the office with curious eyes. Since Joe had taken his Catcher responsibilities more seriously, after the apprehension and redeployment of his sister and the death of his evil sorcerer father, things had become highly organised in the Catcher office. There were wallcharts, multi-coloured stickers, and filing cabinets that were actually filled correctly. Jenni sort of missed the crazy piles of paper on the floor system they'd had before, but it was certainly more efficient these days.

'What is it you do?' asked the short, round cheeked, bald man standing to the left of the fireplace. Jenni noticed he was missing, a couple of fingers on his right hand.

'Yor joking, right?' replied Jenni, looking at him and the tall, thin woman stood beside him. They both shook their heads.

'This is the Thief Catcher office,' she said by way of explanation, only to be met with blank stares. 'You know, Thief-Catchers? People wot catch the bad guys?'

Her clarification was received with polite nods and smiles, but it was clear they had no idea what she was talking about.

'Where you lot from?' asked Jenni. 'Wot's yor story?'

The highly weathered guy reappeared from the kitchen with various flasks clipped to his belt, bouncing around as he brought the tea tray with him. He did not have the biscuit tin.

Jenni dragged a few office chairs over to the fireplace and stomped off to retrieve the biscuits. It had been her experience that people relaxed over biscuits and felt more comfortable in speaking their mind. When she got back, the three guests had all removed their boots and were wiggling their toes before the warmth of the fire. Jenni did a quick digit count. Collectively they were at least six short.

She passed the biscuit tin around, making encouraging noises as the visitors dithered over what to choose and once everyone had a mug of tea and a suitable dunkable snack, she asked again.

'Wot's yor story then?'

It was the woman who spoke.

'I'm Bev. This is Trev and Kev,' she said, pointing first to the short man then the weather-beaten taller one. 'As Kev said, we're founder members of M-TAC, the Meh-Teh Appreciation Club and we're here hot on the heels of a Meh-Teh. We think. There have been sightings on the mountain trail down to Roshaven, through the surrounding countryside and across Coopers Way, but mostly we follow the snow. Meh-Teh snow has a certain resonance to it, if you know what to look for.'

Jenni's ears pricked up at that. Resonance usually meant some kind of magic and if the snow had power, then that might mean she had huge swathes of supply just lying around. Since her tangle with the Sea Witch upsetting her normal access to magic, Jenni now had to tap into abundant natural sources of magic, otherwise she risked drawing too much from one place or, gods forbid, person. After her close call with skimming, she didn't want to risk pulling power from people ever again.

Trev took up the intros.

'We got an invitation from a Fred Jones. He's an honorary member of the M-TAC due to the supply of essential provisions.' Trev stroked the knitted woolly scarf that lay in a huge pile next to him.

It all clicked.

'That ain't Fred, he don't do the knitting. It's 'is mam, she's a bit of a whizz. Made us all fermals.'

The M-TACs looked confused.

'No, I don't think so. These were definitely made by Fred. A personal donation to a worthy cause, I think the note read, didn't it? Based on our written correspondence, Fred doesn't strike me as the sort of person to take credit for someone else's work, does he?' Bev checked with her compatriots, who both nodded in agreement.

Jenni scowled. Fred hadn't mentioned knitting on his resume when he had applied to be her housemate.

What other hobbies was he keeping up his sleeve?

'So you ever met one, then?' she asked.

'A Fred?' Bev frowned.

'No,' Jenni barked a laugh. 'A Meh-Teh.'

The M-TACs looked at each other sheepishly.

'It's very rare to lay eyes on the actual creature. They're powerfully shy and secretive. Not usually found in populated areas, so sightings are thin on the ground.' Kev pulled his rucksack towards him. 'But we have this informative pamphlet…'

He was interrupted by the office door crashing open and Joe coming in. The banging door caused the large clay cast of the giant footprint propped up by the filing cabinets to fall over.

Bev, Trev and Kev immediately crowded round it.

'That is a Meh-Teh footprint!' exclaimed Bev in hushed tones.

'It's amazing, isn't it?' enthused Joe before registering the extra people in the office weren't fellow Thief-Catchers. 'Who are you lot?'

But his question went unanswered as the M-TACs bent nose to clay, examining every inch of the footprint.

'They're experts on Meh-Teh's, apparently. Fred tole 'em to come 'ere,' said Jenni.

'What, here to the office? But Fred doesn't even work here.'

Jenni was saved from replying by the return of Ned and Willow. The relatively small Catcher office was now thoroughly crowded.

Chapter 21

Before Ned could even ask what was going on, he and Willow had to move out of the doorway sharpish at the arrival of Fred.

'Ah, I see you've all met. Lovely.' Fred's apperance was greeted by bemusement and affection in equal measure.

Ned pinched the bridge of his nose. He decided to go for the inanimate object first.

'Joe, why is the clay foot in the middle of my office again? You said it wouldn't get in the way. It looks in the way to me.'

'Sorry, Boss, sorry' said Joe, simultaneously apologising to Ned and the three strangers as he heaved the foot back up off the floor and down the side of the filing cabinet.

The M-TACs watched with longing as the foot was rolled away from them.

'Now, Jenni, what's going on?' Ned picked on his second in command, assuming she'd know for sure who everyone was, but he could see by her immediate bristle that she didn't like being made responsible for the strangers in HQ.

'Right, these three are 'ere looking for 'im.' She jabbed a thumb in Fred's direction. 'They're Meh-Teh specialists wot fink they're on the trail of one. Come down from Coopers Way following clues and such. I wos just being friendly-like and offering them a cuppa and that. They said they wos looking for Fred and that the palace guards 'ad sent em 'ere. That's far as we got afore Joe came rollicking in and knocked over the giant foot.'

Ned turned his gaze to the three unknowns standing barefooted and missing various toes in his office. Eating his custard cream biscuits, no less.

'Bev, Trev and Kev, at your service, sir.' The woman spoke, pointing at her companions. 'Jenni is quite correct. We are the founding members of the Meh-Teh Appreciation Club, or M-TAC, for short. We came here to find young Fred after receiving a tip from him about a sighting of the Meh-Teh and to thank him for his woollen masterpieces.'

Ned had two immediate questions – why did they think it was Fred who had knitted the garments when everyone knew his Mam did all the knitting and how did Fred manage to get a message to the M-TACs so quickly but he quashed them both, turning instead to the young man for his explanation.

'Is it me? Okay then, well, first off, there's a standing forwarding of anyone to the Thief-Catcher's office if they come by the palace guards first looking for me. An initiative from the Highs that ensures people get seen and dealt with. They didn't tell you? No. Well then, that'll be why they came here looking for me. We've been in touch, you see. I sent them some knitted items I figured would come in handy after reading their latest newsletter. Been dabbling a little with the knitting. As you know, me Mam clacks along like a steam train and I thought to meself, it's a wonderful hobby for keeping your fingers busy of an evening plus you make things people can use and it's always a good thing to be useful in your community. Anyway, I was reading the newsletter and powerfully interesting the M-TAC are, what with all the travelling and discovering and the like.

Makes for an excellent read. Especially first thing in the morning when you're ah, waiting.' Fred bobbed his head and looked slightly embarrassed, but realising that no one was about to tell him off, he carried on. 'Turns out that my Uncle Owen, on me Mams side, not the one that married in but the other one, well he happens to know Bev's sister's boyfriend's uncle on account of going fishing together that one time. So we're practically family.'

Bev beamed at him and gave him a wonky thumbs up. Half the digit was missing.

'It's great to see you all, finally meet in the flesh, so to speak. I've got my pin.' Fred lifted the lapel of his jacket up to reveal a M-TAC badge underneath. 'Not allowed to wear jewellery strictly speaking, so I put it under there where it does no harm. Have you got yours, Mr Spinks, sir?'

Ned shook his head and noticed Jenni puffing out her chest. Right there, next to her Catcher badge was a M-TAC pin. He scowled at her and went to get his own cup of tea, but mis-stepped and stubbed his semi-frozen toe. He hurt enough to make his eyes water.

'Why is the kettle always empty?' snarled Ned, his mood further soured at seeing how many of the good biscuits had gone. 'How did you even know it was a Meh-Teh, Fred?' Ned had barely decided that it might be one and until he opened the Ice Book, he had no actual evidence. Apart from the massive footprint that was currently being cajoled to stand between Joe's desk and filing cabinet after half rolling out again. He watched as Joe, assisted by Kev and Trev, man-handled the cast into position.

'It was the last newsletter that tingled my brain, Mr Spinks, Sir. They mentioned how a Meh-Teh could cause extreme wintry conditions, especially when forced away from their mountainous abode. Very territorial, apparently. Linked to their mountain, much like a tree nymph is anchored to her tree. And I thought to myself, Fred, I said, this winter is cold! Way, way colder than we would expect it to be this time of year. I took myself along to *The Daily Blag* to make sure and looked for news reports of bad winter weather this early on. Thoroughly unexpected this early on. We have excessive amounts of snow, way more than we should have, and there's the problem. It has to have come from an unnatural source. It just so happens that I had read the last M-TAC newsletter from cover to cover. That was the one that had been delivered in the summer and it's not always easy to find reading time in the summer, what with our Malcolm and my palace guard duties. Anyway, as soon as the temperature had plummeted, I sent an urgent letter, and it was just pure luck that the M-TAC happened to be at Coopers Way. I told the messenger to start from there and head up North on account of the current location of the Meh-Teh being Mount Firn.' Fred turned to Joe. 'You know, you should consider joining. More than qualified, what with the cast and all. Lots of member benefits.'

Joe beamed and began asking Fred questions in a hushed tone.

Ned was staggered. Fred knew more about the Meh-Teh than Momma K. It made him wonder again whether Fred's talents were wasted in the Palace Guard. He took a moment to gather his thoughts and brewed himself a cup of tea.

'Where are with a location then?' asked Ned once he'd had a few slurps of tea.

'Um… we haven't actually sorted anything out,'

replied Bev, looking at the others sheepishly.

'Yeah, we've been hot on the trail of the Meh-Teh, tracked him right to this city – with the help of Fred's confirmation letter of course - and from the looks of this, we might actually get to see one,' said Kev, jabbing a thumb at the partially hidden clay foot. 'We could help you, be part of your investigation. You know the Meh-Teh has brought all this weather with him, don't you?'

'The snow's magical, innit.' Jenni had a gleam in her eye that Ned decided to pay close attention to later.

'Tell you what, why don't you settle yourself at my… ah, Jenni's place. I'm sure she won't mind putting you up for the night. Like I said, we've got some business to attend to here, then I'll come over and take your statements. See where we are.' Ned looked to Jenni to back him up.

'Wot do you fink, Fred? You 'appy for them to crash wiv us?' She dangled the spare key that she'd taken out of Ned's drawer in front of the lad.

'Oh yes, Miss Jenni. Absolutely. Plenty of room. I can whip up a nice shepherd's pie that will warm your cockles. Do you have anything in?' asked Fred, taking the key and putting it carefully in his pocket.

'Wot do you mean?' asked Jenni.

'Not to worry, we'll stop at the grocers on the way. He's open on account of the guards clearing a path so they could buy important supplies like smokes and the like. But he's bound to have a bit of veg knocking around. Come along, gang, get your shoes back on and we'll head out to Miss Jenni's. I mean, mine. Or even, ours.' Fred smiled so widely, Ned could see every single one of his teeth.

As the M-TAC busied themselves putting semi-soggy socks back on, Ned pulled Jenni to one side.

'You found a housemate, then?'

'Yeah. Fink 'e'll be awright?'

'I think he'll be just fine.' Ned pushed away the thin threads of jealously that tickled him at the idea of someone else living in his wonky house with Jenni. Fred was an excellent choice. He'd make sure she ate something and Jenni, well, she'd probably be a bad influence on the lad, but that wasn't necessarily a negative thing. He was a little wet behind the ears, as it was.

'Um… do you suppose we could take this with us?' asked Trev, pointing at the foot. 'We've got a supplies sled and can lash it down. Put it with the rest of our finds at the M-TAC museum. It's really just Kev's front room, but new pieces are being added all the time. We'll make up a plaque saying you donated it.'

All eyes looked at Joe, whose Adam's apple wobbled at being the centre of attention.

'I don't know… Boss?'

Ned could see Joe didn't want to give away the clay foot.

'No can do, I'm afraid. It's evidence in an ongoing case, so has to stay here.' Which was technically the truth.

The MTAC's hopeful faces fell. Fred leaned in and whispered in Kev's ear, making his head bob up in excitement.

'What about a cast? Could we make a cast of your er… cast? We have some highly effective resin that we can whip up. Won't take long. And we'll still credit you.' Kev's eyebrows were lifted high in hope.

'I mean, I guess so.' Joe thought about it. 'In theory, it should work. But I can't do it with you right now, though. I've got my report on Mount Firn to deliver. I made flash cards to go with my presentation and there are some suggested Q&As for people to ask. I used two coloured pens and underlining.'

Joe seemed torn in half. Half of him wanted to go with the MTACs and his beloved foot cast, but the other half desperately wanted to present the information he'd found about Mount Firn.

'Keep hold of the flash cards, lad. Give me the written report. Go and help them with your foot.' Ned knew there would be a written report. Joe was thorough. But Ned was more interested in clearing out his office at this precise moment. 'Mind you do the moulding outside. There's not enough space in here and I don't think Reg would approve of you using his common room, but you can ask.'

Feeling better at being told which thing to do, Joe handed over his report and began organising the careful removal of the foot. Ned watched in amusement as the M-TACs, Fred and Joe all tried to carry the foot at the same time out the door and down the corridor.

'To me a bit!'

'To you a touch!'

'Watch the wall – watch the wall!'

'PIVOT!'

Ned closed the door with a chuckle and regarded Willow, who was sitting on the window cill, looking at the snow swirling down.

'You okay? You were pretty quiet during all that.'

She turned to look at him wearily, her lips tinged blue.

'I'm so tired, Boss.' Willow half fell from the window ledge, Ned just catching her stiff frame in time to prevent complete timber to the ground.

'Gods, you're freezing.' Ned carried Willow over to

the fireplace. 'SLINKY!' he yelled whilst poking the fire to encourage a more vigorous flame.

The sea dragon sleepily appeared and nudged Ned's back by way of greeting.

'Can you help? Warm her up a bit? I think her sap has frozen.'

Ned moved out of the way, letting Slinky wind himself around the stiffening Willow. He dashed over to the supplies cupboard and pulled out a large fluffy blanket. Wrapping them both up, Ned checked the tea kettle. Empty.

'You ok for a minute while I make some fresh tea?'

The sea dragon nodded and snuggled closer to the tree nymph. Ned was encouraged to see that Willow's lips were turning an odd blue-green colour, which he took to mean that she was warming up.

He stood, leg jigging, tapping his fingers impatiently on the kitchen counter as the water boiled for the teakettle. After what seemed like an eternity, it was finally done, and he brought the tea and some more cups back to the fireplace.

Willow now looked less like a stiff board and more like gnarly old wood. But her beautiful green hair had disappeared, leaving behind straggly branches devoid of leaf and bud.

'Willow love, are you okay? Can you hear me?'

Willow's eyelids fluttered open, and she shivered, taking in her proximity to the fire, the blankets and her own personal hot water dragon.

'What happened?' she whispered.

'You caught a chill. We were out in the forest in all that ice and snow, then we tramped all the way over to the River Whine and stood in the cold checking on Nellie. I was distracted when we got back. I should've realised you were suffering. Here, take this.' Ned pushed a hot cup of tea into her hands and poured one for himself.

Willow nodded her thanks, teeth chattering. They sat in silence, sipping the tea. Ned watched in relief as foliage reappeared in Willow's tresses.

'How do you feel now?' he asked. 'I thought you had safeguards against this sort of thing?'

'Better, thank you. I think my sap got a little icy. My natural defences can only cope with so much cold. We ought to have a chat with the other dryads and nymphs. If it's happened to me, then it's probably worse for them. They don't have the protection of this office. They're in the elements.'

'Okay, we'll make sure we do a welfare check, but no more field trips without appropriate safeguards. I can't risk anything happening to you.'

'But we're already one Catcher down with Sparks being in hibernation,' Willow protested weakly.

'Crime is hardly rife right now. Everyone is concentrating on staying warm. We should do the same.' Ned checked his watch. 'Do you have any dinner sorted?'

Willow shook her head.

'I'll see if I can order a pizza,' said Ned. 'I heard Gariboldi's had a word with Fingers and sorted their supply issues, so it shouldn't be a problem. Do you want me to get Joe back here? And we can all figure out how to find this Meh-Teh.'

'No, it's alright. Let him fuss over his foot.' She tossed her head, causing her fronds to rustle. 'You really think it is one, then? A Meh-Teh?'

Ned ran a hand through his own hair.

'I can't really ignore a giant clay footprint cast now,

can I?'

Willow giggled.

'I guess not.'

'Will you be okay here while I pop over to Gariboldi's?' he asked.

Willow nodded.

'Fungal surprise, right?'

She nodded again and leaned her head on his arm briefly as he patted her shoulder. Ned picked up a fresh pair of thermals from the pile Fred had donated.

'Might as well add another layer, eh?' He closed the bathroom door to more giggling from Willow and leant his forehead on the frame. For the briefest moment, he thought he'd lost her. This winter was kicking some serious butt.

Chapter 22

The double layer of thermals were comforting on Ned's skin as he bundled his coat around him and wiggled his toes within his Gunnington boots. Grabbing a bobble hat and thick gloves, it felt like getting ready to do battle just to step out into winter.

Reg was nowhere to be seen, which was unusual, but no one was drinking in The Noose, despite the initial camaraderie the snow had brought with it. Most people were huddling for warmth at home, trying not to go outside unless they absolutely had to.

Ned had to push all his weight against the door in order to get it open. A snow drift had collected right outside. It was strange that such powdery stuff, that melted in your hand, could be so powerful when it clumped together.

With the door finally opened, Ned was forced to take a long step up to get out. His entrance into the outside caused his nose to tingle and eyes water at the cold snap. Despite wearing gloves, he could still feel the frigid cold, so, shoving his hands into his armpits, Ned made the best foot forward and began tramping through the snow. It had created an eerie wonderland covering everything in what looked like a giant bedsheet. So quiet yet full of a silent menace, Ned's footsteps crunched loudly. His gaze cast about, not sure what he was looking for, but the hairs on the back of his neck were telling him something was there. His breath plumed out, and a shiver gripped him. Still the flakes fell and even though it was daytime, there was little sunlight to see.

145

Just a wide swathe of grey clouds, fully laden and hanging low in the sky.

Getting to Gariboldi's was straightforward enough, despite the snow trying to make everything look the same. Ned let his boots do the walking. They knew their way around their city blindfolded. As he took a corner into Slingshot Row, a voice called out.

'Watch out!'

A torrent of snow flew down from the roof of the nearest building in mini avalanche style. If Ned hadn't paused when the voice called out to him, he would have been smothered by the snowluge.

He spun around, or at least tried to, in the direction of the voice, but his knee decided at that precise moment to twang rather painfully and due to his snow-laden boots having little turning circle, he ended up staggering wider than he intended. His legs disappeared into a deceptive snow drift, leaving him snowed in up to his hips. The treacherous powder instantly fell in around his limbs, gripping him tightly enough that Ned couldn't wiggle himself out. He struggled to gain purchase on the snow in front of him, but it just broke into powdery piles.

'This is ridiculous,' he muttered, trying to ignore the cold seeping into his legs and feet, despite the thick layer of thermals.

'Do you need some assistance?'

It was the same voice that had distracted him in the first place, but try as he might, Ned couldn't see who it belonged to.

'You think?' he yelled, letting his frustration colour his scathing tone.

There was the impression of something massive moving towards Ned from the left. He craned his neck as

146

far round as he could to see shadows coalescing into a looming shape that hovered on the edge of its hidden gloom.

'What are you waiting for? Help me if you're going to,' snapped Ned.

What came out into the snowscape took Ned's breath away, and it wasn't just because his lower limbs had started to freeze.

It was tall and wide and shaggy. Snow white with two enormous eyebrows, a large flat nose and eyes that glittered like ice. It was like nothing Ned had ever seen before.

'Ah… you're… you…' Words utterly failed him.

The Meh-Teh, for that was surely what it was, made a parting motion with its hands and the snow clasping Ned tightly around the legs began to melt away, giving him the purchase to scrabble out. He got to his feet and tried to massage some feeling back into them, regretting the woollen thermals as they hung freezing cold, wet and heavy beneath his trousers. Ned's teeth chattered in earnest.

'You need to find warmth. Is your abode nearby?'

The Meh-Teh had sunk into the shadows and was almost invisible again, but now that Ned had seen it, he didn't think he would ever unsee it.

'Yes,' Ned managed to point a shivering finger. 'Thief-Catcher HQ is just around that corner.'

'Thief-Catcher? I seek one of those. Tell me, do you know Ned the Sorcerer Slayer? For that is who I am trying to find in this confusing place.'

There was a lot to unpack there.

'Yes, I'm Ned. But it's Ned Spinks, not that other thing.' Ned began walking with shaky legs encased in rapidly stiffening trousers back towards The Noose. He didn't look behind him. 'You coming?' He could almost hear the dithering as the creature remained in the shadows. 'Only I need to get out of these icy clothes and you've got some serious explaining to do.'

'I am sorry. I am not good with lots of civilisation.'

'Yeah, no kidding.' Ned waved a hand. 'Is this all you?'

'It is something that happens when we are around. An ancient magic that has no explanation. It just is.' The Meh-Teh had ventured out of the shadows again. It didn't seem as big as Ned had imagined before, but still managed to tower an impressive seven feet.

'Why have you brought it to Roshaven?' asked Ned, unable to control the violent shivering that rattled his bones.

'I came in search of you.'

They had made it back to The Noose. The Meh-Teh was shaggier and wider than the average man, but he was the same height as Ned now.

'You... you've shrunk?' Ned was finding it hard to speak. He was so cold.

'We need to get you inside.' The Meh-Teh pulled the inn's door open easily, the large snow drift melting away at his touch. He put one arm under Ned's and supported him through the doorway and stood for a moment.

Ned realised the creature didn't know where to go. It had probably never been in an inn before.

'Up,' he said, pointing a shaky finger towards the stairs at the back of the room.

Reg had returned to the bar and was wearing both a fetching ultramarine M-TAC bobble hat and badge pinned to his shirt. His mouth had fallen open in surprise.

Ignoring Reg, the odd pair made their way to the stairwell and up the rickety steps. Ned pushed open his office door and used it to pull himself away from the Meh-Teh. He staggered towards one of the chairs by the fire and immediately slumped into it, causing Willow to gasp.

'What happened?' she asked.

Ned jerked a thumb backwards and let Willow have her first Meh-Teh experience. She groped for and found his arm, tapping it wildly.

'Meh-Teh meet Willow. Willow, Meh-Teh.' Ned closed his eyes, letting the warmth from the fireplace soak into him for a moment. The discomfort from his sodden lower half made it impossible to enjoy the interaction. 'Excuse me while I change.' Pushing himself out of the chair, he groped in the supplies cupboard, relieved to find an old set of clothes.

By the time he reappeared from the bathroom, clad in dry yet slightly patched trousers, Willow was still staring at the Meh-Teh, who was standing as far away from the fire as possible.

'Are you going to melt?' Ned asked in alarm.

'I am not. It is just very warm. I do not like being warm.' The Meh-Teh shuddered and snow fell around him, building up into a small, yet contained drift that allowed him to sit down within. Like a giant snow cushion.

'Fred is going to burst,' whispered Willow, finally looking wide-eyed at Ned.

Chapter 23

Before Ned could marshal his thoughts and start questioning the Meh-Teh, the office door banged open and Jenni stomped in.

'Didn't fink 'aving a 'ousemate would be so much bovver so quick. Out of milk. 'Ow can we be out of milk when we don't even 'ave it? And the shops shut now so fawt I'd just nick wots in the fridge 'ere seeing as everyone is back at mine. Awright.' She nodded a greeting at the Meh-Teh and Ned watched in amusement as her brain caught up with her vision.

To her credit, Jenni held it together well. There wasn't much that seemed to shake her and the appearance of a near mythical creature standing in the office barely caused a ripple. She scooted over to a chair on the other side of the room and regarded the Meh-Teh quizzically.

'Wot's going on?' she asked.

'This is… er, sorry, I didn't catch your name?' Ned held a hand out to the Meh-Teh and waited.

'My name can not be pronounced in your language. You may call me Flake.'

Jenni didn't give Ned a chance to ask anything else.

'Yor smaller than wot I s'pected. Wot you doing 'ere? You brung this weather wiv you? 'Ow long you staying?'

'Thank you, Jenni.' Ned interrupted and shot her a look which he hoped she would translate as shush.

'Welcome to Roshaven, Flake. You mentioned you were looking for me. Has there been a crime committed that you need help with?'

Jenni's eyes looked fit to burst. They were so wide, but she held her tongue and fidgeted in her chair, sitting on her hands. A technique Ned knew she used at official council meetings to help stop herself from saying the wrong thing.

'I...' The Meh-Teh cast about for the right words.

'You got lonely up the mountain and came down looking for friends?' asked Willow, a small tendril winding its way out towards Flake.

'Yes, I mean no.' Flake shook his shaggy mane, causing a miniature snow flurry. 'Yes, I came down the mountain looking for someone but no, I am not... was not... loneliness is not my problem.'

The sadness at the back of Flake's gaze said otherwise, but as he was finally talking, Ned decided to call him on it later.

'Yor lost, right? On yor way to some kinda Meh-Teh convention or summink. Took a wrong turn and need us to 'elp you out.'

Ned's imagination ran wild for a moment at the thought of a Meh-Teh convention before pulling his focus back to Flake and his answer to Jenni's question.

'No, I am not lost. Although I am not familiar with my location. I do, however, know how to return to my home.'

Flake's voice broke on the last few words, and his eyes glistened.

'You can't go home, can you?' Ned asked softly.

Flake's enormous eyebrows beetled alarmingly before he slowly shook his head, making his personal flurry scatter snowflakes a little wider than before. He wiped his runny nose on one arm, leaving a snail trail of tiny ice crystals. Realising everyone was staring, he flushed blue and looked down at the floor.

'It's okay. You can tell us, why can't you go home?'
Ned pointed at the bathroom, frowning at Jenni until she
got off her chair and went to get something for the Meh-
Teh to dry his face on. Once the towel had been handed
over and promptly ruined by a frozen nose blow, the
Meh-Teh continued his tale.

'I am a little ashamed to say it, but I have been
evicted by Ice Giants. They will not listen to reason and
are being stubborn in the extreme. They, er... have
declared my home their place and... and will not even
consent to living amicably side by side.'

Ice Giants, thought Ned. That was another new one
on him. He knew nothing about them at all. One glance
at Jenni's blank expression told him she was in the same
boat. And if she had never heard of them before, then
they must be extraordinarily rare or extremely new. Or
old. Considering a myth was telling him about them,
then old was definitely in the running. But it seemed to
Ned that Flake was keeping something back, not sharing
everything with them.

'We have a mutual friend in common. Brogan the
Biscuit-Loving Barbarian. He, er... has spent several
weeks sheltering in the wake of my mountain, and um...
recounted your many er... adventures and exploits.
Um... he said, he said that if I ever had a problem, then
er... you were the man to see.' Flake lifted his sorrowful
gaze towards Ned. 'I er... have a problem, so I have
come to see.'

'And we will do whatever we can to help,' said Ned,
his mind racing. Judging by the number of ums and ers,
Flake was definitely hiding something. 'How many Ice
Giants are we talking about?'

'There are three. Each one more terrifying than the

last. They have escaped from Nowhere and have taken over my realm planning to sow destruction across the land, sending everything into a vicious Ice Age where nothing will survive.' Flake warmed to his narrative. 'They must be stopped before they grow too powerful. The journey from Nowhere has weakened them but as they rest atop the mountain, they will be replenishing their strength.'

'Nowhere?' asked Ned trying to ignore the stone plummenting in his stomach and the wobble in his knees.

'Yeah, you remember, Boss. That's the place in the middle of wot you wos when you followed the rose and that. And all the 'appiness was freatened and stuff. And you like won the day wiv yor magic, innit.'

'Indeed. The retelling of your quest is quite a tale. Such bravery and such magical mastery.' Flake's eyebrow waggled at Ned, who coughed in embarrassment.

'It was really just reacting to the situation. I was lucky, I guess.' The backs of Ned's ears were bright red. 'But, I didn't see any Ice Giants there. Are you sure it's the same place?'

'The tales say you were in the middle of Nowhere. Very fortunate spot to be as Nowhere is vast and unending, featureless and expansive. There is much in Nowhere that we do not speak of.' Flake's voice had grown solemn.

A deep silence fell as people considered what sorts of things might be in Nowhere that you wouldn't want to talk about and also what three Ice Giants could look like. Before Ned had the chance to ask for more details, Jenni piped up, changing the subject.

'I knew it were a you,' she said, cracking her

knuckles. 'I said all along, didn't I? Bloody Meh-Teh doing all this weather and stuff, causing all these problems. Told you.' She looked smugly at Ned, waiting for him to agree.

'Um, Boss…' Willow pointed to the window.

The sky outside had grown darker, and it was raining, but the rain had an odd sparkle to it and clattered more than expected on the pane. Ned moved to take a closer look and realised the rain was ice and it was accumulating on all surfaces quickly. As he watched, a tree branch suddenly gave way under the extra weight of all the frozen water and came crashing to the ground.

'What the…?' Ned glanced left to see the Meh-Teh had shrunk again. He was now more Jenni-sized and had turned bluer. Icicles were breaking off the tips of his fur, tinkling to the floor.

'I am so sorry. I shouldn't have come. I have caused so much trouble for you.'

He finished on a wail that chilled Ned to the bone. He flinched in surprise as the Meh-Teh made a dash for the door. No one was prepared, and the creature successfully escaped.

'What are we going to do, Boss?' asked Willow. 'Is it even our jurisdiction? Should we be interfering in things happening on a mountain we only see on the horizon on a clear day?'

Ned stared out the window again at the treacherous icescape outside.

'Flake came to us for help, so help he will have. We're going to apologise for upsetting him and see if that calms down all this extreme weather and then we're going to go evict his unwanted squatters and ask him to get rid of our snowluge.' Ned jabbed a finger at Jenni. 'Take Willow back to the house, make sure she's warm and has something to eat. Stay there until I come and collect you. I'm locking the office.'

Both Willow's and Jenni's eyes widened. Ned had never locked the office the entire time they had been Catchers. For once Jenni kept her mouth shut and even helped Willow wrap herself up in an extra blanket.

Ned opened the boiler cupboard.

'Slinky, would you mind coming to the palace with me? I'm closing the office. We'll be heading out on a freezing cold field trip that I can't imagine you'd want to come on. Or I can drop you off at the harbour and you can go with the mermaids?'

The palace sounds good. I would like to spend some time with Rose.

Ned had thought the sea dragon would say that. He seemed extremely reluctant to return to the ocean. Ned figured the Sea Witch must have frightened him so much when he'd been her slave that returning to the ocean brought back too many memories.

He opened his coat for Slinky to scamper inside and coil himself around Ned's neck, shoulders, and chest. It was surprisingly comforting, as well as being lovely and warm.

Once Willow and Jenni had gathered everything together, including the milk from the fridge, Ned pulled the door close and locked it with a battered old key he then slipped into his pocket. The icy book he had collected from the library lay semi-thawed and forgotten, balanced above a now three quarters full bucket of water. There was a cracking sound and a handful of icy crystals sparked out of the book, scattering across the floor.

'What about Joe?' asked Willow once they were outside The Noose.

'S'alright, 'e stayed wiv the M-TACers at my place,' replied Jenni.

'Can I stay with you as well? I've been sleeping at the office – it's too cold in the orchard,' said Willow.

Ned felt a pang of guilt. He hadn't even thought about where she was staying in all this weather.

'Corse, no problem. We got room.' Jenni beamed up at Willow.

'Okay you two, take it easy getting home. The streets are slick with ice. Please, no accidents. I'll be back as soon as I can.' Ned watched as Willow delicately picked her way across the slippery cobbles and Jenni slid about like a bar of soap. Hopefully, they would make it in one piece.

Chapter 24

By the time he got to the palace, Ned was warm enough to consider unbuttoning his coat. He held off doing that so as not to alarm any of the palace staff by walking in with a miniature dragon coiled about him.

Rose was in the study looking tired but pleased to see him.

'Tell me you sorted out the Holly and the Ivy,' she asked.

'We did. It's all in my report.' Which was true. He just hadn't written it yet. He grinned at Rose. 'You should've seen Willow. She was amazing, nearly froze herself half to death in the process but they're dealt with and harmony is restored. Fingers' lads will round up the bow wielding idiots. Give them a rap on the knuckles but keep it off our books, which is less paperwork for everyone. They will all be volunteered for seed collection and snow shovelling duty.'

'Seed collection?' queried Rose, happily accepting everything else.

'One of Fred's concepts, actually. He thought it would be a good idea to collect seeds from all the plants in Roshaven and keep them in a safe place. Fingers suggested Griff's warehouse – where the bug hotel is – so we're going to get started on that tomorrow as well. It's worth doing for posterity, and not just because of this wicked winter. I don't know why we didn't think of it before. I know he's officially one of yours, but Fred is wasted in the Palace Guard. I am seriously considering poaching him for the Catchers. Oh, and he's Jenni's new roommate.'

'Is that wise? Won't she be a bad influence?' asked Rose with a wry smile, completely ignoring Ned's comment about poaching Fred.

Ned just grinned and said nothing, opening his coat and allowing Slinky to look about, testing the air with his forked tongue.

'Slinky – it's so nice to see you!' exclaimed Rose, holding her arms out for him. 'Are you alright?'

The lithe sea dragon slinked from Ned to Rose and curled around her happily, eyes lidded, purring like mad.

Rose mouthed at Ned, *Is he ok?*

Ned nodded and his wife looked relieved. With her semi-distracted by being dragon hugged, Ned launched into the state of things.

'All this winter weather is being caused by a Meh-Teh. I just met him, name of Flake. Turns out he's been evicted from Mount Firn and wants my help to get his home back. Knows Brogan as it goes. Bit random.' Ned tried to deliver everything in an even, calm voice, but Rose's head whipped up anyway.

'Who evicts a Meh-Teh?' she asked, cutting straight to the quick and accepting the reality of the myth come to life. After all, this was Roshaven, a magical place.

'Ice Giants apparently.'

Rose nodded. She paced a little in front of the fireplace, absent-mindedly stroking Slinky's scales.

'What's the plan?' she asked.

Ned's heart swelled at how brilliant his wife was. Roshaven was so lucky to have her.

'I lead a team up the mountain. We confront the Ice Giants and get them to move on, returning Flake his home.' He ran a hand over the back of his neck. 'That would leave you to deal with the melt. Unless the Meh-

Teh can remove it when he goes.'

'And you think that's what we should do? What if you said no? Would it just leave and take the snow with it?'

Ned's face fell a little as Rose knocked the wind out of his proverbial sails. He assumed she'd be immediately on board.

'Flake came to me for help. He specifically came looking for me. Asked Brogan for directions and everything. Sought me out. I can't ignore a plea like that. I can't.' Ned braced himself for fighting his corner, which he was fully prepared to do. Rose should know that he couldn't ignore someone who came to him for help. It wasn't in his nature.

'I know you can't. I'm just playing devil's advocate. Making sure you've explored every option. And if you think the best way to lift the severe winter from Roshaven is by helping this Flake, then, of course, I support you.'

Ned pondered for a moment. True, he had leapt straight to helping the Meh-Teh out. And Willow had asked about jurisdiction, but Ned hadn't even been thinking about that.

'Will we be stepping on toes heading over to Mount Firn?' Ned felt he should already have the answer to that, but he hadn't had time to catch up on all the essential reading the Highs said was necessary for the Empress's husband. There was a lot.

Rose pursed her lips, considering borders.

'It should be fine. Provided you don't go in an official Roshaven capacity, so no pomp and circumstance, I'm afraid. A small team, no livery. That sort of thing.' There was a wry smile on Rose's face.

Ned grinned back at her. She knew he didn't like the

livery.

'We should definitely find out if Flake can remove the snow when you leave, but we do have a plan of sorts to handle the thaw, if that's what will happen to it when he leaves the city.' She reminded Ned of the ideas they had brainstormed earlier.

'It all sounds doable to me,' said Ned.

'Where is Flake now? At HQ?' asked Rose, going to sit by the fireplace, still snuggling with Slinky.

'Um... not exactly. I've closed HQ.'

'What do you mean, *not exactly*?' Rose's sharp tone made Slinky's scales ripple. 'And why have you closed HQ?'

'The office was getting frigid. We've run out of biscuits. I nearly lost Willow to the cold and it's not the right environment for Slinky. I sent everyone back to mine... er Jenni's, where they can stay warm by the fire and get something to eat. I didn't think you'd want them all here.' To be honest, it hadn't even crossed Ned's mind that he could have sent everyone to the palace. He forgot he had a lot of spare rooms these days. 'And as for Flake, well, Jenni was just saying how she'd known all along that a Meh-Teh had been behind the entire winter disaster and Flake got a bit er... upset. He set off an ice storm, completely by accident and then, ah... did a runner.'

'You lost it?' Rose looked at Ned in disbelief.

'Him. Fairly sure Flake is a he,' mumbled Ned, inspecting his boots for a moment.

Rose stalked to the windows and pulled the curtains aside so she could get a better look outside. It was glacial. Everything seemed to be covered in icicles and several trees were bent at decidedly painful looking angles.

160

'Great. Not only do we have piles and piles of snow to deal with, we also have a massive ice storm and a weather aggressor on the loose in the city, feeling upset.'

'It doesn't sound good but...' Ned was hit with a bolt of inspiration. 'We have the M-TACs!' He announced proudly.

'The what?'

'The M-TACs. Meh-Teh Appreciation Club. They're in town right now, been on the trail of the Meh-Teh and tracked him here. We've got them staying at mine...' Ned faltered at his wife's frown. 'Ah, I mean my old place. They came because of Fred. He contacted them wondering if a Meh-Teh was behind everything.' Realising he was gabbling, Ned shut up.

'Are these the ones with the aquamarine badges and the eclectic knitwear?' Rose asked coolly. It was, after all, part of an Empress's job to be aware of who was and wasn't in town.

'Yes, that's them.' There was a long pause as Ned waited for Rose to say more. His nerves took over, and he started talking again. 'Interestingly, Fred made them that knitwear. He and his mum have been busy knitting thermals. Brought some over to The Noose. Quite comfy but not so good once they get wet.' He clacked his mouth shut to stop him from babbling on.

'I suggest you use those resources to find this Meh-Teh and remove this winter from my city. If you need any specific mountain supplies, you'd better speak to Fingers. He had some specialist winter equipment delivered in yesterday.'

'He did?' Ned wondered how Rose had that information when Fingers was so very often conspicuously absent from council meetings.

'Spot check,' said Rose by way of explanation. She

randomly checked on different things as part of her imperial duties. Said it kept everyone on their toes, never knowing when the Empress herself was going to come and inspect. 'Griff should be back tomorrow as well. Perhaps he will be a useful addition to your team.'

Ned nodded. If Jenni had no idea who the Ice Giants were, that meant Momma K was unlikely to have any intel and more than likely they weren't fae. There was, however, a good chance that Griff had heard of them before. He was very well travelled, and Ned had hardly even scratched the surface of what his father did and didn't know about.

'We'll need to do some planning. To go up the mountain, I mean. But I can do that tomorrow. Tonight, we can get some supper, just us?' Ned proffered his verbal olive branch.

Rose pulled him in for a hug, which was slightly weird due to her still being draped in dragon.

'That sounds like a great idea,' she said as she rang the bell. 'I'm guessing you want some honeycakes as well?'

Ned bent to kiss her on the forehead and chucked Slinky under the chin. He was a very lucky man. He decided to push his luck.

'Er... there is one thing I wanted to ask. It's about Fred.'

'You want to recruit him for the Thief-Catchers,' replied Rose.

'Yeah, I do. So... what do you think?'

'I was beginning to wonder if you'd ever ask.' Rose smiled at the look on Ned's face. She patted his arm. 'He really is the perfect fit.'

Ned decided not to question further and just accept that he now had a new Catcher who he was very sure would be delighted at his new role.

Chapter 25

It was a brand new day, but Jenni stared moodily into the back garden. It was still snowing. On top of snow. Everywhere you looked, all snow. No other defining features at all. She had no idea if the gnomes were where she left them. Or if gnomes could even survive this weather. Buggers could tunnel, but if the ground was frozen solid, then what would they do? Last time she'd been out here, before the winter arrived, they had congregated mid-left of the garden. She squinted but could only see white. Feeling thoroughly defeated by the weather and wishing she had a gnome or two to torment, Jenni gathered a handful of the stuff together, intending to make a snowball.

What she hadn't anticipated was a surge in magic from the snow and have a sparkly white afterglow in the palms of her hands. There was magic in the snow. Actual magic in the snow. Jenni dropped to her knees and plunged her arms elbow deep. She focused on where she thought the gnomes might be, and the snow parted like a set of doors being slowly forced open.

She was so surprised; she yanked her hands back. Magic rarely did what it was supposed to do for her these days. She was relearning how to access her power, control it and not have it take over. Having been magically hijacked so recently, she was extra cautious at tapping into a new, unknown source of magic. But now that she'd touched it, the lure of the power tickled at her, urging her to scratch that itch. To pull more and more magic into herself. To be the most powerful being in

Roshaven. In all of Efrana. Jenni shoved her hands into her armpits. That wasn't her talking. She didn't know what it was, but it weren't her. She'd learnt that lesson. And she didn't need nobody else's power. And if she did reach out and take it, what would happen? Would she lose herself completely? Could she control it? Would she destroy Roshaven?

Fred yelled for her, making her jump. Scowling at the snow, she turned to go back inside. In her experience, Fred didn't yell. This better not be a hidden fault in his personality, only now revealed because he'd got his feet under the proverbial housemate table.

'Wot?'

'Sorry for yelling, Jenni. It's just that Mr Spinks is here, and he's had a terrible time getting here on account of the ice storm and he looks near frozen to death and I thought what we need here is some hot chocolate to warm everybody up and I bought me mams blend with me from home when I brought some stuff over yesterday only I can't find the cups and truth be told I'm a bit worried about Mr Spinks in that he looks a little blue and his hands are trembling. So I thought I'd better get you.' Fred waited patiently.

Jenni pointed to a low cupboard where the cups were kept. The obvious place for someone of her stature to keep such things, and incidentally, the one cupboard Fred hadn't checked. He busied himself making hot chocolate while Jenni went to see what her boss had done now.

Ned was sitting as close to the fire as possible while Trev stoked it good and proper. Bev and Kev were peppering Ned with excited questions, their voices getting higher and higher as they spoke over each other, not giving Ned the opportunity to reply. Joe and Willow looked on in quiet amusement.

'Wot's going on?' Jenni asked, but her question was lost over the babble. 'OI!' she shouted, and this had the desired effect. All eyes swivelled to stare at her.

'He's met the Meh-Teh,' breathed Kev in a reverential voice.

'Yeah? So did I. So 'as Willow. Wot of it?' Jenni hadn't shared that revelation with the M-TACs on her return. It had been late and everyone was half asleep. Plus it had taken a while to get enough pillows for everyone especially seeing as Willow and Joe stayed the night as well. Besides, she'd been feeling bad about upsetting Flake and still did, hence giving herself a time out in the garden this morning.

Bev and Kev both opened their mouth to speak, but Ned raised a hand to forestall them.

'His name is Flake, and he came down the mountain to ask me for some help. He's been evicted by Ice Giants. The current ice storm is his work, Jenni upset him. She was meant to be asking you for your help in finding him again,' said Ned in an even voice, but Jenni could tell he was mad at her.

She had the presence of mind to look somewhat abashed.

'I wos getting round to it, Boss. Just needed a minute to sort me 'ead out, that's all.'

Fred came bustling in with a tray of hot chocolates. They had mini marshmallows in them and he was wearing a floral pinny.

'It's amazing about the Meh-Teh, isn't it? Meeting an actual myth. In real life. And Ice Giants! Who knew?' Fred was chuntering away to nobody in particular. 'Are they made of actual ice? Or do they just live in icy places? Can they manipulate ice or do they have magical ice power? Do they melt like normal ice when left out in the sunshine?'

The others ventured a few ums and ahs, nobody really having any answers. It was a bit too much for Jenni.

'I can do magic!' she shouted, speaking much louder than she intended.

'Yes, we all know you can do magic, Jenni. You are fae, after all.' Ned took a slurp of his hot chocolate, licking his lips at the velvety smoothness of it.

'No, you don't understand. I can do Meh-Teh magic. With the snow. I can controls it. Come and see.' Jenni abandoned her cup untouched and bolted for the back garden.

She stood, foot tapping, waiting for the others to gather round her. When she was happy that she had everyone's attention, she flexed her fingers and dug them deep into the snow. A swirly pattern of snowflakes began dancing upwards.

'Um, Jenni?' Ned's voice sounded strained, but Jenni was too close to temptation to listen to him.

She moaned softly to herself and closed her eyes.

A cold gust of wind blew loose snowflakes together, forming a ball-like shape. It was joined by three others as they spun around the garden, gathering flakes as they went until Jenni had two large snowballs and two smaller ones. The smaller ones levitated onto the larger and smooshed down. Then an unseen force whipped four branches over, two into each snow pile, and finally some pebbles shot out of an oscillating snow drift, forming a smiley face on the two snowmen. Jenni made the snowmen dance.

'Enough,' said Ned in a strangled voice. 'Jenni! Release the magic, now!'

Jenni scowled, but did as he asked. It made her gasp as the power left her. It was almost painful. Ned grabbed her by the shoulders and peered into her eyes.

'How?' he asked.

Jenni wiggled out of his grasp and shivered. She was suddenly chilled to the bone.

'There's magic in the snow, innit. I came out 'ere cos I felt bad about scaring off the Meh-Teh and that got me finking about the gnomes and if they wos awright, so I just shoved me hands in it and the snow moved.'

She shivered again as the full enormity of how easily the foreign power had invaded and taken over.

'But why hasn't this happened before now? This isn't the first time you've touched snow since the bad weather started – is it?' asked Ned.

'Nah but it's the first time I touched it wiv emotional intent,' explained Jenni.

'Emotional intent?' Ned looked nonplussed.

'Intent is when you know what you got to do and you know how you're going to do it, so you just get on with it and get it done, Mr Spinks, sir. Comes in handy with vegetables at dinner time, I find. I expect emotional intent is when you feel so strongly about the vegetables, it becomes a mental challenge not to give them names and personalities.'

'Yes, I know what intent is. Thank you, Fred.' Although he wasn't entirely sure Fred had it right on the emotional side of things. Ned looked at the piles of snow, frowning.

'She's turning white,' commented Trev. 'Is she meant to do that?'

Jenni watched as Ned peered at her more closely. She spread her hands out in front of her to see for herself and saw that they were covered in a sparkly white residue.

'I think maybe we should go talk to Momma K, yeah? Give her an update on the Meh-Teh. See if she knows anything about the Ice Giants. Okay?' Ned was making shushing motions with his hands to encourage the others to get back into the house.

Jenni dropped her arms and a heavy flurry of flakes fell, beating gravity to the floor. Whilst what had happened had given her the willies, she was still reluctant to head indoors and leave the snow behind. Then she perked up at realising she would have to walk through it to get to the Fae Grove. Jenni shuddered again. No, she was not excited about walking through snow. What was wrong with her?

'My question is why is the snow out there like powder when the Meh-Teh triggered an ice storm? It should be like a skating rink. Not fresh and fluffy.' It was Kev. He'd been quiet for a long time.

Jenni eyed him suspiciously. It was always the quiet ones.

'I didn't want it to be frozen solid,' she said in a small voice. She started picking the side of her thumb with her index finger, an anxious habit she thought she'd grown out of.

'State manipulation, interesting,' murmured Kev as he joined his compatriots around the fire and began talking to them in hushed tones.

'Shall I come with Mr Spinks, Sir?' asked Fred. Joe and Willow also made noises about accompanying them.

'No need. You guys hold the fort here. Keep M-TAC together in one place. We'll go looking for Flake once we've spoken to Momma K. Won't be long.'

Jenni could tell Ned was forcing the cheeriness into his voice and glanced down again at her sparkly hands.

It wasn't fading. As she looked down, a lock of hair fell over her eye. Only it was several shades lighter than it should have been. She held it out in front of her to get a better look. Yep, her hair was lighter. Odd.

'C'mon Jenni. Let's get a move on. It'll probably take us half an hour to get through the ice storm,' said Ned in his fake cheery tone. It was normally only a few minutes' walk to the grove.

'I might be able to do summink about that,' said Jenni softly as they walked out the door. She stuck her hands resolutely in her coat pockets. 'But I ain't gonna. No, I ain't. Not gonna do nuffink wiv this snow.' She continued muttering under her breath in the same vein, talking herself into not doing anything.

The impressive storm was still beating the streets of Roshaven but was it Jenni's imagination that the snow fell in a slightly softer pattern around them and the icy wind didn't howl quite so loud in their ear as Ned and Jenni made their way to the Fae Grove.

'How are you doing, Jenni?' asked Ned, his voice laced with concern.

'I ain't... I dunno... s'weird.' said Jenni.

'What is?'

'This power, it gotta be wot the Meh-Teh is using, right? But it ain't... natural. Like, it feels nasty and icky and stuff.' She shuddered. 'I mean, I fink the Meh-Teh wos using magic, but he ain't fae, so mebbe it ain't magic like wot we got. But the fing is, there's lots of magic in this snow, right, and I can sorta scoop it out and recycle it. I fink it's a bit like when I draw natural magic from the fings wot is around us. Wots around us right now is snow so when I was in the garden I fawt give it go, see wot 'appens. And yeah, bit of snow magic. But it's got a mind of its own, Boss. It's tickling me head,

170

telling me how good it'll be to use it. Calling me. And it's so easy. All I gotta do is just reach out. That's all. Just reach.'

'Are you, er… safe?' he finally asked.

'I ain't gonna turn into an eleven-foot monster if that's wot you mean,' Jenni snapped. 'I got some self-control.' Her insides were quailing at the effort of ignoring the magic. She wondered if the Meh-Teh had the same struggle. It hadn't looked like it when he'd been gently flurrying in the office.

'Good, good.' Ned was trying to get a good look at her without making it too obvious.

Jenni hunched into her coat and tried to ignore the massive amounts of magic swirling around her, begging her to reach out and touch it. It was so weird. A few hours ago, walking in the snow had just been cold and crunchy. Now she felt like she was fighting for her sanity. But it was only a short walk to the grove. All she had to do was put one foot in front of the other. Momma K would know what to do.

Chapter 26

The fae grove was a tinkly icescape. There were sparkly icicles hanging throughout, catching the light, and artistic snowflakes fell in lacy perfection. Everything had a blue tinge with icing sprinkled on top.

There was a soft glow from Momma K's inner sanctum and the thief-Catchers hurried towards it, hoping for heat. It was freezing everywhere else.

What met his eyes stopped Ned in his tracks. Hundreds of fae huddled around small fires. They were all wrapped up in blankets and hats, scarves and gloves and every single one of them looked miserable. Most didn't even look up to see who had arrived.

Momma K was so bundled up, Ned could barely make out it was her.

'Catcha?' Momma K tilted her head as much as the woollens festooned about her would allow.

'Are you alright?' Ned frowned. The last time he'd been here, it had been tropical.

'We not… doing so good Catcha. Me sent as many fae away as can go. Stay wid friends elsewhere but dat weaken de realm. No fae here, no realm. Dose dat stay are too weak ta go. And me tired. Bone cold. Tell me ya know what causing de winter.'

'It's being caused by a Meh-Teh. Did you know about him? He says the Ice Giants kicked him out, and he's come to find me to help him get his home back.' Ned paused, but there was no immediate response from Momma K. 'I'm here to see if you have any information about the Ice Giants. How we can encourage them to move on and if that doesn't work, how we defeat them.' He waited again. 'Momma K? Were you aware of the Meh-Teh?'

But Momma K's attention was firmly on her daughter.

'Wot ya got?' she sucked her teeth, eyes narrowed as she stared.

'The snow magic is calling me,' replied Jenni miserably. She lifted one of her sparkly white hands, twirled her fingers, and made mini snowflakes dance in intricate patterns around her.

'Stop dat! It no yor magic. It no yor blood. It no for fae!' Momma K pushed several layers off, emerging from her blanket cocoon and came to stand in front of her daughter. She placed her tiny hands on either side of Jenni's head and closed her eyes. The whole grove hushed. You could hear the ice sparkling.

'Enough,' hissed Momma K. Lifting her face to the sky, she blew a blast of icy air out of her mouth, visibly slumped once the energies had been expelled. Jenni's hair returned to its usual dirty straw colour and her hands lost their snowy countenance. 'I pulled out de magic for now but it no keep it out. Dere a connection now. Catcha-man, ya need de Book of Ice. Dere a spell ta return de Ice Giants, send dem back to Nowhere. But it take a lotta power. More den yours. But she can't do it. You hafta find anuder way.'

'Why can't I do the spell? Wot's wrong with me? Why is the snow magic calling me so bad?' Jenni looked small and deflated.

'Daughta... Me been worried at dis. Afta de Sea Witch, me worried and now me see. Ya changed. It permanent, me doh know. Me tink maybe yes maybe no. But dis uder power, it call ya and it be hard for ya to

173

resist. Ya must. Ya must resist wid everytink ya got. Udderwise it will be de end.'

'Whaddya mean changed? I'm just using magic from me surroundings like wot I'm supposed to, ain't I?' Jenni sounded scared.

'Me can no draw dis power.'

Momma K's words fell into silence as all fae eyes regarded Jenni.

'Me daughta... ya no longer just fae. Ya sometink mixy mixy. Two worlds pushed togetha, no fighting, just growing, changing. Me doh know how good, how bad. Me do know ya no just fae. Not no moh.'

Jenni turned to Ned, ready to scoff in disbelief, and stopped at the look of shock on his face.

'Wot? You fink she's right?' Jenni was almost in tears now. She didn't want to be mixy mixy nuffink. She just wanted to be plain old Jenni.

'I think your mum knows more about this than I do.' He came and gave her a hug which blindsided her so much, the tears started to fall. 'But I am confident that we'll get to the bottom of it. I won't let you turn into some kind of ice queen. Promise.'

Jenni wiped her snotty nose on her sleeve and smiled shakily up at her boss. She knew he would always have her back.

'We got some good news then. We got that book, ain't we? It's the one you got from the library, right?' She regarded Ned, waiting for confirmation.

Ned smiled sheepishly back at her.

'You're right. We do have it. I forgot all about it and left it at the office. We'd better go pick it up.' He turned to Momma K. 'Any idea how we open it? It's frozen solid, no sign of defrosting.'

Momma K was still regarding Jenni, visibly

weighing and measuring her in some way. Then she abruptly turned away from her daughter and addressed Ned directly.

'When de time right, de book will open. Butcha must pay for de knowledge. Dere always a price. Always.'

'How come you didn't tell us about the Meh-Teh?' asked Ned, determined to get an answer.

'It a myth.' She flicked a glance at Jenni once more. 'But de myth sometime walk among us. Catcha-man, hurry. De fae no survive much more winter. Hurry.' A plume of dragon breath huffed out of Momma K's mouth as she snuggled herself back into her blanket cocoon, almost disappearing from view.

Jenni shivered, realising that the surrounding temperature had fallen since they'd arrived. She could see Ned's teeth chattering and felt utterly useless. There must be something she could do to help. Throwing caution to the wind, Jenni clenched her fists and pushed her arms out to either side of her, moving slowly as if they were pressing against some enormous weight. Gradually, the icy bite in the air lessened and the oppressive snow moved backwards. It was still tinkly and full of icicles, but there was an invisible line around the huddling fae keeping the bulk of the cold at bay. The effort of bending the snow magic to her will and then letting go of it dropped Jenni to her knees and had her gasping for breath. Ned helped her back up to shaky legs and stayed close in case he needed her again.

'It ain't gonna last for ever but it should 'elp.' Jenni spoke to her mum, ignoring the incredulous looks from everyone else.

'Tank ya daughter. But ya got to be safe. If ya try to do too much, de snow will no let ya go. Me advice?

Leave it be. Even for de sake of anuder. Me doh tink ya'll be able to hold on next time.' She regarded Jenni with huge, shining eyes. 'Me doh want ta lose me daughta.'

Jenni sniffed and nodded and for once it was Ned hurrying after Jenni as she made a swift beeline for the exit.

'You sure you're ok?' He asked her as they arrived back in Roshaven and before the biting cold drove his breath away.

'Yeah. Let's go get this book.'

Ned's confident stride was somewhat marred by the huge slide his boots took on the cobbles but by windmilling his arms like his very life depended on it, Ned was able to maintain his balance and it was with smaller, more cautious feet that he headed over to Catcher HQ.

Chapter 27

On entering the office, Ned breathed an icy breath of relief and immediately started coughing. All this cold was really getting to his chest. The Book of Ice was still on the bucket on the chair. In fact, instead of continuing to defrost, it appeared to have changed its mind and had now turned the bucket and the chair into an ice block upon which the book rested, looking innocent. If books can ever be called innocent.

Remembering how cold the book had been when he first got hold of it, Ned made sure his gloves were firmly pulled on and went to pick it up. Nothing. The book was welded to the bucket, which was stuck to the floor in a determined manner. After a few moments of heaving, Ned very nearly couldn't pull his gloves off the damn thing. It was a lot colder now than it had been.

'We are going to have to rethink this one,' he said, wondering whether the old boiling hot water trick might, well, do the trick.

'I could have a go,' offered Jenni, but her hands were jammed deep into her pockets and she was eyeing the book with deep mistrust. 'If you wants.'

'Do you think it will come free because you are fae?' Ned asked the question, but he already knew the answer.

'Nah, the snow magic is pulling me towards the book. It wants me to pick it up. It weren't doing this afore, but it's awake now.' There was a note of yearning in Jenni's voice and she'd taken an involuntary step forward. 'And I wants to but I don't neiver. I fink... I fink, Boss, if I picks this up then it'll 'ave me.' She dragged her gaze away from Ned. 'I don't want the power to take over again.' Her body betrayed her with another step towards the book.

Ned edged himself between the two and felt the cold radiating against the back of his legs.

'Maybe you could wait downstairs? Have a little check on Reg, make sure he's got everything he needs.'

Jenni nodded, but it was clear she had to physically pull herself away from the book, bucket and chilly office. It wasn't until the door clicked shut behind her that Ned let out a sigh of relief. Well, half relief. He still had to pick the blasted thing up. Ned tried to remind himself that it was just a book, nothing to be afraid of. He nudged the bucket with his foot and was surprised when it wobbled a touch. Bending down to inspect it further, Ned realised the frigid conditions had lessened somewhat. The magic had turned on to lure Jenni, but now that she'd gone, it had relaxed again. Ned really hoped it was a proximity reaction rather than a conscious thought. He didn't like the idea of a thinking book. Somehow, Ned was going to have to keep the two of them as far apart as possible. Inspired, he picked up the furry coat everyone had teased him about and carefully wrapped it around the book that he could now lever off the bucket.

Confident that he would not turn himself into a human popsicle, Ned found one of Willow's indestructible hemp bags and stuffed the icy parcel into it. The fur was getting stiff already. Speed was going to be important, but where should he take the book?

He stopped at the bottom of the stairs and called over to Jenni, who was sitting on a barstool, Reg nowhere to be seen.

'Look Jenni, I've got the book here, but I think it's reacting with you somehow, and the closer you get to it, the more frozen it becomes. We won't be able to open it if you're nearby.'

Jenni nodded miserably.

'So I'm going to take it back to the Palace. You go home, tell Fred and the M-TACs to meet me in the study.' Ned paused and considered how the young palace guard was likely to react to that. 'Make sure Fred knows he has permission to cross the inner perimeter and that I'm counting on him to escort our special guests.'

'K.' Jenni wiped her runny nose on her sleeve. 'Wot do I do?'

'Look after Willow. She caught a nasty chill yesterday, and we nearly lost her.'

'Yeah, she told me. Fawt she had inbuilt fingies wot stopped all that?'

'So did I, but apparently her natural defences aren't enough to guard against this severity of winter. Keep an eye on her, please. And ask Joe to help you put together a supply list for a trip up Mount Firn. And then, between you, with the assistance of Fingers, sort out the logistics for setting up the seed bank and fielding the animals out of the city.' Ned felt relieved. There was plenty there for all three Catchers to be getting on with and it should take Jenni's mind off the snow power.

'I can't come, can I?' asked Jenni.

Ned could only shrug his shoulders. If Jenni and the book were reacting that strongly already, it was unlikely that she would be able to come on the mission with him. It would be the first time they had not quested together.

'You go ahead. Get home, wrap up warm and crack on with your jobs. I'll catch up with you later, yeah?'

Jenni nodded and slid off her barstool. A blast of cold air dashed inside as she let herself out of The Noose. Ned waited a couple of minutes before crossing the floor and leaving. Jenni was nowhere to be seen, so he hunched his shoulders against the weather, which was mostly ineffective, and began tramping over to the Palace. It was times like this that Rose's continual mentioning of moving Thief-Catcher HQ to the Palace gained merit.

Hopefully, he would be able to open the book and find out how to deal with the Ice Giants. The M-TACs would figure out how to find the Meh-Teh, who would agree to leave Roshaven and return home. Then everything would just melt away. Hopefully.

Ned didn't notice that he was leaving shiny footsteps behind in the snow. The snow magic was turning them into pure ice. Unable to bend Ned's magical will in the same way as it could with Jenni, it was trying to change the environment immediately around them. Ned only noticed when he paused to change hands on the hemp bag and his foot slid abruptly. He looked down and saw the prints.

'No, no, no, no. Don't start trying anything with me. I'm not your man.'

He began walking a good deal more gingerly than before, making sure he didn't slip on the ice. A broken leg would be the very last straw. All around him, the flakes whirled like dervishes and the wind shouted.

At least Fred would have a roaring fire going and some hot beverage of some kind. That should help to make Jenni feel better. Ned's stomach growled, and he perked up. He had Ma Bowl's kitchen to greet him and there was bound to be some warming soup and perhaps even some honeycakes.

Chapter 28

'Come in, come in! Let's get you warmed up. Where's Mr Spinks? It's a rum one out there, that's for sure. Bigger than the storm in '84 and our Mam says that was the deepest, darkest winter Roshaven ever had. They had nothing for weeks. Lived on sucking snow and making their own entertainment. Although she always gets rather vague on the ins and outs of that whenever I ask her. Not to worry. I've been keeping some notes of events this time around. For posterity, you know. Might be interesting reading in a few hundred years. You never know, do you?' Fred finally stopped for breath as Jenni sidled past him and headed straight for the fireplace.

The entire brunt of the winter storm was battering the door, and it took an almighty heave for Fred to get it closed. In the sitting room, the MTAC were sprawled like human cats on the rug in front of the fire, with toasting forks speared with sausages and bread dangling in the blaze. Joe and Willow filled one armchair, and the tree nymph appeared to be back to her full plant glory.

They all greeted Jenni cheerfully and when they saw how cold she was, got her quickly settled facing the flames with a snuggly blanket wrapped around her. A mug of hot chocolate with marshmallows was pushed into one hand whilst a toasted sausage sandwich was pressed in the other. Hunger and the desire to feel warm took over, and she tucked in.

Fred did a good job of waiting for Jenni to finish eating but he kept leaning forwards, opening his mouth, lifting a finger then returning to sitting, legs jigging away like anything. As soon as the last morsel of sandwich had been demolished, he unleashed his tirade of questions.

'Jenni, what's happened to Mr Spinks? Did you go see Momma K? Has she kept Mr Spinks there? What did she think was happening to you? Will Mr Spinks be coming back here? Are you going to turn into a snowman? Do we need to cook some more sausages? Should you be out in the snow? Can Momma K solve the winter? Does Mr Spinks have a plan? Won't you die if you get too cold? Do you want another sandwich? Can you control the weather?'

Jenni squinted as she tried to process all the questions.

'Nuffink. Yeah. Nah. Stuff. Not yet. Don't be silly. Always. Probably not. Nope. I fink so. Maybe. Yes. Not yet.'

It was Fred's turn to figure out the answers to his questions. After a good five minutes, he sat back with a pleased smile on his face, then quickly leant forward, gesturing for Bev to get another toasted sausage sandwich on the go.

'I'm glad Mr Spinks is ok. Did he have a message for us?'

Jenni eyed the sausage sandwich greedily before dragging her focus back to Fred.

'E says you and the M-TACs gotta go to the Palace and meet 'im in the study. E says you got permission to cross the inner wotsit.' She turned her attention to Willow and Joe. 'We gotta put a list togever of wot we fink we need to travel up Mount Firn and sort the plan for the seed fingy and the deer fingy.'

Fred felt that her relay of Ned's instructions might not be quite as detailed as those originally given to her.

'He actually said that I can cross the inner perimeter? You're sure?' Fred needed to double check. Palace guards, unless specifically ordered to do otherwise, stayed on the outer perimeter. It was their job to keep undesirables out and, on special state occasions, look smart and imposing. Fred had discovered it was quite difficult to do both at the same time.

Jenni grinned at him and nodded, gratefully receiving her second sandwich with glee. It seemed her delivery had been sufficient for everyone else. Trev handed over a list he'd been working on of supplies needed for a mountainous climb in the snow to Joe, who added it to some paperwork on the small table beside him.

'Willow and I have already been talking about the seed bank and how best to use our volunteers. We both agreed we should flush the deer out of the city first and then we can split Roshaven into zones, provide each volunteer group with a list of plants and what to be aware of seed-wise. Then me and Willow will set up in the warehouse and ensure correct labelling and storage. All we've got to do is let Fingers know the plan.'

'K,' said Jenni thickly around her sandwich and gave the pair a thumbs up.

Bev, Kev and Trev had been pulling on their winter wear and with a jolt Fred realised he would be the one holding them up if he didn't start doing the same. And it was his job to escort M-TAC to the empress's study. A huge honour. He began frantically winding his extra-long scarf around his neck and by the time he pulled on his snow boots – just ordinary palace-issue boots but with snow still on them – everyone was ready to head over to the palace.

'Ready, Miss Jenni?' he asked, perplexed that she

wasn't.

'Nah. Just youse. Off you go.'

There was a slight stiffness to her words, but Fred had no time to dwell upon it. He had been summoned to the imperial inner perimeter and he would deliver his special guests in one piece, snowstorm or no snowstorm.

Chapter 29

Ned watched Fred. He was actually oscillating from standing so straight.

'The M-TACs, your Empress,' he announced, then took the customary palace guard retreat steps towards the study door.

'Where are you going, Fred? We need you at this meeting.' Ned smiled at the consternation that flashed over Fred's face, swiftly followed by intense pride.

'Yes, Sir, Mr Spinks, Sir.'

Rose beckoned them all to join her at the large table in the study and once everyone was seated, she made sure they all had a beverage.

'Sorry, but can I ask? Why is Miss Jenni not here? Surely she is integral to any and all Thief-Catcher meetings?'

Ned could see Fred looked almost like he was about to burst into tears.

'She's… linked to the snow somehow. It's not magically safe for her to be around anything to do with the abnormal weather.' Ned held his tongue from saying more to Fred, but all he really wanted to do was talk about how worried he was about Jenni. He'd told Rose everything he'd learnt from Momma K, but between the two of them, they hadn't been able to come up with any solutions. Yet. His wife gave his hand a quick squeeze. He took comfort from that and cleared his throat. 'This is the Book of Ice,' he said, gesturing to the now thawed book on the table. Occasionally, a tinkle indicated the descent of a tiny icicle to the floor. 'It's meant to have the spell we need to defeat the Ice Giants and get the Meh-Teh back home. Get winter under control.'

Fred clearly couldn't help himself. His naturally enquiring mind let loose.

'Why is Jenni affected by the snow? Did she get zapped by the book? Is she turning into an icicle? Will she have to go and live in the mountains? Do you think the Meh-Teh will know what's wrong with her? What if she gets so cold her heart stops working? Don't you die if you get too cold? Is she now controlling the weather? Will she turn into an Ice Giant? Do you want a biscuit?'

Ned desperately leapt onto the one question he could confidently answer, despite the fact that it was unrelated to all the others. He'd spotted the biscuit plate making its way around the table and was keen to secure for himself the two chocolate digestives, partially hidden by the plain hobnobs. The honeycakes had already gone.

'Yes, I will have a biscuit.' He looked at Fred's worried face and did his best to reply. 'I can't answer all your questions, lad. But trust me, we will get to the bottom of it and solve this winter as well as what's happening to Jenni. She always pulls through for Roshaven. And this time, we'll make sure we do the same for her. I'm confident we can sort it out.'

Fred's entire body relaxed. Ned was surprised. He wasn't sure he'd sounded that convincing. Then he realised the young lad trusted him implicitly and if Ned said it would be alright, then it was going to be alright.

'The first thing we need to do is locate the Meh-Teh. That's where you come in.' Rose smiled warmly at the M-TACs who had just begun to remove their bobble hats and woolly scarves.

'Bev, Trev and Kev at your service, Ma'am,' said Bev with a bob of head, the others following suit.

'Honoured to be able to help in whatever way possible.'

The study's fireplace kept fizzing as snow fell at random moments down the chimney. Ned couldn't decide whether that was normal or if it was the snow magic messing around.

'What can you tell us about the Meh-Teh?' prompted Rose.

'A Meh-Teh is a very shy creature, not one for socialising at all,' began Trev. 'In fact, it's astounding that he even came to this city and spoke to people. It's never been recorded before. We are truly breaking ground in Meh-Teh investigation and discovery. Exciting times, don't you agree?'

Ned smiled weakly, trying to muster the enthusiasm for scientific advancement, but he was more worried about Jenni and his city.

'We just need to find the Meh-Teh and hope he'll talk to us again. Any ideas?' Ned cast a hopeful look over the MTACs, who all beamed back but said nothing.

'I have an idea,' said Fred, but then Kev started speaking so he stopped.

'The thing you have to understand about Meh-Teh's is they are very set in their ways. They like their own company, they like their own habitat and they're damn near impossible to see in the wild. I mean, we've never had the opportunity for eyes on observation. Everything we know has come from second-hand accounts and our own extrapolation. MTAC is our life's work. We have dedicated every waking moment...'

Bev interjected, 'And several digits.'

'And several digits to the pursuit of knowledge in the faintest hope that we would one day get to see a Meh-Teh in real life.' Kev took a shuddering breath, emotion threatening to overcome him. 'This is a historic moment. We really should be documenting. Are we documenting?'

Trev waved the pen and paper he had been scribbling furiously with just moments ago. Bev held up the pencil sketch she'd made of them sat in the Empress's study. Ned had to admit, the likenesses were uncanny.

'So with all this knowledge, how are we going to find Flake in Roshaven?' Ned asked again.

And was again met with a smiling yet apologetic silence.

'I might have an idea...' began Fred, but this time was cut off by Rose. Manners dictated he wait his turn, especially as it was his empress talking, but Ned noticed Fred's legs had begun jigging in impatience. He put a hand out to him to let him know he could talk next and the lad bobbed his understanding.

'Can't we just lure it? Into some kind of anti Meh-Teh trap where we can immobilise it and transport the creature back up the mountain, deal with the ice giants and get back to normal.' Rose made it sound so easy and matter of fact, but Ned knew that it wouldn't be. Besides, he'd met the Meh-Teh, spoken with him. He had no intention of trapping him like an animal.

'I'm not sure that's a good idea. For one thing, we owe Flake an apology. He came here for our help. It's the least we can do after scaring him. I think we'll make more progress with a mutual understanding and agreement moving forwards. And Momma K said we'd need a lot of power to cast the Ice Giant spell. So that needs working out.' Ned didn't know if Flake's innate magic might come in useful, but thought it was unlikely. Things were never that straightforward.

Rose's eyes sparkled at him and he felt like she

looked somewhat proud at the fact that he had the gumption to counter her suggestion.

'Fred here has an idea. What do you think we should do?' Ned turned to the lad, pulling with him the focus of everyone else. Fred gulped.

'Well, I've been thinking about what I want to do when it's cold. I go and find the warmest place there is right? And I get all snuggled up with blankets and our mam brings me cocoa and the fire is roaring and the cats are purring and it's just lovely. A wonderful way to unwind from a hard day's shift. Our Malcolm spends most of his time in front of the fire. Me Mam says he's part cat and part sloth and one of these days he'll get the shock of his life which I suppose means that a hot coal will bounce out of the fireplace but we're very careful about that, what with the fire guard and all.' He paused minutely for breath before continuing. 'So if I was going to go somewhere super warm and snuggly, surely a creature of ice and snow would go somewhere super cold and snowy. That would be their comfort spot.'

At first, Fred's triumphant smile was met with confused faces. Ned had noticed this happened a lot when people listened to Fred. The lad liked to waffle, but Ned had clearly been getting more and more used to the way he spoke because he caught on to his notion almost straight away.

'You're right, Fred. That's a brilliant idea. Let's figure out where the snow and ice are thickest or deepest or coldest or whatever the measure is and that's where we'll find our Meh-Teh. Good work.'

Fred blushed beetroot, and the others gave up trying to unravel his train of speech and instead added their approval to the idea.

'What do you reckon, guys?' Ned asked M-TAC.

'Do you think you can figure out the coldest part of Roshaven?'

There was a long pause as Bev, Trev and Kev shared uneasy glances.

'Maybe, but I don't think you're going to like it,' said Trev finally.

'Well, would you share that information with the rest of us, please? So we can make an informed decision.' Ned didn't mean to sound so snippy, but he was ready for answers, not more cryptic clues.

'We believe it will be Jenni. If she opens herself up to the snow magic, she'll become its power centre and the Meh-Teh won't be able to resist that lure. He will be drawn to it as sure as eggs is eggs.'

Ned didn't have the foggiest what eggs had to do with it, but he was one hundred per cent adamant that there was no way Jenni was going to let in the snow magic.

'No, I'm sorry. That won't work. What else have you got?'

Rose half frowned at Ned but didn't push him on the decision for which he was grateful.

'We'll have to do a grid walk,' said Fred.

'Grid walk?' queried Kev.

'Yes. A grid walk. It's where you get lots of people together and they all walk in a straight line, spaced out a bit, and they look for things. It's a tactic often used in the search for mispers – that's missing persons. Very effective when it's children as they like to hide in odd places. First of all, the place you're looking gets gridded, easy enough to do with a map, but even if you don't have one of those, you can draw an approximation. Joe has lots of large sheets of paper. He showed me the other day when he was explaining his organisational process.

With enough people, the grids could be easily searched for a drop in temperature, which I imagine would be obvious. I mean, we could ask everyone to walk without their gloves on. Our mam says the fingertips are one of the most sensitive parts of the human body, which is why it hurts so much when you get a paper cut along the tip.'

Ned was considering the logistics of such a grid walk when he had an epiphany and clapped his hands together, making the others jump.

'And we have lots of bodies gathering right now for the deer drive and seed collecting. We're bound to find the Meh-Teh. Well done, Fred.'

'Yes, a grand idea but completely unnecessary, eh?' said Griff, walking into the study and nodding towards the windows that opened out onto the Rose Garden. The Meh-Teh stood in the flowerbed.

Chapter 30

Ned could've sworn that one moment the Meh-Teh wasn't in the garden. The next he was.

'How did you know he was there?' he hissed at Griff.

'Pure luck. He caught my eye as I walked in,' replied Griff with a whisper. 'Don't spoil the effect, eh?' And he dug his son gently in the ribs.

Ned couldn't help but grin back. It usually was all about the timing.

'Let's go and speak with him,' said Rose. 'But maybe just me and Ned to start with. We don't want to scare him away again. Everyone else can stand in the open doorway, but not one footstep in the snow. Got it?'

The M-TACs, Griff and Fred all nodded earnestly. Ned decided they'd make it thirty seconds before they wouldn't be able to resist the urge to come closer.

Rose beckoned Ned towards her as she wrapped herself up in a nearby coat.

'Is Jenni going to be alright?' she asked quietly.

'She's worried. So am I. But one problem at a time. You ready?'

Rose nodded and together, they entered the snow-clad garden, the spectators hot on their heels and just about managing to stay inside.

'Hello Flake. This is my wife, Rose, Empress of Roshaven. Thank you for coming back.'

The Meh-Teh stared at Rose with a sort of longing in his eyes before bowing low and proffering a frozen rose, which she took carefully with a graceful nod of thanks.

'I apologise for my behaviour earlier. I have come to realise how severe the implications of my being here will be for your city, and I can assure you, that was not my intention.' As Flake spoke, the ice storm was lessening, losing its oomph.

'We understand. But it won't be possible for you to stay here very much longer. And we are going to need your help to deal with the melt that is bound to occur when you leave.' Rose squared her shoulders, ready to negotiate.

'Snow and ice are my medium. It's a part of who I am. If you help me, I can remove my winter,' replied Flake.

'Even all the snow that has piled up? And the ice and frost?' Ned was surprised. 'How will you manage that?'

'Yes. I can lessen it, stop the snow from falling but you may need to deal with meltwater, a natural side effect of snow leaving. Provided, of course, you return with me and defeat the Ice Giants first.'

There was a slight hitch in the Meh-Teh's words as he spoke which set off the hairs on the back of Ned's neck. Flake wasn't telling them everything, although Ned did think he was being honest about removing the snow.

'Can you come in? It's a little... chilly out here.' Ned thought about the inner blaze going on inside. 'We could bank the fire.'

'I would rather not, if you do not mind. Insides make me nervous.' While Flake was talking, he was eyeing the open door with all its gawkers with an equal measure of distaste and wariness.

Ned glanced back and saw that he'd been wrong

earlier. The people inside had lasted about twenty seconds before venturing outside. Every single one of them had a matching sheepish grin plastered on their face.

'These people are just curious to meet you, Flake. They mean you no harm. If it makes you uncomfortable, I can send them away.' The warning note in Ned's voice was aimed at Bev, Trev and Kev. He wasn't sure how far he could trust them. At least he knew that Fred and Griff wouldn't try to steal a toenail or start performing tests.

'And on behalf of Jenni, I would like to extend our sincere apologies for upsetting you earlier. We are honoured to have you visit our city.' Rose spoke calmly, as if she were used to talking to mythical creatures regularly.

'Thank you. I accept your apology. And I am very sorry for my manners. Being indoors unsettled me. In fact, your entire empire puts me ill at ease. No offence.'

'None taken.' Ned reassured him before Rose could reply. 'The Empress has given me imperial approval to assemble a team and go eliminate these Ice Giants, get you back home. We have the Book of Ice, which I believe contains a spell to help us.'

At the mention of the spell, the Meh-Teh twitched violently, causing all its fur to ripple. The temperature fell momentarily, and Ned shivered. When the Meh-Teh cocked his shaggy head to one side, Ned wondered if he'd said the wrong thing at the lack of reaction until he realised Flake was emotionally overcome. He could tell because a small snow cloud had formed above him and was silently raining a steady flurry of tiny snowflakes.

'Can I ask… about the magic in the snow? Is it yours?' Ned needed to know if Jenni was attracted to Flake's energies or whether something else nefarious

194

was going on.

'As I said, we Meh-Teh have a natural affinity with wintery weather. We can exercise emotional intent and have the snow or ice react in line with our mood. It is innate. We are born with it. Are we magical creatures? I cannot answer that. There are degrees of wonder in our world. I am seen as a mythical being therefore practically everything about me could be perceived as magical.'

'So that's a no, then.' Ned scratched his head, thinking. 'Do you know where the magic in the snow has come from?'

Flake's eyebrows beetled as if they were warring with each other.

'I... do not.'

It was so obviously a lie, everyone fell silent. Ned waited to see if anyone else was going to call the Meh-Teh out, but when even Rose said nothing he realised it would be up to him.

'Uh... are you sure? No clue at all?' he asked gingerly, not wanting to set off another snowsplosion.

Flake shook his head mutely.

Ned rocked on his heels a little. It had already been agreed that they would go with Flake and help him, so there was going to be a journey ahead. Travelling companions on the road, campfires... well, in theory, maybe not actual fires. Opportunities for camaraderie, at the very least. Flake knew something, and it was clear he wasn't comfortable sharing that information at the moment. Could be he was scared, more likely a trust issue. Ned would just have to show him he was the most trustworthy person in Roshaven.

The quiet that had followed Ned's queries about snow magic was destroyed by an excited explosion of noise from the small group of people standing next to Ned.

'Can I come?'

'Can *we* come?'

'This has to be documented! It's the greatest event in the history of winter.'

'Who are you going to leave in charge?'

'I really think we should come.'

'I really think I should come.'

There was a momentary pause as people tried to turn and see who had said what before Fred made the final declaration.

'Anyway, you need people of intelligence on this sort of mission...'

'Quest,' interrupted Kev. 'Or possibly a geas.'

'There's no geas,' Ned said sharply. 'And this has got to be a finely tuned mission in order to succeed.'

'Quest,' muttered Kev, nodding to himself.

Ned turned back to Flake. 'We require some time to get together our supplies for a trip up Mount Firn. Would it be acceptable if we left tomorrow morning? How do we reach you?'

Flake looked mournful.

'Is there any pressing reason why we can't leave now? Why just you and I can't traverse the miles to my mountain upon this moment?'

His massive eyebrows had descended in a genuine plea that seriously tugged on Ned's heart strings.

'I'm sorry Flake, my husband is not equipped to survive the harsh conditions as he stands. He requires specialist equipment, and it is my imperial wish he travels with companions, should something untoward occur.'

There was a sharpness to Rose's innocuous sounding

request that even Flake had to acquiesce to. The Meh-Teh nodded sombrely.

'I accept your timeline and appreciate your unflinching assistance. I will meet you on the North Road out of Roshaven. Shall we say when dawn crests the horizon?'

Again, there was the slight hesitation behind the Meh-Teh's words. Almost as if he didn't really want Ned's help, and yet he sounded so sincere.

'Er… let's say around 9-ish. Give the sun a chance to rise a little,' suggested Ned.

Flake huffed but said nothing, leaving behind a flurry of agitated snowflakes and disappearing from the garden. A very excited yet perplexed group of people were left standing outside.

Chapter 31

'When did you get back, Griff?' asked Rose, leaving the M-TACs and Fred to converse in hoarsely excited whispers by the now closed French windows.

'Moments ago, my Empress. I came straight here. As swiftly as I was able in this weather, eh? It's got worse.'

'And this odd snow. Is it only in Roshaven?'

Ned noted the hitch in his wife's question. If the snow was only here, then at least sending Flake back up the mountain would hopefully solve that problem, but if the weather was more widespread, then there were more significant connotations to consider.

'It is localised. Fidelia is just coming into winter, no frost yet and definitely no snow. This is very much a Roshaven special, eh? But you have a plan, I see.'

'We do. Flake – the Meh-Teh – came down Mount Firn with his snow magic to find me and ask me to help evict the ice giants from his home. Momma K told me there is a spell in the Book of Ice that will vanquish them.' Ned liked that word. Vanquish. It made him feel like he was going to win and that nothing could go wrong.

'Ah, so Jenni is going to cast the spell and we all come home in time for tea, eh?' He looked around. 'Where is Jenni?'

Ned exchanged a glance with Rose.

'Ah, not exactly. The snow magic is trying to corrupt Jenni. We need to keep her as far away from it as possible, so no, she won't be casting the spell.'

Griff narrowed his eyes at his son.

'Is that what all that questioning was about? The magic in the snow? You think something else is going on?'

Ned shrugged.

'Jenni says there is a powerful magic in the snow, calling to her, but she knows if she gives in and lets it sweep her away then she will lose herself in the power so I'm doing my best to keep her out of its reach. No spell casting and no questing,' he said.

'Right, so the combined might of the rest of the Thief-Catchers will win the day?' Griff did not sound convinced.

'Um... no. Willow will have to stay here. The intense winter almost killed her once. I don't want to put her in danger again. Besides, she is setting up a seed bank and together with Joe, they are in charge of getting the deer out of Roshaven.'

'So who is going with you?' asked Griff.

Ned realised the rest of the room had gone silent. Bev, Trev, Kev, Fred and Rose were all waiting to see what he would say next. He decided to bite the proverbial bullet.

'Bev, Trev, Kev, I'm sorry, but it's just too dangerous for us to take civilians into the field like this. There's no telling what will happen. We will potentially be dealing with highly volatile magical forces. I can't take the risk that something might happen to one of you. You do understand, don't you?'

M-TAC nodded miserably.

'You will document, though, won't you? A first-hand account is worth more than its weight in gold.' Trev looked at Ned anxiously.

'I will do my best. And I promise to talk to you

199

about it once we return.' Ned felt the first fluttering of nerves in his stomach and that voice at the back of his head add, *IF*.

'Um, Mr Spinks, Sir? I have all my copious notes from all my correspondence with M-TAC and our conversations here in Roshaven. What do you want me to do with all that? I can type it up and put it in a colour coded ring binder. With an index. Or I can get things laminated. Alternatively, I know your man, Joe, likes a bit of etching. Would take a while to etch everything, but where there's a will, there's a way, me mam always says.' Fred radiated helpfulness.

'I want you to gather those notes together and bring them with you. You're on the team. Griff obviously. And I'm bringing Fingers.'

It was a bit of risk saying he was going to bring Fingers with him when he hadn't actually asked the man yet, but he'd done well with the quest to find the Sea Witch – baring the crabs – and Ned was positive there were no such things as ice crustaceans.

Fred looked fit to burst with pride. Griff acknowledged Ned with a nod, but there was a thoughtful expression on Rose's face.

'Do we really think you should take Jimmy as well?'

The use of *we* gave Ned a clue that he was on dangerous ground. Wisely, everyone else turned back to the fire where Griff launched into one of his impossible tales in an attempt to give Ned and Rose some privacy for which Ned was very grateful.

Rose continued.

'He plays a pivotal role in the smooth running of Roshaven. And for all we know, you could be going on a wild ice chase.'

Ned hated to admit it, but Rose had a point.

'We do not want our entire A team swanning off on a dangerous quest.'

Ah, thought Ned. That's what this was about. Rose wanted to come as well.

'Did we agree on quest, then?' As ever, Ned's avoidance to fight with his wife led him to focus on the minutiae.

'You can't have Fingers and Griff. With all three of you gone, I am left with just the Highs and it's not enough. I need more than bureaucracy to deal with the aftermath of this winter.'

'I'll take Griff then,' suggested Ned, observing his wife's face as some of the frown lines relaxed and her nostrils stopped flaring.

'Very well.' She caught his hand. 'But for gods' sake, you will be careful, won't you?'

Ned brought her hand up to his lips for a kiss.

'Of course I will.'

There was loud laughter at one of Griff's tall tales from the fireplace and at a quick nod from Ned, Griff led the others back to the table where the Book of Ice sat innocently.

'Let's have a look at this spell, eh?' suggested Griff, and before anyone could caution against it, he picked the book up and started turning the pages.

'Any, er… side effects?' asked Ned.

'Not that I can tell. Why?'

'Huh. It was just a lot colder earlier. What does it say?' Ned craned his neck to get a look at the pages as Griff flipped through. 'There, what was that?'

Griff turned back, and they perused the page.

'Spell to return Ice Giants to Nowhere. Convenient,' said Ned, reading aloud.

'Isn't that where you went? Nowhere. Middle of,'

asked Griff, smoothing his moustache and looking grave.

'Yeah. I guess if you want to get rid of something, sending it Nowhere is the best place. Hard to find.' Ned was trying very hard not to have a flashback. Echoes of bleakness and black sand as far as the eye could see, were tugging on his consciousness. He refocused on the words in front of him. 'Says it opens a portal. Huh, the spell ingredients are a bit... unusual,' he said, reading through them. 'The heart of a stalwart. The breath of regret. The fickleness of indecision. The courage to do what's right. The strength of belief and three tears from a Meh-Teh.'

Trev scoffed loudly.

'You'd probably be able to finagle the rest of that, but you'll never get the tears of a Meh-Teh. They can't cry. Famous for it. It's in all the literature.'

Ned blinked in surprise. Meh-Teh couldn't cry?

Fred was nodding sagely.

'He's right, Mr Spinks, Sir. All the books say the same. No tears from a Meh-Teh. Something to do with evolution removing the ducts what leak liquid in sub-zero temperatures. I mean, it makes sense when you think about it. Our Mam says our Malcolm ought to evolve into a sofa given his complete dependence upon it.' He leaned conspiratorially towards Ned. 'I think she is pulling my leg on that last one, Mr Spinks, Sir.'

'I'm more worried about the heart,' murmured Rose. 'Do you think it means an actual heart?'

'I reckon these things are very often open to interpretation, eh? What we need to do now is get a supplies list together and gear up. One does not simply walk up Mount Firn.' Griff smoothed his moustache.

'Where's the spell? There are no words, no

incantations. Just the ingredients.' Ned flipped the page back and forth several times, but there was nothing else.

'It doesn't need an incantation,' explained Rose, peering over his shoulder. 'Look, it says combine and cast with intent. I'm guessing the ingredients provide the intent and the focus, so it's up to the spellcaster to essentially throw it in the right direction.'

'And the different things will just mix together?' Ned sounded sceptical.

'It's old magic. Less waving around. Probably why the ingredients sound so unusual, and in the case of Meh-Teh tears, so hard to come by.' Rose looked to Griff for confirmation, and he nodded.

Ned shut the Book of Ice with a bang.

'We should already have a supplies list. The M-TACs have told Joe what we need, and he was going to speak to Fingers about getting kitted out.' Ned ran a hand through his hair. 'I've got to touch base with my Catchers.'

'I'll come with you, lad. We can visit WGI Emporium with the supplies list. I'm sure I'll have everything you need, eh?' Griff was re-wrapping himself up to face the weather outside.

Ned tried not to smirk. His dad and Fingers had a semi-friendly rivalry on being the only one able to supply unusual and hard to find objects. He should have known Griff would want to kit out the trip from his own stores.

'And I need to be getting back home, so I'll be heading the same way, won't I, Mr Spinks, Sir? Can't believe I get to tell everyone I met a Meh-Teh. Me! An actual myth. Amazing.' Fred's beaming face suddenly fell. 'What about Corporal Hobbs? I haven't filled in a leave of absence form, and it hasn't been approved and ratified so I will essentially be going AWOL, which is a punishable offence.'

'I think I can help you there, Fred,' Rose said with a smile. 'You are officially released from your position as Palace Guard.'

Ned spoke hastily as the tears pooled in the lad's eyes.

'And can now call yourself a Thief-Catcher. Welcome to the team.' He held his hand out to Fred, who took several moments to catch up on the meaning of what had been said and then get his emotions under control.

After shaking Ned's hand vigorously, Fred snapped a sharp salute at his Empress.

'What do I do about my old uniform?' he asked anxiously. 'And the new one?'

'Don't worry, we can sort all that out later. For now, let's go tell the others the good news,' suggested Ned.

'What about us?' asked Bev.

'You are welcome to stay here in our guest quarters,' said Rose. 'I know the imperial librarian is keen to update our records on the Meh-Teh. It seems you are the experts to talk to.'

Ned thanked his lucky stars for his wife. It would've been crowded and potentially complicated to try to organise everyone if the M-TACs came back to his, sorry, Jenni's house. By asking them to stay here and get involved with a project close to their hearts, it should keep them busy and not tempted to follow Ned up the mountain. At least not right away.

Chapter 32

It took twice as long as usual to travel through the wintry weather back to Jenni's house. Now that they had found and apologised to the Meh-Teh, the previous blizzard had calmed down significantly, but the results of that storm meant treacherous footing and even larger snow mounds. There were several snowmen dotted along their path, and Ned eyed each one carefully. You never knew.

Everyone knocked the snow off their boots as best as they could before entering the crooked little house. Willow, Joe and Jenni were dozing by the fire – relaxed, warm and from what Ned could smell - full of hot chocolate and toasted sausage sandwiches, so it was hardly surprising.

They all looked up sleepily at the new arrivals, taking a moment to realise Griff was with them.

'Hi Griff! How are you? What was the weather like in Fidelia?' asked Joe, shifting over to allow the others closer to the fire.

'Fine, fine. No snow. So once more Roshaven is the unique jewel, eh?' Whilst talking, Griff shook the hot chocolate pot to discover it was empty and made encouraging gestures to Fred to go replenish. He also found the covered dish with a few gently charred sausages within and set to putting some curly bread onto a toasting fork. Bread wasn't usually curly, but it had been left out for a while – the host overcompensating for the amount of toast required by bringing out too much in the first place. It would be fine once toasted.

Whist Fred was clattering in the kitchen, Ned spoke

to his Catchers.

'We found Flake. Or rather, he found us. He has agreed to meet me on the North Road tomorrow morning so I can go help him out and get rid of this weather. He claims that the snow will disappear once we've successfully evicted the Ice Giants, but I'm not so sure about that, so Willow, you stay here and man the office with Joe. Report directly to the palace in order to help with the melting strategies if needed.' Ned paused to make sure she was okay with those orders. Willow responded with a cheerful bloom. 'How did the animal relocation turn out? I take it you have met with Fingers.' For a moment Ned imagined his Catchers having spent the entire morning in a comfy daze, gently toasting themselves by his old fireplace.

Joe straightened in his chair.

'It went very well, Boss. Fingers' lads had rounded up all the volunteers to help with the herding. There really wasn't very much for us to do except give the official thumbs up. We; me and Willow and Fingers, went to the warehouse where the bug hotel is and sorted out the other side for the seed bank. We need to cool it down for optimum storage. Not a problem right now, obviously but this winter will lift eventually and then we'll want it to stay cold.'

'Yes, Fingers has a plan. And I've sent feelers out on The Vine to request seed donations from the plants we didn't already collect. They're going to deposit them at the warehouse.' Willow beamed at Ned. 'It's all in hand. Is it just you headed up the mountain?'

'Good, good.' Ned nodded at the progress they'd made. 'No, Fred will, ah, be coming with me.'

'Wot? Not Fingers?' Jenni asked in surprise.

'No, he will be staying here, assisting the empress,'

replied Ned stiffly, remembering Rose's response to his early assumption.

Jenni sniggered but soon stopped when Ned glared at her, but inwardly he noted that she hadn't complained about Fred. Worth knowing that she already counted him as one of them.

'Is Fred your imperial liaison, Boss?' asked Willow.

'No, he's…' But Fred had returned from the kitchen with fresh hot chocolate and as he set it down, he puffed his chest out proudly.

'I am the newest Thief-Catcher.'

For once he didn't run on in usual Fred fashion. A testament to how emotional he was still feeling about everything.

The others made lots of happy noises and congratulated him loudly. Jenni shook him energetically by the hand and gave Ned a thumbs up with the other.

Once everyone had settled back down and armed themselves with fresh drinks and snacks, Jenni spoke up.

'I guess I ain't going then.'

Ned shook his head.

'We can't take the risk that the snow magic won't overtake you.' Ned pointed at Griff. 'He managed to open the Book of Ice at the palace. We've seen the spell and are aware of the ingredients. We wouldn't have been able to do that if you'd been there. I think the book was reacting to your potential strength.'

Jenni's shoulders fell and her little sprite ears drooped. It made Ned's heart ache at how unhappy she looked.

'But… but… 'ow will you manage wivout me? I mean, I ain't even 'ad chance to show you everyfink yet and yor still a bit wonky on the whole summoning fing and you ain't got the pulling of magic out the ground sorted. You got yor light fingy down, but you need a bit more than just light Boss. Gotta be vigilant on these sorts of quests. Cos you know, you never know. And, and... I'll be 'ere. 'Ow am I gonna keep you out of trouble? I mean, you don't even remember that it's *adhuc manEre* not *adhuc mAnere* when keeping criminals in one place.'

Ned flushed at the unexpected outpouring. And then felt somewhat picked on at his limited spellcasting ability. He meant to do the exercises, but he'd been busy, and they were always the last thing on his never-ending list. He was also very conscious of the others trying hard not to look like they were listening closely to their conversation.

'You've been a brilliant teacher, Jenni.' Ned risked a white lie. 'And I've been practising as much as I can. It'll be odd without you, but I need you to stay here as my deputy. Make sure everything runs smoothly. Keep an eye on Fingers.' Ned rummaged in his coat pocket. 'Here's the key to the office.'

Jenni wiped her nose on her coat sleeve and took it.

'Yeah, corse I will. Plus, you need me to check in on Momma K and that. Make sure 'er realm goes back to normal once old Flakey boy leaves.'

'Exactly.' There was a long silence which Ned had to commend Fred on in particular.

'Err... so 'ow you gonna get the juice to do the spell?' asked Jenni. 'Cos you ain't got enuff magic to pull that off. And unless Fred's bin 'iding immense magical prowess, he ain't gonna be able to 'elp you neiver.' She squinted at Griff. 'And you ain't magic, are you?'

'A smidge of power runs in the family but it skipped generations when it got to me. Ned won that lottery, eh?'

Ned's ears pricked up. He had very limited knowledge about his heritage or the rest of Griff's family. They had been meaning to have a conversation but never quite found the time. All eyes turned to him, and he realised that chat would have to wait for another day. Right now, they were curious how he was going to generate enough power to be all vanquishy.

'And I can't be much help in that area, Mr Spinks, Sir,' said Fred. 'Not an inkling of magicalness runs through my family. Not one single smidge. Shame really, imagine what we could accomplish if we have a little bit of magic helping things along?'

Everyone took a moment to consider Fred with powerful magic behind him. Ned gave a slight shake to get rid of that terrifying imagery.

'Well… I thought… we might ask Mia. Joe's sister,' he said.

There was a stunned silence so Ned expanded.

'Flake mentioned he'd already spoken to Brogan so there's a good chance he'll be wintering in Blyz, at the foot of Mount Firn. And the last I heard Mia is still working with him, learning the barbaric craft and such like.'

'Wot about 'er restriction on power?' asked Jenni. 'Momma K set that, it ain't likely to just disappear.'

'True but by my estimation, it should have fully worn off by now. And according to Brogan's letters, she is sticking to using her magic for good.'

'Brogan writes you letters?' Joe sounded hurt. 'Mia doesn't write to me. And anyway, if you're going to ask Mia, shouldn't I come with you? After all, as her twin, I amplify her power.'

'Nah, Momma K broke the twin fing when she did the power block. Did no one tell you? Fawt they 'ad.'

209

Jenni watched the consternation flow across Joe's face and kicked her feet uncomfortably. 'Ere, sorry bout that. But it's a good fing though, right? You don't wanna spend yor life stuck to 'er. Be yor own person and that.'

Tears were forming in Joe's eyes and Ned felt bad for him, but he too had assumed someone had told him about the power break when it happened. Willow enfolded the lad in a gentle catkin embrace and looked at Ned.

'I thought you'd told him,' she mouthed.

Ned shrugged back. He'd figured she'd told him. Apparently, they'd all thought someone else had done it.

While Willow comforted Joe, Griff leaned in to talk to Ned in a low whisper.

'I didn't know you were going to ask Mia.'

'Me either,' Ned whispered conspiratorially. 'It just sort of came to me. She's the only other powerfully magical person I know – beside Momma K – and I can't see the fae queen coming on a quest with us.'

They both chuckled as they imagined that scenario and sipped on their delicious hot chocolate, waiting for Joe to pull himself together.

'You know,' Joe sniffed. 'When you think about it. It's actually a fantastic thing. Right? Not to be tied to her anymore. I mean, she'll always be my sister. That will never change. But who knows, perhaps my magic will settle and return.'

Ned shot a warning glance to Jenni as she opened her mouth, shaking his head, urging her against speaking out. She saw Ned's look and quickly closed it again. If no one had told Joe that the magical connection between him and his twin had been broken when Momma K restricted Mia's power, then it was a good bet that no one had told him that breaking that connection had

210

removed his power completely. The lad was so used to being a negative counterweight to his sister and had been so desperate to not unleash any warlock juju when they'd been fighting against his dad that he'd spent most of his life ignoring it. He was better off without it in the long run, but that was definitely a conversation for another day. Willow was looking at Ned wide-eyed as if to say, *how could you not tell him*, but… it just hadn't been the right time.

'Um, Boss? Should we tell Neeps what's going on?' asked Joe. 'I said we would keep her in the loop.'

'Mmm.' Ned thought for a moment. On the one hand, he didn't want to cause mass panic in Roshaven by telling everyone there was a Meh-Teh roaming the streets, bringing the winter, but… he didn't want to upset press relations either. 'Give her the update but wait until we've left. That way at least Flake won't be the centre of any mass attention.'

'Speaking of, do you have the supplies list, lad?' asked Griff.

'Yes, it's right here.' There was a scramble of paper leafing before Joe found and pulled out the right one. 'This is based on the M-TACs suggestion on what we would need cross referenced against my own research from the Imperial Library.'

Griff cast an eye over the items, smoothing his moustache with his other hand.

'Mmm. I think WGI Emporium will have most, if not all, of this, eh? Shall we go and see now? That way, we'll have time to acquire anything we might be missing.' Griff's tone was suggestive that it was highly unlikely he wouldn't have everything on the list, but he didn't like to boast.

Ned felt reluctant at leaving the cosiness of Jenni's

front room, but he told Fred to stay put with the other Catchers while he and his dad wrapped back up to trudge down to the docks and the WGI Emporium warehouses. Griff completely failed to see the hurt look on Jenni's face at being left behind again, but for Ned, it was like a punch to the stomach.

Chapter 33

After trying to open the door to the bug hotel and being shouted out by the diminutive old caretaker for letting in Jacks, Ned discovered WGI Emporium had done well with Joe's list. They had nearly everything they needed except for enough pairs of woolly socks. Griff shrugged when he saw what was left on the list.

'Demand has been high, eh? Do you think we really need this many pairs?' he cocked his head on one side as he looked at Ned.

'I think Rose will have conniptions if I don't take the right number of socks. Plus, we should probably get a couple more coils of rope. Can't hurt to have a few spares. In case of disaster.' Ned was feeling pensive. There was definitely a cloud over this quest and not just a snow filled one. It was weird not having Jenni by his side.

'Mmm, rope has been scarce of late. Supply issues on the chain for some reason. Shall we go see Fingers? Find out what he has?'

Ned nodded, and they headed off. Jimmy Fingers was found tucked away in the back room of his office at the docks, shuffling paper. The space previously belonged to Two Face Bob, and Fingers had finally removed the remaining vestiges of a man with two heads. Nobody in their right minds needed that excessive number of mirrors.

It had ruffled quite a few feathers that Fingers refused to work from the palace, but with so many appendages in numerous business ventures and opportunities, it would have been madness to conduct business anywhere else. Here at the docks, Fingers could run the semi-official operations he had set up with ease, his network of lads doing the dirty when needed and keeping it all copasetic. He could also perform all of his imperial duties with efficiency and aplomb. Yes, Jimmy Fingers was aware of who was coming into Roshaven, who was going out and almost everything in between.

Before his elevation to Lower Circle, Ned knew Fingers had been grooming himself to take over from the recently deceased Two-Face for years. That Fingers was now officially several rungs higher than Two-Face ever had been was not lost upon him. Fingers was very grateful for his new position.

He did, however, seem to be a little bemused by Ned's request for socks and ropes.

'You're actually going to go up Mount Firn with this mythical Meh-Teh, destroy some fabled ice giants and get rid of all this winter? And you don't have enough socks?'

'The Meh-Teh will remove the winter once we help him. At least that's what he said,' said Ned. 'And just because you didn't see Flake, doesn't mean he isn't real. Griff saw him.'

Fingers murmured non-committedly. For two gentlemen who ran in similar circles, they didn't seem to care much for each other. Ned had always put it down to professional rivalry.

'And you don't want me to come with you?' asked Fingers.

Ned could feel the back of his ears heating as he explained, again, that the Empress had requested that Fingers stay in Roshaven and assist her with the running of the city, especially if the snow didn't magically disappear as claimed, which to be fair no one was expecting.

'And Jenni's not going because…?'

Fingers couldn't help it. He always wanted to know the ins and outs of everything.

'The magic in the snow is tempting her and if she comes with us, she might not be able to resist.' Ned felt inspired. 'Don't let her know I asked you to, but can you keep an eye on her? In case the snow doesn't leave Roshaven and...' He left the unspoken hanging between them and waited to see what Fingers would say.

Jimmy hesitated. Ned could tell that part of him wanted to saddle up, so to speak, and have another grand adventure, but he was aware that Fingers still had the odd nightmare about the crabs he'd encountered when he had been the official Roshaven envoy to the Sea Witch.

'There's hazard pay,' offered Ned. 'Should things get tricky with Jenni.'

Fingers narrowed his eyes, trying to determine whether Ned was lying, so Ned tried to look as innocent as possible. He didn't actually have any hazard pay, but if something happened while he was away, he'd make sure all parties involved were looked after.

'Okay, fine. Try looking down the far aisle for the socks and rack B for the rope. We should have everything you need.' He paused and grinned. 'A gift between businessmen?'

Ned realised he was not included in this part of the conversation and there was a tense moment before Griff inclined his head, agreeing to Fingers' proposal. Once that had happened, Ned knew it was safe for him to talk again.

'Look, thanks for what you did for Sparks and the others. It was really good of you. There's not many people who would think about setting something up like that for insects. It wouldn't even occur to them that all this cold weather would affect them.' Ned gestured in the general vicinity of the bug hotel. 'Appreciate your help with the animals and the seed bank. Joe said you had it all under control?'

'Yes. It went smoothly. My lads were... persuasive at dispersing both hunters and animals. I think nearly everything has returned where it should be.' Fingers leant back in his chair. 'Clever idea about the seed bank but, is it necessary at all if the snow is going to magically disappear tomorrow?'

'It would actually be a very important evolutionary act. To preserve nature in our ever changing environment and became an attraction that our visitors can be encouraged to add to when they weigh anchor, bringing their own exotic plants. It would quickly gather international renown. Possibly even become a sight of scientific excellence, eh?' Griff smoothed his moustache.

Ned had to hand it to his dad. He always knew how to stoke a man's pride. Fingers looked thoughtful and began slowly nodding.

'I guess. Something that can be left behind for younger generations. It makes sense to set it up in the hangar next to the bug hotel. They can both be permanent fixtures. A unique licensing opportunity for other cities to consider.' Fingers eyes gleamed at the potential business opportunities. Whilst the bug hotel was officially set up in one of Griff's warehouses, he leased that space from the Lower Circle so they would both profit from such an enterprise.

Ned knew the bug hotel was in Jimmy's own self-interest. A lot of the bugs in Roshaven worked for him.

216

Fingers had told him once that they were cheaper to use than carrier pigeons, didn't get seasick travelling across boats and were usually ignored by almost everyone. Yes, there were the occasional, unfortunate casualties, but the Hive, as he called it, was an invaluable resource for someone in his position. Jenni had informed Ned that Fingers could talk to the insects as well. She had been very impressed. He really was a man of many talents.

He and Griff set off to collect the socks and the spare rope, calling farewell to Fingers, who was back at his desk, sifting reports. It looked like everything was coming together.

Chapter 34

All the mountain gear was piled up on the floor of the third best meeting room. Ned looked doubtfully at the three rucksacks that it was all meant to fit within.

'Do you think we could ask Flake to carry some stuff?' he said.

Griff arched an eyebrow. Perhaps not.

'We could always leave some socks behind, eh?' Griff winked and carried on rolling clothes into small sausages that he could squeeze in the bag.

'Rather you than me,' muttered Ned as he tried to figure out if he should hang the cooking pots on the outside of the rucksack or ram them inside. He peered over at what Griff had done. Hanging on the outside it was.

Fred came clattering in, despite no longer being a Palace Guard and not having a helmet or ceremonial pike to clatter with.

It must be his boots, mused Ned while giving the lad a small wave.

'What are you doing here? I thought you'd bunked in for the night at your new place?'

'That was indeed the plan, Mr Spinks, Sir but then I got talking to Joe about the kit list and how there was going to be quite a lot of it and I thought to myself, I said Fred, there's a very good chance that Mr Spinks, Sir will need your help and perhaps doesn't have the breadth of folding experience that comes from living with our Mam. She is a champion folder. Six times winner at the Easter fete. It's all in the wrist. Excellent wrists has our

Mam. I started to get an itch in my tummy at the thought of not being here to help and I said to myself, I said Fred, you are a Thief-Catcher now. It's your duty to go above and beyond and ensure the folding gets done. The folding could be key to the whole quest. And then when I spoke to Miss Jenni about the folding and such like she said I should please meself and I realised that as a Thief-Catcher, it's important that I don't please myself. Oh, no no no. It's my duty to please you. At least, to do my duty with the utmost of respect to the individual and to uphold the law of Roshaven and enforce justice and order upon the populace under the direction of my Empress, long may she rule.'

Even Fred had to take a breath after all that.

'Okay. Well, over here then, lad. Get your rucksack – we're just sorting out how best to pack them.'

Immediately Fred set to packing his bag at twice the speed of Griff and Ned. He offered several helpful tips on how to maximise folding and stuffing so that the vast pile of stuff really did make it into the three rucksacks. Ned surveyed the bags with some pride.

'What about the spell ingredients, Mr Spinks, Sir?' asked Fred.

'Mmm? You can just call me Boss now. Umm… there aren't any actual physical ingredients. It's all metaphysical by the looks of things.' Ned scratched his head. 'We left the Book of Ice in the study for safe keeping. I don't think we should take it with us up the mountain, though. Who knows how a book all about winter is going to react in such wintry conditions, especially given that we know there will be Ice Giants. But we need to write out what it says for Mia to cast the spell.'

'Well, at least we've sorted out the physical

mountain climbing side of things, eh,' said Griff. 'Now we can figure out the magical spell side of things. Come on.' Griff led the way out of the third best meeting room and over to the study.

The Book of Ice was indeed laying on the desk in the study where Ned had left it. The entire room held onto a chill at the edges, but the book itself had remained thawed. Ned quickly flipped it open to the relevant page, surprised at how cold the pages felt.

'So we had the heart of a stalwart. The breath of regret. The fickleness of indecision. The courage to do what's right. The strength of belief and three tears from a Meh-Teh. And it just says combine the following and cast with intent.' Ned flipped back and forth. But there was nothing else about the spell.

'There's that intent again, Mr Spin… ah Boss, Sir. Powerful thing intent. Me mam says it's enough to get you through anything given the right mental focus. But I'm sure we've got buckets of the stuff. Intent all over the place. Bound to have.'

Ned hoped Fred was right. Intent was all well and good, but what if everyone had a different kind of intent? What would happen then? Would the spell just unravel before it came together? He looked at the page for a while, hoping Griff or Fred would jump in with some ideas, but neither was forthcoming.

'Right, well. The tears of a Meh-Teh are straightforward enough. I mean, I know Trev said they don't cry…'

'It's in all the literature, Mr Spi… ah Boss, Sir. All the literature.' Fred bobbed his head.

'Books don't always hold all the answers. And we have the trip up the mountain to talk to Flake about his tears and whether we can have three. Perhaps he'll stub his toe or get a paper cut.' The backs of Ned's ear blushed, but he pushed on. 'And I'm fairly sure we have the strength of belief now that we've seen the Meh-Teh for real. That myth has most certainly been busted.'

'What about the myth of the Ice Giants, Mr Boss, Sir?' asked Fred.

'Griff?' Ned swung that one over to his dad.

'It's true that they are creatures of mythology and yet, as we have seen, myths are walking the streets of Roshaven. If Flake says the Ice Giants are in his mountain home, then I see no real reason to disbelieve him, eh? I don't think he would travel all the way down here, so far out of his natural comfort zone, to risk finding Ned and asking for assistance if it were something he could handle. The chap certainly knows his snow magic. Why would he lie about needing help?'

It was such a simple question, but it niggled at Ned immediately. His naturally pessimistic view of people in general launched into action. What reasons would Flake lie? To lure them up the mountain, sure, but to what end? If they disappeared, what would happen? Rose would probably send a search party and Jenni would definitely come looking for them. She would be infected by the power of the snow magic, lose control and become an all-powerful ice queen who would terrorise Efrana on whim and Ned wouldn't be able to save her because he would've been eaten by a Meh-Teh... No. Ned forced his thoughts to slow down. This was all conjecture. Flake wasn't going to eat him. Besides, he had Griff and Fred with him. And they were planning to find Brogan and Mia. Brogan was a famous barbarian with a great deal of muscle to throw around, while Mia had magical firepower. He wasn't going to be eaten.

'Are you okay, Mr Boss, Sir?' asked Fred. 'Only

you've gone ever so pale. Have you had something to eat and drink recently? Me mam says it's crucial during times of high stress to remain hydrated and to eat little and often. Regulates everything apparently. And it is so very important to be regular. Helps with all kinds of processes.'

'I'm er... fine, thanks. Just letting my imagination run away with me. Back to the list. Courage. I'd say we have plenty of that between us. Plenty of courage. We wouldn't be going up the mountain with Flake if we weren't brave, right? Can't say that we don't have courage.' Ned tailed off, aware that he was babbling. Now that he'd had the thought, he just couldn't shake the idea that this whole quest was a giant trap.

'I imagine we'll have buckets of regret once we get up the mountain, eh? Regret for carrying all those pairs of socks we didn't use.'

Ned smiled weakly at Griff, grateful that he was trying to make light of the situation, but not really feeling very comforted at all.

'If all these spell ingredients are metaphysical... I mean, we're not going to have to sacrifice an actual heart, are we?' Ned wasn't sure he wanted the answer to that question.

'It makes sense for them to all be metaphysical. That's why you need the potent magic, in order to pull these abstract forces together and bind them with the Meh-Teh tears, eh?'

Ned nodded. Griff made sense. And if Meh-Teh tears were scarce, it would fit that they would be used to pull the ingredients of the spell together. He tried to breathe a little easier. Really, all they had to do was make Flake cry.

'And then, once everything is mixed together...'

Ned paused. 'I guess it will open a gateway to send the Ice Giants back from where they came. I mean, the spell is called *Return The Ice Giants to Nowhere,* so let's assume it does what it says. And swirling vortexes are always cool.'

As the others nodded their agreement, Ned hoped he was right.

'Okay, I'm going to copy out what's here, so we can leave the book here. I suggest you both try to get a good night's sleep and we'll meet in the courtyard in the morning. Are you alright getting back home, Fred?'

'Oh yes, Mr Boss, Sir. It's almost a straight ice glide from here to there. See you tomorrow!' He waved cheerfully and Griff walked out of the study with him, leaving Ned alone with the Book of Ice.

He pulled parchment and pen to him and began scratching out the spell details. He really hoped they were right with all their conjecture.

Chapter 35

'Are you sure you're going to be alright?' asked Rose for the umpteenth time.

'I'm sure,' replied Ned. 'But are you?'

'Oh, I'll manage somehow.' She gazed at him fondly. 'I shall worry about you. You will be safe, won't you?'

'Doubly safe.' He scratched his nose. 'Did you, er... get the coat?' Rose had been in complete agreement with Ned when he had suggested that Jenni get a new coat, in the right colour.

'Yes! It's...' Rose searched in the various piles of things on the far side of their bedroom before pulling out a large white box. 'Here. Here it is. What do you think?'

She lifted the lid and Ned peered in. The coat looked very new with super shiny buttons, but it was the absolute perfect shade of red. And double breasted. Which made it look a lot more upmarket than the last one. Ned didn't think Jenni would mind about that. It was the colour that was key.

'What about the pockets? Did you make sure the pockets were super deep?'

'Of course, just as you asked. And I made certain they put in an internal pocket as well. It should be spacious enough for Jenni's various bits and bobs.' Rose popped the lid back on, looking pleased with herself.

Ned kissed her on the top of her head, taking a moment to breathe in her caramel perfume that he loved.

'Thank you. It's perfect. Umm...'

'Yes?' Rose cocked her head to one side, waiting for

Ned to expand.

'You will keep an eye on her, won't you? Jenni, I mean. I'm worried about this whole snow magic thing and how it's calling on her. I've put her in charge of the Thief-Catchers, but really, I need you to make sure she stays away from the snow.' Ned let out a small laugh. 'If that's even possible.'

'I will, I promise. I'll have her liaise with us on the melt, when it happens and ask Fingers to keep an eye as well.'

'Yes, I asked him too.' Ned felt slightly relieved. There wasn't much more he could do, short of scrapping the whole quest and he couldn't do that.

'But…' It was Rose's turn to hesitate.

'Yes?'

'What do I do if she does succumb? To the snow magic, I mean.'

Ned looked rather helplessly at his wife.

'Honestly? Hit her with all the magic Roshaven has and hope it's enough to break the connection,' he finally said. 'She's fighting it and she's strong. You know how strong she is, but… she's scared.'

They embraced again. Ned knew Rose understood how much Jenni meant to him and he had faith that she would look out for Jenni while he was away, but he still felt rubbish for leaving in the first place.

They were both quiet for a long time as Ned finished double checking he had everything.

'And you've got extra socks?' Rose asked quietly.

Ned half smiled.

'Yes. I made a point of getting spares.'

'And you will make sure your feet don't get wet, won't you?'

'I will do my best.'

'Which boots are you taking?'

Rose had him there. Ned considered lying for a brief moment but knew he would never get away with it.

'My street ones.'

Rose tsked in an alarmingly good impression of Momma K, making the hairs on the back of Ned's arm prickle.

'Those won't be any use in snow, or up a mountain. Your feet will be wet. No, you need to take these.' She proffered a giant pair of padded boots that had a white fur trim around the top that she'd been keeping somewhere. 'Snow boots!'

Ned eyed them suspiciously but slipped one foot into the boot. It was a bit of a mission to get his feet in, but he couldn't deny the result was very comfortable. And dry.

'What about everyone else? I can't be the only person wearing these... snow boots.'

Rose smiled in triumph.

'Fingers made sure you all had some. Said it was a good luck gift. So really, not wearing them would seem odd. Seeing as everyone else will have the same.'

'Fine. Give me the other one.' And Ned encased his feet within the snow boots.

There was a knock at the door and a palace maid popped her head in.

'Delivery for you, ma'am.'

She handed over a small bag with a handwritten label before bobbing her way out again. Ned eyed it curiously.

'Oh, it's from Kendra,' said Rose. 'It's your mistletoe tincture. For your knee?'

'Brilliant, that will definitely come in handy,' said Ned as he took the bag and tried to find a place for it.

226

'The deer and that are all sorted now. Joe said it was an extremely efficient operation and if he thought that, then you know it was spot on. Oh, and I told you about the seed bank, didn't I?' He was trying to make sure he'd kept everyone up to date on everything.

Rose nodded.

'Yes, you did. It's a wonderful project.' She narrowed her gaze at him. 'You have got your thermals on, haven't you? The ones Fred knitted?'

Ned looked at the chair where a neatly folded pair of thermals lay. He sighed.

'Help me get these blooming boots off, would you?'

Rose giggled and gave him a hand. And with a couple of other layers as well. Half an hour later, a rather flushed Ned met up with the rest of the team in the Palace courtyard.

Chapter 36

'Everyfink awright, Boss? Yor a bit late,' asked Jenni, tipping Rose a quick wink, but her voice trembled and Ned could see she was putting a brave face on. It brought a lump to his throat. This would be the first time he and Jenni had not worked on the same case since... since they both started as Thief-Catchers. And that was more years ago than he'd like to remember.

'I forgot to put my thermals on.' Ned fake coughed to cover his embarrassment. 'This is for you.' He proffered the coat box and waited nervously while Jenni took and opened it.

'Oh, Boss.'

It was all she said, but he knew she loved it by the way she hurled the box to the floor, shrugged the blue coat off as fast as she could, put the new one on and did a few twirls.

'Pockets!' she yelped as she discovered their depth.

Ned grinned at Rose and had to raise his voice over Jenni's delight to check in with the rest of the team.

'Has everyone got everything? All ready?' he asked.

There were muted nods from the group. Ned was satisfied to see Griff and Fred had snow boots on their feet and that they too were all topped with fur. Griff also had a fur trim on the hood of his puffy jacket and some bulky looking gloves that looked like they were probably fur lined as well. Fred was bundled into various outer garments. Ned wasn't entirely sure they were all supposed to go together, but as long as he was warm, that was the main thing. The young lad radiated eagerness, the bobble on his woolly hat bouncing around like anything. The Meh-Teh was nowhere to be seen, but he had said he would meet them on the North Road out of Roshaven. It was a bit much to expect him here, especially with so many people gathered.

He nodded at the M-TAC, who were looking both forlorn and excited as they stood slightly off to one side. They took this as permission to all speak at once.

'You have got plenty of paper and spare pens for documentation, haven't you?'

'You will take rubbings, won't you?'

'Document, document, document. And anything you can bring back for validation is key.'

Ned decided on the smile and nod approach to their barrage. He lifted a hand as if to say, absolutely – totally got this – no need to worry – and it seemed to do the trick.

Ned realised Rose's teeth were chattering. It was rather cold in the courtyard, despite palace staff having cleared some of the snow and installed a few braziers.

'Right, love, we'd better be off. The Meh-Teh is…'

'Meeting us outside the city gates,' supplied Fred helpfully.

'…meeting us outside the city gates. Right.' Shouldering his pack, Ned felt a small pang at leaving Rose behind. 'I'll be as quick as I can.'

'Please take care, alright. Keep your feet dry.' She kissed him soundly on the lips, which he returned with passion.

As they moved apart, Ned saw that Rose's eyes were extra bright and shiny.

'I'll be fine, promise.'

She nodded.

'Go on. You'd better get going before you lose too

229

much daylight. Be safe – all of you. And come home in one piece.'

Ned turned to Jenni, not sure what kind of farewell to expect and was surprised when Jenni nearly knocked him off his feet in a sudden hug attack. Being sprite sized, she wasn't tall enough for Ned to hug her back properly, but he wrapped his arm around her as much as he could and squeezed.

'I know I ain't coming wiv you cos of the magic and stuff but just, just, just don't do nuffink stupid, yeah? Watch out for tricks and don't agree to fings. Make sure you wear all them socks.' She sniffed. 'Socks is important.'

Rose put her arm around Jenni, who was momentarily looking very small and lost. It was an almost physical wrench for Ned to pull himself away from the two most important people in his life.

'Nearly forgot – 'ere, take this wiv you.' Jenni shoved a red leather-bound book at Ned. 'S'travelling book wot you can send messages in. You write summink and then it shows up in our one.' She held up another one identical in size and colour. 'It won't do essays, but you can let us know 'ow yor getting on and that.'

'Wow Jenni. These are expensive. How did you manage to get your hands on a pair?' Ned turned the book over in his hands.

'Borrowed 'em. Don't worry. You can give 'em back when you return,' said Jenni airily. 'Just be safe and come back wiv all yor fingers and toes. And don't lose the books.'

'We will!' called Fred as he led the way, stomping out the courtyard, his bobble bobbling. 'I mean, we won't, but we will. Won't lose but will come back. Well, we will win, but…' Fred had walked too far away to really hear what he was saying.

Griff fell into step with Ned, giving him a brief nod.

'Simply need to go up a mountain, get rid of some Ice Giants, and come back down again,' he said. 'Easy peasy, eh son?'

'Easy peasy,' murmured Ned back at him, not for one minute believing it was going to be anything close to easy.

Chapter 37

Ned wasn't sure whether to be relieved that Flake was actually there waiting for them or not. If he hadn't been, then his claim that he needed Ned to go up the mountain and defeat Ice Giants was a lie – some unfunny joke. And the snow was a weird weather phenomenon that they would figure out and sort. However, if he did show up, then it wasn't an elaborate hoax and Ned had some vanquishing to do. Either way, Ned didn't like the options.

'I must say, Boss, I didn't know if he was going to be there or not. A bit touch and go, wasn't it? You never can tell with Meh-Teh whether they're going to show up or not. Part of their mystery. Talking of, do you think they still count as super mythical creatures now that we've met one? Or do they become a bog-standard creature which seems a bit deflating. Shall we tell him that he'll always be mythic to us or is that the worst possible thing to do? We don't want to big up the myth unnecessarily.'

Pleased that Fred had finally got the hang of calling him Boss, Ned fell back on the classic non-committal mmhmm. It was the easiest way to respond to Fred when your attention wasn't really on what he was saying.

The Meh-Teh stood calmly, watching them walk up the road towards him. He seemed more relaxed out here in the countryside, unfettered by buildings and lampposts. There was still snow here, but it was a mere few inches compared to the massive drifts filling the streets of Roshaven.

'Thank you for coming. My heart is relieved that you are a man of your word, Ned the Sorcerer Slayer,' intoned Flake. 'But... why does someone of your calibre need to bring additional people? An entourage is not necessary where we are going.'

'Just Ned is fine. I brought with me Fred Jones, Thief-Catcher, and Griffin Bartholomew, our Ice Giant expert, at the insistence of the Empress, if you remember.' Ned knew that Fred would be puffing out his chest in pride, but he hoped that Griff wasn't raising his eyebrows in surprise. He dare not look and check.

'I thank you both for taking on this risk, but I urge the two of you now to turn back. If Ned the Sorcerer Slayer cannot defeat the Ice Giants, what can you do?' Flake looked at the duo mournfully.

Ned felt a prickle of unease. Why was Flake so adamant that no one accompany them? Surely he could see the value of extra people. They were going to fight Ice Giants for goodness' sake. He was saved from answering by Fred.

'Well, right now, we can carry the equipment and when we have a pit stop, I can brew us all a cuppa. Nothing like a cuppa to warm the chilly old cockles. I think everyone will be happy to nibble on one of me Mam's rock cakes. Legendary they are for nibbling on. Keep you going for hours, they do. And when we get to Blyz, we can meet up with Brogan and Mia and finalise the spell. It's good to have support personnel on a quest like this.' Fred beamed at Flake who did a sterling job of listening attentively, right up until he mentioned meeting up with more people, then his eyebrows beetled and a flurry of snowflakes whipped up.

'Additional people. Why is this necessary? Are you not mighty enough to defeat the Ice Giants upon your own?'

Ned was trying his best to ignore the now incredulous look plastered on Griff's face, probably from being called support personnel but also quite possibly at Ned being called mighty.

'I find in these situations it's a good idea to use everything at your disposal, including experts and the like. And anyway, it can't hurt to have a bit of extra fire power against the Ice Giants, can it?' Ned had that odd feeling in his stomach again, that sense that perhaps Flake wasn't exactly telling them everything. They would all have to be hyper alert.

Flake harrumphed and his eyebrows remained agitated.

'Let us begin. It is a long walk to the mountains.' He strode off, snowflakes dancing in his wake.

'We need to find out everything Flake knows about these Ice Giants. I think he's holding out on us. Might be a good idea to keep our wits sharp, eh?' Griff murmured to Ned, who nodded his agreement.

Ned jogged to catch up with Meh-Teh.

'Ah, Flake? Can I ask you about the Ice Giants? Get a bit more intel.' Ned matched his stride with the Meh-Teh, who had thankfully slowed down a little for Ned.

'I will tell you what I can.'

A significant pause filled the air as Ned waited. The Meh-Teh opened his mouth a couple of times and shook his fur, almost as if he didn't know exactly what to say. It was unnerving.

'It is my understanding the Ice Giants have been brought back to our realm for reasons of discord and terror. They will sow destruction wherever they go, but they need time to gather their energy and leave my mountain.' Flake gestured to the countryside. 'It is too warm for them at present. They do not have access to my snow magic, however, they are brutal in their interactions.' The Meh-Teh growled, shaking his shaggy fur vigorously, spraying snowflakes widely. 'They are cruel and merciless and will stop at nothing to achieve their goal.' Flake was nearly shouting now but stopped speaking to take some deep breaths through his wide nostrils, calming himself down. 'When it became impossible for me to stay in my home any longer, I did the only thing I could do. Came to you for help.' His voice was gruff with unspoken emotion.

Ned knew, without a doubt, that Flake was hiding something. And it wasn't just being kicked off his mountain. The anger and hurt that had momentarily spiralled out of the Meh-Teh had been terrifying. He obviously had good reason for not sharing all the facts and after that display, Ned was hesitant about pushing him too much, too soon. They had some time before they reached Mount Firn.

Regarding the Ice Giants, everything Flake had said matched the little Ned had found out for himself. Not wanting to push the Meh-Teh on something so sensitive, Ned changed the subject.

'Why isn't the countryside covered in deep snow like it is in Roshaven?'

'Because the sun has melted it, and I was not here to maintain my connection and lower the chill factor to optimum. Snow can only occur at optimums.'

'Then, with you leaving Roshaven, the winter really will melt.' Ned was relieved. Obviously he would double check with Jenni in the message book, but he was hopeful that the snow would leave.

'It will,' confirmed Flake. 'Once I release my hold on maintaining the winter.' For the first time, the Meh-

Teh looked sheepish. 'I needed to ensure you would come with me to the very end. Eventually the magical aspect of the snow will gradually disappear on its own, and the flakes will melt in the usual manner. I anticipate that Roshaven will not be overly burdened with melt, should the proper precautions be taken.'

'Can't you release your hold now? I mean, I am here, as promised.' Eventually sounded like it could be a very long time.

Flake regarded Ned solemnly.

'I will release my hold once my home is returned,' he spoke so softly, Ned had trouble hearing him.

They walked in silence for a while. Ned felt he ought to push Flake on the subject of the Ice Giants as there was definitely more to learn, but for now he decided to see if the Meh-Teh would answer the other burning question he had previously avoided.

'Um, well, you know, you can trust me — us. We're completely in your corner, ready to fight for your home and everything. So... er... about the magic.' Ned tried to keep the desperation out of his voice, but he was very worried for Jenni. 'What do you know about the magic in the snow?'

Flake was silent for a very long time. Ned kept opening his mouth to ask again but kept stopping himself, feeling that if he could just hold his tongue, he might get some answers.

'I regret that I cannot tell you what you want to know. The magic that your fae could be sensing is different from the winter I am able to control. There is an undercurrent within. It came with the Ice Giants. Further to that...' Flake lifted his hands in that universal *I don't know* gesture.

Ned nodded. It felt a bit closer to the truth than last

236

time, and it could very well be that he really didn't know where the magic had come from. The fact that it came out of Nowhere with the Ice Giants was worrying. He would have to update Rose and the others in the communication book when they stopped. He decided to leave the questions for now.

The next few hours passed with little incident. They were an odd looking group should anyone have been out and about, but they met nobody. With all the inclement weather blanketing Roshaven, local visitors were giving the city a wide berth. And it was winter. Not the bone clenchingly cold winter that was magically adhered to Roshaven but winter, nonetheless. The sun fell low in the sky quickly and the temperature began to drop.

'Where are we?' Ned asked, looking around, trying to orientate himself. He didn't recognise any landmarks. They had travelled much further than he'd thought they would.

'I can quicken our pace a little. The journey will only take two days,' replied Flake.

Ned was impressed.

'How does that work?' he asked.

Flake gave him a small smile.

'Another question I cannot answer. I believe it is something to do with our dependence on our mountain. We Meh-Teh can stray, but not far. We can leave, but not for long. We can visit other places, but we must always return and recharge. And so, our feet will carry us swiftly home. It has always been this way.'

Ned mused on Flake's reponse. Could it be that Meh-Teh had some sort of homing spell that gave them a kind of seven-league boot effect? And it was strong enough to affect those around them? That was beyond impressive. No wonder the Meh-Teh had faded into myth, they would've had been used as a glorified pack animal otherwise. Also… did the use of *we* mean there were more Meh-Teh living on Mount Firn? Or was it like the imperial *We* Rose employed from time to time? That had taken some getting used to.

'Ah, Mr Flake, Sir? We may want to think about striking camp soon. Before we lose the light?' Fred piped up.

The Meh-Teh slowed his stride and turned to regard the three men.

'You cannot see in the dark?'

'A little, but not well. And it's got nothing to do with the amount of carrots you eat, despite what they tell you. In fact, it has been my experience that most food related tales are false. Eating your crusts does not give you curly hair.' Fred pointed to his very straight head of hair. 'Case in point.'

Flake regarded Fred quizzically before turning and striding off again. The others had little choice but to fall in.

'Are we ever going to stop, Boss?' Fred asked Ned quietly. 'Only I might not look like it, but I have to refuel regularly, otherwise my blood sugar falls into my boots and I'll be of absolutely no use to anyone if that happens.'

'Here, chew on one of these, should tide you over, eh?' said Griff, handing over a ship's biscuit that looked reminiscent of Fred's mams rock cakes. Fred had bought some into the office once and Jenni had tried juggling with them, quitting when one fell on her foot.

As the light continued to fail, Ned plucked up the courage to tackle the topic of stopping for the night again.

'Ah, Flake? Sorry to bother you, but we really do

need to stop. As Fred said, we can see in the dark to a certain extent. Of course we can, but we have to have a break. Eat something, drink something, sleep. All that sort of thing. You understand?'

Flake stopped walking and Ned nearly walked right into him but managed to just about veer out of the way.

'It will take us three days to reach the mountain at this rate.' The Meh-Teh leaned down to Ned and lowered his voice to a loud rumble that the others could clearly hear. 'Are you sure we can't leave these fine gentlemen here to rest and continue upon our way? It is most imperative that we reach the mountain top at the utmost speed.'

'I'm afraid I require rest and recuperation as well.' Ned had a flash of inspiration. 'You want me to be at full strength when we face the Ice Giants, don't you?'

Flake crumpled round the edges and Ned realised that the Meh-Teh's shoulders beneath his shaggy fur had dropped.

'I suppose you must do what you have to. I shall leave you to your camp and your *fire*.'

The word fire was laced with such dislike that Ned almost cringed at wanting to have one.

'I will return in the morning, at first light. I assume that will be acceptable? Then we can continue our journey north. There is little time to delay.' Flake glanced up at the sky. 'We must be quick.'

Ned frowned. Why was Flake trying to rush now? Sure, he'd always been keen to leave, but at the same time had accepted the fact that Ned would need to gather supplies and get ready for this trip. Surely he didn't expect them to trek through the night as well.

'We'll make it, don't worry.' Ned tried to gauge Flake's reaction, but his furry complexion made it tricky.

'A decent night's sleep and something to eat, and we should cover a good distance tomorrow.'

Ned watched as the Meh-Teh walked away, fading into the deepening gloom. Shivering, he turned back to the others and clapped his hands together.

'Right then, camp here, shall we?'

Fred instantly began happily chattering away as he started to set up a bivouac tarp between two handy tree trunks.

'This will do just fine, Boss. We can make camp here. Use this here tarp to keep the worst of the weather off us while we bed down beneath it. It'll be close, but that's where all the warmth comes from. I take it everyone remembered their roll mats. Terribly important is a roll mat. It's really the best thing you can do before putting down your sleeping bag. Helps to keep the damp and such from rising into the bag. Some protection against worms but burrowing beetles are going to burrow, it's not their fault, it's in the name. Snakes too. Well, they won't burrow but they will come and investigate the warmth although there isn't much warmth going around at the moment given all this winter but even so my suggestion would be to zip up those sleeping bag all the way to the neck and make sure we sleep with all our clothes on and possibly a few additional layers. Those extra socks will come in very handy now, Boss, very handy indeed.'

'What about winter snakes, eh? Don't they enjoy slithering in the snow?' Griff asked Fred with a glint in his eye, and Ned tried his best not to grin.

'Interesting you should mention winter snakes, Mr Griff, Sir. They are an unusual anomaly that I wouldn't expect to see this far south, but after all, we have met a real-life myth, so who knows what else we will run into on this quest. They are actually called snow snakes and can blend in with the snow because of their white scales, their little black eyes peeping out so small you'd mistake them for tiny pebbles. They even have white tongues! Amazing. But you really, really have to be careful of snow snakes because although they like it cold, they are very nosy and like to come and see what's going on. When you think about it, travellers in the mountains and through the winter are usually very cold as well and with the risk of frostbite and digits falling off all over the place the snow snake really only needs to lie in wait, and it's got an easy meal. A lot of people aren't very sensible when it comes to hiking in the snow, you know. They don't prepare properly, and they aren't equipped to handle the frostbite of a snow snake. Tragic, really. They just need to educate themselves. I could recommend some excellent pamphlets.'

Ned and Griff stood to one side, letting Fred crack on with setting up the camp and listening with a wry smile to his continuous commentary, waiting for the opportunity to get a word in edge wise and lend an offer of help. Fred finally paused for a breath and Ned leapt at his chance.

'Where did you learn all this campcraft, Fred? Is there anything we can do to help?'

Fred stood rapidly to attention, three fingers in salute at the side of his forehead.

'Junior Forest Ranger Jones at your service!'

'They still have those?' whispered Griff to Ned, who shrugged.

'How did you manage to be a Forest Ranger in the city?' Ned was curious.

'Ah, well, you see Boss, sent away for registration and as I was the only one in my area, I got to be in charge of choosing which badges we did first and where we camped. Spent several lovely evenings on the riverbank of the River Whine in my tent. Learnt a lot about mosquitos. And the importance of making sure you cook your sausage all the way through and not just to the point where you think it's probably done on account of the level of charring you're experiencing. Charring does not equal cooked.'

Fred stood back proudly so that Griff and Ned could survey the campsite he had created. The bivouac looked oddly inviting, and he had dug beneath the thin layer of snow to reach the dirt beneath, arranging a series of small rocks together in a circle to act as a firepit.

'Excellent work, excellent.' Ned fished through his own rucksack for the tea bags as Fred rummaged for the kettle. 'Great minds think alike. Do we have water to make tea?'

'We can use the snow, Boss. As long as we boil it right good, it'll be fine for tea making. A lot of people think rain is clean and that you can just open your mouth open and let the raindrops fall in and that's how you get a drink, but I can tell you now that rain is not clean water. Oh no no no. It is caused by the collection of particles of pollutions – dust and tiny bits of stuff that clump together and rise up in the sky. Then they gather together, attracting each other and bits of water and stuff and suddenly you have a cloud and then when that cloud gets super heavy, all that water falls on down. I read about it in one of my pamphlets.' Whilst delivering his impromptu science lesson, Fred had scooped up copious amounts of snow, pulled out any obvious leaves and twigs and set to filling the kettle with it.

'I think I'll have a spoonful of sugar with mine, eh?' remarked Griff, who had taken his ease on some handy logs nearby.

'We'd better start a fire, otherwise it'll be a long time before we even get to that stage,' said Ned, showing off his limited campcraft knowledge. 'Gather dry twigs and any moss that you see. Nothing wet which I appreciate will be tricky, but I'm sure if we forage properly, we'll find what we need.'

'That's right, Boss. We need dead wood ideally and dry moss for sure. Look under any fallen trees for bigger branches and if we go a bit further into the treeline, there might be some dryer material we can use. Collect as much as you possibly can because we can take it with us for future fires. Always a good idea to have a kindling bag, I should have thought of it before, but I was so focused on getting ready on time that I didn't stop to pick mine up. I do have my flint and cotton wool though, so starting the fire won't be any trouble at all. This is such a fine adventure, isn't it, Boss?'

It was hard not to get swept up in Fred's enthusiasm, and so Ned found himself whistling jauntily as he looked along the road for anything dry they could burn. They were lucky that this side ran alongside woodland that hadn't been cut down for farming. That was the case on the other side of the road. Bare fields topped with snow stretched out like a barren wasteland. Ned shuddered as some flakes fell down the back of his neck and he returned his attention to gathering firewood.

When he dumped what he had managed to find at the fire pit, Griff and Fred had already returned and Fred was sorting the kindling into piles.

'It's important, Mr Griff, Sir, to sort your kindling into sizes so that you can accurately build your fire with the right materials. We want match sized, pencil sized, finger sized and thumb sized to start with.' He was whittling while he talked, shaving some of the larger pieces of wood into smaller pieces. 'Then we need the wrist to forearm stuff. That's what will be our fire fuel. All that stuff over there will maintain the fire once we've got it going.' He pointed to the larger logs that had been uncovered. It reached as high as Ned's shins. 'That's not going to be enough for the whole night, but it'll do for making us some dinner and a hot drink. We can always huddle together for warmth.'

He began building up the kindling, leaving plenty of room for air flow, and reverently pulled out a small bag from his pocket. It smelt strongly of paraffin. He took out one ball of cotton wool and placed it in the centre of the fire. Returning the bag to his pocket, Fred took his flint and striker from the top of his rucksack and began making sparks. The cotton wool caught almost instantly and after several tense moments of blowing on the spark, small flames licked the kindling.

Griff and Ned clapped enthusiastically.

'Well done, lad! Well done,' said Griff.

Ned's estimation of Fred rose yet again. The lad was full of surprises. All that was left to do was check in with the team back in Roshaven. He opened the message book and started to write.

Hi, made good progress, set up camp, everyone is still in one piece. How are things? How's Jenni? Ned

There were a few tense moments where nothing happened. Ned jiggled the pen in his hand, waiting.

Hello! All is good here. Still snowing. And nothing is melting yet, but the volunteers have been shovelling and people are adapting. Jenni seems to be okay. We are all keeping an eye on her and keeping her busy, away from the snow. How are you? Rose x

Ned bit the end of the pen, trying to find the right

words to explain why the snow hadn't started to melt in Roshaven yet before deciding to just say that the snow would melt once he'd helped Flake. He also wrote down everything Flake had told him about the magic in the snow, asking his wife what he thought the unknown quantity could be. There was a long pause as his lengthy message was read.

I'm not sure... let me ask Jenni. Hang on.

A massive ink blot appeared on the page.

Awright Boss – could be anyfink, really. Probably just summink wot came out of Nowhere when the Giants did. Mebbe it's gonna just disappear when the snow melts. Fingers give us a pair of gloves wot never get wet so I can touch the snow and it don't make no difference. Well good. Be safe!

Ned was surprised at how relieved he felt. He knew the team would pull together and look after Jenni, but it was still a relief to know she was alright. He wondered briefly at what the gloves were made of to never get wet but was soon distracted by reading and replying to a goodnight message from Rose.

Chapter 38

True to his word, Flake return at sunup. The men had taken turns on watch to keep the fire alive so they could quickly cook some porridge in the morning and were just taking down the camp. It didn't take long, but it was certainly disconcerting to have a Meh-Teh watching them, especially as his presence lowered the temperature.

'Do you always make it cold, Mr Flake, Sir? Or does it require effort, like a conscious thought? As if you got up this morning and said, do you know what? I'm going to make it snow today.' Fred asked as they hefted their backpacks onto their shoulders, ready to set off.

'It is both young Fred. A Meh-Teh has a deep connection with winter, so it typically runs cold when we are around. However, if I focus my energies, I can influence the weather. These things are tied to emotions, of course. A Meh-Teh always tries to be in control of their emotions.'

'So that's why you don't cry, then?'

Ned winced at Fred's directness. He had hoped they could broach the subject of Meh-Teh tears a little more delicately.

'Ha!' The Meh-Teh made everyone jump with his exclamation but said nothing immediately. He looked to be struggling to find the right words. 'We cry,' he finally said softly before pulling away to walk in front of the others.

Ned huddled in with Fred and Griff.

'Good thinking about asking directly, Fred. At least

now we know they can cry,' said Ned. 'Maybe it's like dragon's milk, a mystical, magical ingredient that is so surrounded in secrecy, people assume it doesn't exist.'

'But, Boss, it's in all the literature that they don't cry,' said an anxious sounding Fred.

'Books don't always tell the whole truth, lad. Very often it's a just the most popular version at that time, eh?' Griff patted the dumbfounded Fred on the shoulder.

Ned could see that the cogs were turning in Fred's mind, given the intense expression on his face and the fact that his lips were moving silently.

'So, does that mean that dragon's milk exists then, Boss?' he eventually asked.

'Nope. I checked with Slinky. That one is definitely a mystical, magical mystery,' replied Ned.

'Indeed, I think that one is the result of a sharply minded businessman, looking to take advantage of a situation, eh? Would require a little grandstanding but I can see how it could be done.' Griff smoothed his moustache.

Ned grinned. Trust Griff to know that. From what Ned had gleaned from his father's operations, there was a definite scope for a fair amount of grandstanding.

They settled into a companionable walking group. Flake leading the way, setting the pace with Ned, Griff and Fred striding behind and Fred peppering the others with random questions on whatever seemed to enter his head. Each evening Flake left them to it and Fred took charge of the campcraft. As predicted, it took them three days to walk to the village Blyz at the foot of Mount Firn.

'We have made remarkable time, eh? With your assistance methinks,' said Griff, inclining his head at the Meh-Teh, who had stopped walking and was eyeing the village in the distance warily.

'Yes. Although it has taken three days instead of two because of your evening rests. But as I said I would, I lengthened our steps with a touch of magical intent. It is tiring to do so but we needed to make haste. And now we are here, we must not delay. We must head up the mountain.'

Ned shook his head. It was late afternoon. They would be crazy to start climbing now.

'No, I'm sorry Flake, but we need to go into Blyz and try to find Brogan and Mia. Convince them to help us and then we can start planning how we tackle the Ice Giants. Besides, I wouldn't mind a decent night's sleep in a proper bed tonight.'

Griff and Fred added their agreement, but Flake's eyebrows were beetling again, and a furious flurry of snow began.

'No! I insist. Leave the others behind but you, Ned the Sorcerer Slayer, you must climb the mountain. We have little time.'

'Flake, calm down. I'm here, aren't I?' said Ned. 'I told you I would help you evict the Ice Giants and I will. I've brought my best men with me. We're going to ask one of the finest warlocks around to cast the spell. We got this. Don't worry, you'll get your home back. I promise.'

Flake looked at the ground and the furious snowflake flurrying slowed down. But the uneasy feeling at the back of Ned's mind that had tried to rear its head from time to time was now in full force, threatening to overtake Ned completely. Flake was definitely hiding something.

'I haven't been entirely honest with you,' Flake said.
Aha! thought Ned, although he immediately

regretted being right.

'I must deliver you to the Ice Giants. Then they will release my son.'

Chapter 39

It had taken a while for everyone to calm down. Flake had promised to wait for them at the base of the mountain as long as they could leave at first light and Ned, despite Griff and Fred's urging not to, had promised to go with him up the mountain. As they settled themselves at the local inn, nursing warm mead and bowls of steaming stew in seats close to the fireplace, Ned repeated his decision whilst having a near identical argument with Rose in the Travelling Book.

'The way I see it,' he said, 'nothing has changed. We have the spell. We'll soon have the magical firepower. We're still going to defeat the Ice Giants. If anything, we have the advantage. The Ice Giants don't know we know.'

Furiously scribbling in the book, he wrote:

I understand that you're worried, but don't be. If anything, we're even more motivated to help Flake and get his son back. We're expecting Mia and Brogan to turn up any minute, so let me talk to them and I'll let you know what they say later.

Griff pursed his lips.

'What if Flake still hasn't told us everything? Sure, he's admitted the Ice Giants have his son, but what if there's an army of Meh-Teh's up there, ready to rip us all limb from limb in sacrifice, eh? And what does a trio of mythical Ice Giants want with a bog-standard man? No offence, eh? I'm just… concerned. Why doesn't Flake know why they want you? Why would they trade a mystical Meh-Teh for you?'

Ned frowned. It wasn't like Griff to fall into a worst-case scenario. He was usually the one looking on the bright side. And he wasn't offended. He had no idea why Ice Giants would want him. Even Flake hadn't known specifically when they'd questioned him after he'd revealed the real reason for getting Ned up the mountain. He glanced down, Rose had replied.

Fine.

Okay, that had gone about as well as expected. He looked up at Griff.

'Look, Brogan frequents this inn every evening. The barkeep said so. Once he's here, we can talk to Mia and find out more about the Ice Giants.'

As if on cue, a huge shape filled the doorway and Brogan, the biscuit-loving Barbarian, entered followed by Mia who glared down on the inn's inhabitants with a haughty gaze. As she clocked Ned, Griff and Fred, she beamed and waved, tugging on Brogan's arm to bring them both over.

'What are you two doing here?' she asked. 'Is Joe alright? Where's Jenni?' She glared at Fred. 'And who is this?'

Ned felt a pang at the questions. Camping with Griff and Fred had been fine, but he was missing Jenni something fierce. He missed her wisecracks and her sense of humour. He missed how she could always make light of a situation, roll her sleeves up and get on with it. Hell, he even missed her stinkiness. You could depend on it.

Fred made his chair screech as he pushed it back to stand. He gave a little bow.

'It is my absolute pleasure to make your acquaintance Ms Mia, or should I address you as Warlockess – is it an ess? And Mr Brogan, Sir, we met once, in Roshaven. It was that time you were holed up at *The Daily Blag* offices, but I was there in my official capacity as a palace guard which I am not any longer. A palace guard, not official. Now I am an official Thief Catcher. Newly recruited and proud to wear the pin.' He adjusted his scarf to show off his TC badge that sat next to his MTAC one. 'It is such an honour, really, a true honour.'

'Yes, thank you, Fred.' Ned cut him off before he could gush anymore and addressed Mia himself. 'Joe's fine, don't worry. And Jenni's back in Roshaven. And now you've met Fred. But we've actually come to find you. We need your help.' Ned waited for Brogan and Mia to get themselves sat at the table and for Griff to order more drinks before continuing. 'Flake came to Roshaven.'

'Who's Flake?' asked Brogan, bringing out a packet of shortbread biscuits that he offered around.

Ned was confused and mini alarm bells started ringing in his head. The others from Roshaven sat very still, serious looks on their face.

'The Meh-Teh? The one you sent down the mountain in search of me. Ned the Sorcerer Slayer?'

Mia laughed so hard she snorted out her drink halfway across the table.

'Is that your new nickname?' she asked when she finally stopped sniggering.

The backs of Ned's ear were firmly ruddy.

'No. That's what Flake, the Meh-Teh, said Brogan called me. When he told Flake how to find me. To help him defeat the Ice Giants. Any of this ringing a bell?'

'Nah mate. Sorry. I mean, I was aware the Ice Giants had appeared but pretty sure I would've remembered meeting a Meh-Teh. Stuff of legend. Good for the BSS,' said Brogan.

'BSS?' queried Griff.

'Barbaric Skills Sheet. It's a new thing, all the rage up in the big cities. A job comes up and you hand in your skills sheet, then whoever is the best fit for the quest gets the gig. Evens out the competition, lets you play to your strengths and ensures the job gets done by the absolute best man…'

Mia interrupted. 'Or woman.'

'…woman, or indeed person. Mythical encounters get added under Personal Experience, sometimes Additional Knowledge. It's all about selling yourself in the best possible way.' Brogan leaned close towards Ned. 'You know, if you do start using that nickname, confirm it with me. I'll add it to my BSS under Personal Connections. Already got your wife.'

Ned took a long swallow of his drink to allow himself a moment to digest everything. The world of barbarian hiring was changing. But more importantly, Flake lied. Again.

'Regardless of whether you sent him or not, the fact remains that Ice Giants have invaded Flake's territory, and he wants my help to get rid of them,' said Ned.

'That's not strictly true though, is it, eh?' Griff held up a finger. 'The Ice Giants want you and blackmailed Flake by kidnapping his son to force him down the mountain and bring you back. Apparently, it's not cold enough for them to do it themselves.'

'Oh!' Brogan slapped his thigh. 'That Flake. A Meh-Teh, huh? Cool.' He pulled out a scroll and pen and scribbled something down. 'Proper legend.'

Ned was gobsmacked. How could you meet a Meh-Teh and not realise what it was? I mean, the guy practically radiated snow!

'You never told me you met a Meh-Teh! Where was I?' asked Mia.

'Oh, ah, I was very drunk, my sweet. It was a passing exchange of pleasantries whilst staggering back to our rooms at the guest house. I barely remember it at all.'

Mia crossed her arms and shifted her body away from Brogan. Ned decided to forge onwards with his request, addressing her directly.

'We have a spell to vanquish the Ice Giants and we need your power. We were hoping you would cast the magic for us.'

Mia stiffened.

'Why haven't you brought Jenni with you to do the spell? She's much stronger than me.'

'Too strong for her own good. There's power in the snow. It was affecting Jenni. She couldn't maintain control.' Ned picked at the tabletop. 'You heard about the fight with the Sea Witch?'

'Felt it. Huge magical imbalance. She was lucky to come out of it alive and in one piece. Really lucky,' replied Mia.

'You should have seen Mr Spinks in action.' More gushing from Fred. 'I was in charge of guarding the kelp forest entrance to make sure nobody interrupted things and Miss Jenni was up at the top of the hill at Justice Heights. And Mr Spinks just walked in. Just like that. He walked into the kelp forest without a by your leave. Determined to go rescue Miss Jenni and armed with nothing more than what you see before you today, ready to face danger.' He lowered his voice dramatically. 'Her eyes had turned black on account of all the dark magic leaking into her soul.'

'Yes, thank you, Fred.' Ned was a touch

embarrassed now. 'Jenni might not have been so lucky. The fight changed her magical ability completely.' Ned realised who he was talking to. 'Hey, have you sensed anything in the snow? Any new magical disturbance?' In his urgency, he had leaned forwards causing Mia to bend away from him.

'Um… I mean, I thought I felt the Ice Giants arrive. There was very definitely a disturbance, but you know, we're at the foot of a mountain, nestled in a mystical convergence. There are ley lines of power all over the place. Surely even you must have noticed that?'

Ned considered that for a moment. Now that he thought about it, there was a faint buzzing in the air. He'd assumed it was something to do with mountains, this being his first time climbing them and being in their general vicinity. It was proper outdoors air. All sorts of things in that. Not like your city smog. At least you knew where you were with your city smog.

'Yeah, I guess,' he admitted. 'So, you might have sensed something?'

Mia turned to see if Brogan was paying close attention, but he was chatting with Griff about one of their recent jobs and Fred was hanging on to every word.

'I've been having… dreams. Nightmares, really. About… well, about my dad.'

Ned stiffened.

'The Sorcerer? But we got rid of him. Sent him to… Nowhere…' He tailed off. A very bad feeling brewing in his stomach.

Mia stared at Ned for a long time, and he was uncomfortably reminded of facing her on opposite sides before, back when she was the infamous Rose Thief working for her evil sorcerer father who Ned banished to Nowhere.

'You're not… he's not…?' Ned didn't really know how to ask the question. 'We came here for your help.' He whispered, wondering if everything was about to fall apart.

'They are just dreams. Let me look at the spell,' she finally said, holding out her hand.

Ned let out a shaky breath and dug the instructions out of his bag.

Mia read through it a couple of times, then handed it back.

'Seems relatively straight forward. It's all metaphorical, except for the tears and I'm guessing the rumour about those is fake?'

Ned nodded.

'We'll help but… Ice Giants… it's going to be tricky to get close enough to whammy them with this spell and this is a onetime cast. It'll have to be pre-mixed and then held in stasis until release. The closer I am, the more effective the spell will be, but I'm not even sure I've got the oomph to send three back from whence they come, plus… you're aware this opens a portal, right?'

Ned nodded.

'The thing about portals is, they open both ways. We send the Ice Giants back and… who knows what comes through? It's the magical price for casting the spell.'

The pair of them stared at each other, neither one willing to speak aloud at the possibility that someone or something might try to get through the portal. Mia changed the subject.

'It's a shame about Jenni. We are probably going to need that extra firepower. Have you been… practising?' Her tone was withering as she raised an eyebrow at Ned. Being a warlock meant she had natural access to her power, whereas Ned was a spellcaster which required him to learn how to unlock his power. Which was why he spent most of his time magically blocked.

Ned had been aware of Fred bobbing about on his chair, desperate to speak but unsure of the etiquette for interrupting. Both Brogan and Griff had turned their attention back to Ned as well.

'Fred, did you have something to add?' Ned turned to the lad, eager to take the attention away from whether he'd been practising his spell exercises or not. Fred shot him a very grateful smile.

'Thanks, Boss. I was just wondering why Mr Brogan and Ms Mia were still here when clearly their interaction with Flake was that much less impactful than it was on him. I mean, from the way he was speaking, it was like they were the best of friends and had spent a significant amount of time discussing your prowess in dealing with the evil sorcerer. Begging your pardon, Ms.' Fred actually stopped talking to tug his forelock at Mia, to which she bestowed a dazzling smile upon the lad that meant it took him several swallows to get his bobbing Adams apple back under control.

'Oh, we're staying here for the winter. Just missed out on a big job due to not having all the skills on my BSS and there will be a huge convention at Kriburgh in a few weeks' time offering all kinds of training and access to specialist skills. The perfect place for polishing your BSS. Figured we'd rest and recuperate beforehand,' explained Brogan.

'And then we found out about the Ice Giants,' prompted Mia.

'Oh yeah. Then we heard the Ice Giants had returned and were camping out on this mountain. Imagine that. A coincidence if ever there was one. And because we were already here, we ticked the BSS box for being on site and got the contract. Or at least the future contract because someone is bound to want to hire a barbarian with Ice Giants about. Maybe multiple contracts which will be a decent payday. Speaking of paydays... who's paying for this quest?'

The backs of Neds' ears started to redden.

'I was, er, rather hoping you'd help us out of the goodness of your heart,' he said.

Brogan actually guffawed loudly.

'But we're barbarians!' he bellowed.

Ned rallied.

'Exactly.'

He waited and prayed that Fred wouldn't pipe up.

Brogan looked at Mia, who gave him the smallest of nods.

'Fine, we'll do it for old times' sake, but we want a glowing testimony for the BSS. And future quotes whenever we ask for them.' Brogan thought for a moment. 'An official seal of Roshaven would look nice.'

Ned exhaled in relief.

'I'll see what I can do,' he said. 'You must know all about the Ice Giants. What can you tell us?'

'It seems they've invaded this mountain and evicted a Meh-Teh,' said Brogan without a trace of irony.

Ned looked at the barbarian's gentle face and weighed up whether the man was trying to annoy him on purpose or whether he just happened to be the most forgetful barbarian in the business. At least Mia looked embarrassed for the both of them.

'Sorry,' she said. 'We don't have much information at all. Except how they got here. That was the talk of the tap room. A chap travelled through here a few weeks back, just before your man was evicted, and said he wanted a guide up the mountain. Odd though, he had no coin, so I was sure he'd never get anyone to take him up. Turns out the top tracker, Ferdinand, took him in the end. Free of charge. We thought that was odd, didn't we?'

Brogan nodded and took over the tale.

'Well, Ferdinand came down the mountain in a bit of a daze. The chappie he went up with nowhere to be found. Took a good day and half before we could get any words out of Ferdie. Turns out the bloke – Norm was his name – was a vessel for some higher power who channelled through him to open a portal and release the Ice Giants. The guy was pretty small, probably why they only managed the three. Mind you, three Ice Giants is a darn sight more than I'd want atop a mountain. Even I felt the power surge. Thought it was a bout of indigestion to begin with. It's not a clever idea to eat too many biscuits before bedtime.'

Ned had gone cold at the mention of Norm.

'Huh, that's ever so funny, because we know someone called Norm. Well, know is a strong word. More of an acquaintance, I'd say. Turns out he's Jenni's dad and in servitude to the Sea Witch. Or was at least until Miss Jenni defeated her and cast her out in a terrific magical battle. I was there. Guarded the kelp forest entrance. Pivotal role. Oh, and Norm is a wanted criminal. Stroke of luck that we're here really when you think about it. We can kill two birds with one stone.' Fred beamed.

'Maybe not so defeated, eh?' Griff looked worried. 'Is Norm still about?'

'No, we never saw him again. There's a possibility that he's still atop the mountain, but I can't imagine he would've survived the immense magic flows. Not without a huge amount of power skimming to build up his defences and we all know that skimming is illegal,' said Mia, taking a sip of her drink. She looked at the stricken faces in front of her. 'What? What did I say?'

'Magic skimming is a particular speciality of Norm,' said Ned with a sigh. 'If he didn't come down the mountain with Ferdinand, my guess is that he's long gone. Mischief managed and all that. On to the next thing.'

'It's still the best lead we've had, eh?' muttered Griff.

'I'll be sure to ask the Ice Giants if they've got a forwarding address before we vanquish them,' replied Ned waspishly before turning back to Mia. 'Look, Flake is meeting us at the foot of the mountain, first thing tomorrow. Will you be able to cast the spell by then?'

'Should be fine,' said Mia. 'Who's going to represent what?'

'Er…' Ned scratched his head. 'Um…'

Chapter 40

Ned really didn't want to be the one to choose which person represented which metaphorical aspect, so he was stalling for as long as possible.

'Um…'

'I will be the breath of regret, eh? Got plenty of those to choose from. Shouldn't be too difficult to come up with one.' Griff spread his hands out, sounding chipper despite the metaphorical item he'd just volunteered for.

Again, Ned wished he had the time to unpack his father's past and find out more about him. What sort of things could he be regretting? Was one of them not being around when Ned was growing up? He pushed those thoughts aside sharply as Fred plucked at his sleeve.

'Yes?'

'I reckon I should be the fickleness of indecision. I know it sounds like it could be a negative trait, but sometimes not knowing what to do for the best can be a great strength. It gives you options and allows you to look at something from every angle. Weigh up the pros and cons. Decide what's going to work for you.'

Fred unusually paused for breath and Ned opened his mouth to cut in, but he was too slow.

'And then there's the whole matter of changing your mind and dealing with large amounts of choice. Sometimes I think life would be so much easier if there just wasn't huge amounts of choice to deal with. We could all get along better if there was only one type of cake in the bakery but whenever I come out with stuff like that, me mam raps me knuckles and tells me that variety is the spice of life and wouldn't it be boring if we all liked the same things, said the same things and did the same things. We'd be sheep rather than people. I kind of like sheep.'

Fred looked to his audience for any immediate reactions to sheep before sweeping on.

'They have excellent chewing skills, and their wool is very good for knitting thermals, so sometimes I think that being a sheep wouldn't necessarily be a bad thing and maybe we should all try being a sheep for a day and see what it's like. That's usually when me mam gives me a clip round the ear.'

He beamed as the others took the customary Fred pause to catch up and figure out exactly what he'd said.

'You got it, kid,' said Mia. 'Brogan, you can be the courage. You've got buckets of it, especially when the odds are stacked against you.'

'You think the odds are stacked against us?' asked Ned, relieved to not have to feel courageous about the whole thing, while Brogan nodded, looking as pleased as punch to be metaphorical courage.

'Us against Ice Giants? I think we're operating on a wing and a prayer, but more has been done with less, so let's give it our best shot and see what happens.' She tapped a finger on Ned's chest. 'You've got the heart.'

Ned nodded. He'd figured as much.

'Pardon me, Ms Mia, but what about the strength of belief? We don't have another team member on account of leaving Jenni in Roshaven because of her magical wobbliness and leaving Willow in Roshaven on account of her inability to deal with the deadly low temperatures – deadly to her being a tree nymph despite putting on two woolly vests and wrapping up against the weather with an extra thick set of thermals I knitted myself – and we didn't bring Joe on account of him staying in Roshaven to help Willow set up the seed bank to save all the seeds of Roshaven from being frozen and destroyed and us losing all the plants and not having a Vine anymore.'

Ned listened in dazed amazement as Fred threw out all grammatical use of commas and held his ground firmly against using them.

'We didn't bring Fingers because Empress Rose, long may she rule, said he was integral to the running of the city, and she couldn't do without him and anyway Ned couldn't have the whole A team and he already had Griff who you've just assigned something to. I'm guessing a person can't be two metaphorical aspects? Because if that was the case then you wouldn't need any of us and you could just cast the spell yourself but then does using a metaphorical aspect drain the power from your actual aspect and do we all need to make sure we have a good breakfast tomorrow before we get going because as much as Mr Brogan's biscuits are very enjoyable, I'm not sure they lend themselves to being large, deep wells of resourceful energy.' Fred picked up his drink and took a long, noisy slurp.

'We don't need another person. We've got everything we need,' replied Mia.

Ned blinked in surprise. He hadn't expected Mia to keep up with Fred so easily.

'Who's going to be belief?' Ned asked.

'The same person who is going to give us his tears,' replied Mia. 'I take it you copied this spell down exactly from the book?'

Ned nodded. He'd learned that lesson the hard way

in the past.

'Then if you actually read it, it says *The strength of belief and three tears from a Meh-Teh.* Your Flake will have to provide both those things.'

Ned frowned. That put them in a pickle. Quite a pickle indeed.

'There's something else you need to know,' he said. 'It turns out the Ice Giants are holding Flake's son hostage and that they will only release him for me. I don't know why.'

'I think I do,' said Mia. 'It's because you can control access to Nowhere.'

Griff clapped his hand on his knee.

'Of course! That makes sense, eh?'

'Well it certainly doesn't make sense to me. Why on earth do the Ice Giants think I control access to Nowhere?' asked Ned.

'Probably because it's where you sent Father. Where you went yourself when love died. It's where you saved the world.' Mia regarded Ned critically for a moment. 'You are the only human to purposefully entered and then successfully left Nowhere and survived. There must be something about you, something hidden deep within your core. Some buried magical ability.'

Ned remembered. He remembered being in the middle of nowhere. It had been black and there had been a lot of sand. It was where the rose of love had been sent and where he'd gone with Jenni to get it back. But he didn't have any special connection with the place. Jenni had found the magical signature Mia had left behind after she banished Brogan to Nowhere. She'd opened the portal, not him. He'd only gone there because Jenni thought they could find the rose and bring it back. But it had been his love for Roshaven and Rose that had brought them back. It had been a fluke really that he'd ended up sending the sorcerer there when they'd fought at the final showdown.

'I can't access Nowhere. Jenni opened a portal there last time, and that was only because she followed your magical signature. If anyone's going Nowhere it's you.' Ned jabbed a finger in Mia's direction.

She flushed.

'That wasn't me. I mean, it was me, but I was drunk on warlock power. Out of control and being used by my father. Half the time I didn't even know the spells I was casting.' She gave the group a pleading look. 'You have to believe me. That part of my life is behind me. I have no idea how to open a portal to Nowhere, I promise.' She waited for them to respond. It was slow in coming, but there were slight nods and smiles from everyone, except for Ned. Mia rallied. 'You punched a hole out of Nowhere to come back. I bet that's what the Ice Giants are betting on. That you can get... the rest of them out.'

Ned had a horrible feeling he knew what Mia was going to say. That he could get one person in particular out of Nowhere. The person he sent there in the first place.

Fred had been quiet for a long time, but now he'd raised his hand.

'You don't have to raise your hand, lad,' said Ned, gesturing for him to speak.

'Mr Spinks, Sir, Boss, what if... what if the Ice Giants want you to release the sorcerer so he can return the Sea Witch's power?'

It was the most succinct sentence Ned had ever heard from Fred and it had been delivered in a tense, breathless style that gave him goosebumps. The scariest thing was it was also exactly what Ned was thinking.

What if indeed?

'Why would the Ice Giants even know who the Sea Witch is, eh? Or even care about her lost powers?' Griff rubbed his goatee. 'Seems to me they are powerful enough without having to get involved with anything like that. We don't need to be worrying about the Sea Witch, eh?'

Despite the intent, Griff's word didn't make Ned feel particularly comforted.

Chapter 41

They had spent the rest of the evening arguing. Ned refused to be moved on his decision. The snow in Roshaven would only be lifted if Ned went up the mountain. It was his duty to his city and his Empress. The fact that he was going into a hellish hostage scenario set up by the disembodied Sea Witch working through Norm, using the threat of Ice Giant destruction and a perpetual snow-bound Roshaven with the possibility of being made to release the Sorcerer out of Nowhere was really neither here nor there. They didn't even know for certain that the Sorcerer was trying to escape. As he had said many times to the rest of the group, he was prepared to sacrifice himself to save Roshaven, but it wasn't going to come to that. They had a plan. They had the spell and the ingredients, mostly. All they had to do was convince Flake they would win. They just needed his tears and his belief.

As it turned out, the tears weren't the problem. While he had been in Roshaven and during the journey to Mount Firn, Flake had been a pillar of stoic calm, unruffled even by Fred. Now that they were on the verge of confrontation, he was an emotional wreck, alternating between relief and terror. It was odd to see him so afraid. And Ned finally understood why the books said Meh-Teh's didn't cry – instead of tears, Flake made opals. Beautiful teardrop shaped opals. Ned collected them from the floor and patted a furry shoulder.

'Come on, Flake buddy. It's alright. It's a brilliant plan. We can't lose. They're not expecting us to come armed with the power to get rid of them. They're not expecting you to tell us about your son. What's his name?'

The Meh-Teh blew his nose noisily.

'Nix. His name is Nix. We thought about calling him Khion, but my wife liked Nix more. Said it matched him better.'

'It's a great name. And your wife, where is she?' Ned wondered if they had a double rescue on his hands.

Flake's hands shook and when he answered, his voice was tight with anger.

'Eira died when the portal opened and the Ice Giants came through. She was in the wrong place. That is all. Standing in the wrong place. The man who opened it could have told her to move. There was no reason why not. He must have known where the portal was going to open. He was in charge of activating it. So what that he had black eyes and claimed to not be in control? No one could accidentally miss a seven foot Meh-Teh.'

Ned grimaced. It certainly sounded like the Sea Witch was meddling, trying to cause chaos, and that she still had her claws deep into Norm. They knew he'd been working for her before, but Norm had made that sound like a purely contractual agreement, procuring hard to come by items and the like. Not being a magical vessel responsible for killing innocent creatures.

'I'm sorry I didn't tell you before. About my wife,' Flake spoke quietly.

'Oh no, it's alright. I knew you were keeping something from me, but I had no idea it was this. I am so, so sorry. I can't imagine the pain you're in, but I promise you, we will get Nix back for you.'

'I appreciate that, but...' Flake's tone turned bitter. 'You are only a man. A mostly non-magical one at that.

268

What can you do against the might of the Ice Giants and the Sea Witch?'

Ned wished the others were with him. He'd asked them to stay in the pub until he'd had a chance to talk to Flake, but he could have done with some Fred optimism right about now.

'Well, we defeated her once before and don't forget it was me that sent the Sorcerer to Nowhere, so I'd say you were very definitely on the winning side. We got this. I've got the spell to return the Ice Giants, I've got all the ingredients and you've got an entire team of people committed to saving your son.'

Flake managed a tiny smile.

Ned held up the handful of Meh-Teh tears he had.

'I'm going to go give this to Mia and we'll meet you here in about ten minutes. Is that alright?'

Flake nodded, his shoulders still drooped and looking utterly defeated before they had even begun. Ned hurried back to the others. They had their work cut out to get this Meh-Teh to believe they could win. But then, a thought occurred to him, and Ned grinned.

'What kind of belief does it have to be?' he asked as soon as he entered the tavern.

'What?' Mia looked confused.

'What kind of belief? It's non-specific, right? All you need is the strength of belief. That's what the spell says, right? Strong belief.' Ned was so keyed up he was speaking very fast.

'Er… yeah, I guess. Why?' Realisation dawned on Mia's face. 'Oh… he doesn't believe we can win. He thinks we'll lose. Yes, that might work. Did you get the tears?'

Ned dropped the opals into Mia's hand and she put them into a spell vial she had ready.

'Let's do this,' he said, clapping his hands together.

'Okay, hold still while I extract your heart.'

Ned blinked before feeling his heart pound out of his chest. It was beating a million miles an hour, thrumming loudly in his ears and he could barely take a breath. Then, as quickly as it had started, it stopped, and he gasped for air, like he'd just run as fast and as far as he possibly could. Mia was holding up the vial that now had a tiny beating heart inside it. It was pink and glittery.

'Did you...?' Ned didn't have the words to talk.

'Yeah, I made it look like this. Pretty, don't you think?'

'I guess.' Ned flopped down into a chair, getting his breath back. He pulled the travel journal towards him and flipped it open to a new page.

'Who's next?' asked Mia, grinning wickedly at the others, before crooking a finger and beckoning Fred over.

'Oh, is it me next, Miss Mia? Are you sure? Do you think that maybe someone else should go first? Because we want to make sure we extract them in the right order. If they come in an order. What order do you think they should come in? Is that something we should know? Or maybe it doesn't matter what order they are extracted, and it just matters what order they are put back together again? Will they all be glittery or...? Shall I stand over there or...? Do I need to...?' Fred's usual flow of chatter and questions skittered and stuttered to a stop. His mouth gaped open, and his eyes glazed over, fingers twitching before two little glittery green arrows pulsed out of his mouth and floated gently into the open vial in Mia's hands. One arrow pointed in one direction whilst the other took the opposite one, each of them swinging back and forth, up and down, in and out. Fred shook his head, looking a little dazed, and stepped back without saying a word.

'You okay, lad?' asked Griff, as he walked closer to Mia.

Fred gave a thumbs up and sat on the edge of the table. Griff raised an eyebrow at Ned. It was weird for Fred to not talk. Ned began writing into the journal.

Hi   love
The extractions of the metaphorical aspects are going well, with no lasting side effects so far. But we've discovered something – I'm not sure you should tell Jenni. The thing is, it was Norm. He let out the Ice Giants, started this whole thing. But from the sounds of it, someone or something is controlling him. Apparently, he has black eyes. I'm not jumping to conclusions, but...

Ned stopped writing and looked up as Griff was next to be extracted.

'Come on then, extract away.' Griff squared his shoulders and looked Mia right in the eye. Nothing happened immediately. Then Ned noticed Griff's feet were twisting left and right. He wrung his hands, his shoulders slumped, and he bit his lip, tears forming in his eyes. A small, glittery blue pirate ship floated out of his head towards Mia's waiting vial. Griff let out a tremendous sigh and sniffed loudly, wiping his eyes before stepping back to join Fred perched on the table. The two of them leaning into each other for moral support.

Ned was concerned. He hoped they were both alright. It looked like the extraction had knocked the pair of them sideways. Some writing appeared in the book in front of him.

Hey   x
Bit hard not to tell Jenni - she's here with me, keeping

out of trouble and playing sprite tricks on the maids.

You ain't got proof it's me – could be anyone.

There was a sizeable ink blot as Ned imagined Rose and Jenni wrestling for control of the pen. His attention turned to Brogan, who stood in front of Mia in an easy stance, ready for anything. Radiating confidence.

There was no noticeable difference to the barbarian as several sparkly yellow stars shot out from his muscular arm and landed in Mia's vial with a tiny clink. Brogan clapped a hand on Ned's shoulder as he passed him and leant down to whisper something at Griff and Fred, who both started nodding and stood up, looking a little revived.

Ned scribbled a quick message in the travel book.

Okay, look, don't do anything rash. Wait for me to get all the facts. We're about to head up the mountain and get this done. Speak to you when I get back. Love you.

He closed the pages before they had a chance to reply, choosing instead to keep the image of Rose and Jenni exasperating each other in the palace in his mind. He tucked the book safely into his backpack.

'I just need to get Flake's belief and then we're good to go,' said Mia.

'He's waiting for us outside,' replied Ned. 'Look, can I take a quick minute to say thank you – to all of you. I really appreciate you giving your time and expertise on this quest, and I know that if we work together, as a team - no, a family - we can absolutely win the day.' Ned wasn't sure what was coming over him, but he felt all gushy.

The others picked up their kit and there was a lot of shoulder slapping and grinning at each other as the side effects of having the aspects extracted wore off.

Just outside Blyz, Ned introduced Flake to everyone and watched nervously as Mia pulled out the Meh-Teh's belief. It was a glittery purple snowflake that wobbled. He guessed that was because Flake didn't believe they would win, but belief was belief and hopefully it would do for the spell.

'Okay, so thinking about it, we've got the spell and obviously that's the plan. Get the Ice Giants sent back to Nowhere, but… what about fighting tactics? Other than Flake's snowbility, what do we have in terms of additional weapons?' asked Ned, feeling a little embarrassed at having left the discussion of weaponry until just before they were due to walk up the mountain.

Brogan pulled a double-headed axe over his shoulder with one hand and a barbaric-looking scimitar from the other. The simple action of drawing them was definitely menacing. Griff twirled a couple of wickedly sharp knives in his hands before disappearing them up his sleeves again. Mia thunked a throwing star into the ground in front of Ned's feet, making him flinch, and Fred pulled out a small bottle of black powder.

'What is that?' asked Ned.

'It's bang-bang powder, Boss. Sister Eustacia gave me some ages ago when we were having problems with the rats. It makes a massive noise and creates sparks, a real distraction to your opponent in a fight and should make the Ice Giants look the other way if we wanted to create a sneaky diversion.' He pulled another bottle out of his pocket. 'I have two bottles if you want one.'

Ned stretched out his hand and took the bang-bang powder. While he was grateful for it now, he would have to have a word with Sister Eustacia about handing out incendiary devices without a permit. Especially to the more accident-prone citizens.

273

'What about you, Boss? What do you have?' asked Fred.

The backs of Ned's ears heated, and he pulled out his trusty collapsible baton. With a flick of his wrist, he snapped it out and then back in again.

'Awesome,' breathed Fred. 'When do I get one of those?'

'When you've completed basic training,' replied Ned, hastily making a mental note to create some basic training for Fred and to ask the dwarves for a couple more batons. He decided against showing the impressionable lad the trusty set of illegal knuckledusters he also had. If it came to it, they would come in very handy, and he could explain later.

'Um, Flake? If the Ice Giants know that we're coming... do we stick to the lie you told me? Or do we use the fact that I know you're planning to exchange me for your son?' asked Ned.

'I am unsure what you mean.' Flake's eyebrows beetled furiously.

'Well, we could do the classic fake prisoner walk. You know, pretend to bind my hands and bring me in, looking all defeated. Give the others time to spread out and assume a decent attack formation and then throw everything we've got at the Ice Giants while Mia casts the spell.'

There were murmurs of agreement about his plan. Flake considered it for a moment.

'This seems like a good surprise attack, as you say. I am content to go with this strategy. Whilst the others mount their attack, I will rescue my son. I trust you are all capable of casting the spell without me. You have everything you need from me. My son... my son is my focus.'

'Absolutely. We understand and yes, we can handle the rest.' Ned looked over at everyone. 'Mia, you find some protective cover in order to cast. Fred, you throw the bang-bang powder and distract the Ice Giants, giving Flake the opportunity to grab his son. Brogan and Griff, you attack them, keeping them off balance. Then, once Nix is clear, Flake can immobilise the Ice Giants in snow, and we can send them back to Nowhere.'

'What are you going to do, Boss?' asked Fred.

'I'll cover Flake. I've got the second bottle of bang-bang so I can create another diversion, if need be, and I'll protect Mia.'

'And you've got your magic, Boss, which is bound to spring into action once we're in the thick of it, as it always does.' Fred beamed with completed confidence.

Ned's stomach roiled. His magic had always leapt into action in the protection of either Jenni or Rose, and neither of them were with him. He wasn't sure his magic would do anything at all, but he checked his spellcaster's belt to reassure himself that it was still full to capacity should he require it. He'd made certain he filled it before he left Roshaven.

Chapter 42

Ned was mostly confident as they set off up the mountain. The path was gentle to begin with and the sun shone in a cold yet clear blue sky. Fred was whistling tunelessly, giving the impression they were just out for a walk.

'I've had a bit of an idea, Boss,' said Fred. 'I'm a keen pamphlet collector and I've been learning ever so much about all sorts of things. It being winter, I've learned about igloos and the Snieg and I discovered lots of winter facts such as all snowflakes are different. Can you believe that? It seems daft, doesn't it? You would think that Mother Nature would keep them all the same, make it easier to churn them out, but every single one is unique. Sometimes the different is the tiniest nth of an angle of a fractal, but a difference it is. Did you know that it's almost impossible to tell with the naked eye that they aren't the same? Up at the Fae University, they have some special microscopes to look at small things and make them seem bigger. These microscopes are fascinating bits of equipment. I attended an open day and had the chance to see the tiniest part of a leaf. It was amazing under there, Boss. Amazing. No wonder The Vine is so good at what it does. Nature blows my mind. Absolutely.'

'The idea?' prompted Ned.

'Oh yes. I was thinking how snow can't melt ice. It just can't. In fact, unless we get a lot of heat up there, we won't be able to melt the Ice Giants, if indeed they are even made of ice at all which is a shame really because if we could light some fires then boom, job jobbed but nothing is ever as simple as it should be. Me mam says that all the time. Anyway, did you know snow can insulate ice? Basically trap it in a steady state. So if we can somehow get the Ice Giants in a precarious pickle, crack 'em or put them in a position of weakness and then Flake can manipulate the snow over them it should stop the Ice Giants from moving, getting thicker and protecting themselves and it should improve their weaknesses. That is as long as the Ice Giants are in fact made of ice.'

By this point, everyone was listening in.

'How do you improve a weakness?' asked Brogan. 'Do you mind if I take notes? This could be a brilliant case study for the BSS.'

Fred opened his arms expansively.

'Cover it in snow!' He beamed at the group.

Ned's brain took a moment to process the fact that Fred had spoken a single sentence.

'The talkative one is correct. Snow is a great insulator – good for burying and smothering.' Without exactly meaning to, Flake sounded sinister.

Privately, Ned though he could carry on with his life quite happily not seeing Ice Giants up close and personal, but he tried to digest the information Fred had supplied. It seemed unlikely to him that an insulating layer of snow would break ice, so he decided to ask Flake for a demonstration. They'd been walking up the mountain a little while now and it was definitely getting colder, snowier, and icier.

'Flake? Could you cover this ice in snow?' Ned asked, pointing to a fairly deep puddle that had iced over but had a divot in it.

Flake obliged with a sudden flurry, and they all

watched to see what would happen. At first, nothing at all, and then there was a groaning noise followed by a loud crack and the snow flumped down in the middle of the puddle. Scraping the snow aside, Ned discovered that the ice had indeed been broken.

'Well, I never. You might be right there, Fred. Good job.' He gave the lad a thumbs up. Who knew pamphlets would save the day? 'You see, Flake, you do have power over your domain. Just because they're Ice Giants, doesn't mean they're in charge.'

Although Ned reckoned it was unlikely Flake would suddenly be filled with self-belief at being able to defeat the Ice Giants, it wouldn't hurt to reinforce everything they had going for them. Confidence could carry you a long way.

'I cannot say for certain that the giants are, in fact, made of ice, so this may be a pointless exercise.'

Ned revised his opinion on Flake's level of confidence. At least he hadn't said they were walking to their death.

The terrain got more intense, requiring greater attention to foot placement, so all conversation halted while everyone focused on making it up the mountain in one piece. After climbing for ages, Flake finally drew them into what looked like a crevice in the rock face. It turned out to be a decent sized cave.

The humans stood clustered in the entrance, trying to take in all the icy wonders within the cave. There were ice stalagmites and stalactites that sparkled when the sun's rays caught them, casting rainbows on the shiny walls of the cave. Every now and then, there was a tinkle as one of the smaller spikes fell from the ceiling. The walls shone from the groundwater that had seeped through and been frozen in place. Tiny snow spiders scuttled across the shiny surfaces to the safety of their crystallised webs up in the corners. Flake's footsteps into the cave disturbed snowapedes and ice scorpions which click-clacked across the floor, stinging tails held high, ready to attack anyone who came too close.

'This will be the best place to refuel. There is an old hunter's fire pit where you can make...' Flake shuddered. 'Where you can prepare food. I would suggest you all at least hydrate. It is important to drink enough fluids, even in the cold. Watch out for the ice snakes.'

As the group ventured further into the icy cave of wonders, Fred had his notepad out and was sketching some of the unusual animals, true to his word to M-TAC in documenting everything. He wasn't paying attention to where he was going, tripped on a stone, and stumbled. Fred managed to keep his balance, thanks to a steadying hand from Griff, but his half fall set off the hanging saucepans on his backpack, which made an almighty clatter, startling a colony of snowbats. They wheeled, like flying white furry mice, through and round them all, making nearly everyone squeal in fright.

Flake looked nonplussed.

'The bats will not hurt you. They have excellent spatial awareness. As I said, it is the snakes you must watch out for. They possess exceptional blending skills.'

Indeed, the Meh-Teh was peering nervously into the gloomier corners of the cave, trying to get a good look without getting too close.

'I believe we are safe for now. After pausing here, we must face the Ice Giants. They will be aware we are on the mountain. We must hurry. Half an hour here, no more.'

'They know all of us are here?' asked Ned. He had

been hoping they would have the element of surprise.

'I expect so, yes. They are Ice Giants.'

The way Flake made that statement suggested he believed there was nothing Ice Giants couldn't do.

A spine chilling, tingly snow wail sounded in the distance.

'What was that?' asked Ned, trying to keep the city boy fear out of his voice.

Flake had stiffened.

'Dire wolves. Be on your guard.'

Chapter 43

Brogan took charge of the fire making, and Ned was happy to leave it to him, the wolf howl had put everyone else on edge. Fred hovered around the barbarian for a little while, watching his methodology but for once keeping his thoughts to himself. He nodded happily as smoke began to appear and wandered over to where Ned was sitting.

'It's a bit weird this, isn't it, Boss?' remarked Fred.

'Weird?' Ned wondered exactly what part of the whole escapade Fred thought was particularly peculiar.

'Well, this is like that time you went up the mountain to defeat the evil sorcerer, isn't it? You even have some of the same team as before so that's a good sign, and it's not like we need to say second time lucky because you were successful in the first time, and we don't even know for sure that the evil sorcerer is trying to escape. For all we know, it could just be Ice Giants and, to be fair...' Fred lowered his voice. 'We don't even know that for sure. I mean, we are risking life and limb climbing up Mount Firn on the say so of a mythical creature that I was sure really did actually exist but had no idea that I would ever get to see with my very own eyeballs. It's so weird.'

Ned digested this. He hadn't thought to draw any parallels. Back then he'd just been reacting to events, trying to keep his city and wife safe, look after Jenni and do his job to the best of his ability. He could count the differences; his feet were a lot colder now – despite the double socks – and he missed Rose, was feeling more than a little lost at not having Jenni by his side and whilst Mia seemed very confident about the spell, Ned knew from experience not to completely rely on magic.

'What was it like, Boss?' asked Fred.

'Mmm?'

'Going on that quest with Jenni and Rose and everyone. Defeating the Sorcerer. Any tips?' Fred was leaning forward, on the edge of his rocky seat and the rest of the cave had quietened, waiting to see what Ned had to say.

'Um, I mean, yeah, it was more a hill on that one rather than a mountain, but there are definitely parallels. We had a magic potion to use in order to defeat the Sorcerer, which we all dipped our weapons into.' He laughed softly as he remembered. 'In fact, Rose – or Fourteen as she was then – had dipped her arrows into the potion and none of us saw her do it, she wasn't supposed to be fighting. The Sorcerer had a protective bubble and our weapons bounced off, it was touch and go. He locked us all. We couldn't move, except for Mia.' He thought about it for a moment. 'Joe was hit first, then Mia had her magic ripped out.'

'I remember,' Mia whispered. 'It hurt like hell. I never dreamed I'd get my magic back, but the block that Momma K put on me protected the root, so it could return.' She flourished her hand, causing sparkly stars to dance.

It reminded Ned of Jenni. He really missed her.

'He bound Willow and Jenni together. That was a big mistake.' Mia glanced at Fred. He was enthralled. 'Everyone always underestimates the gentle ones, but Willow, she was amazing. She called on the surrounding plants, to feed into Jenni's power but also to help them get free and to break the Sorcerer's protection.'

282

'He sent me away. Just like that.' Brogan slapped a hand on his thigh. 'I had absolutely no power whatsoever. I was desperate to join the fight, to see if Mia was alright but I had no control at all.'

Ned picked up the tale.

'He threatened to drain the love out of me and Rose and use her as a figurehead. It made me so angry, suddenly I could move. I was free of the spell, so I threw my best knife at him, but it bounced off the shield, obviously.'

'It broke his attention though,' said Mia. 'And Jenni was able to start hurling fireballs at him while Willow's plants managed to make a crack in the shield.'

'Yeah, she got a ball in the balls and the plants trapped the Sorcerer in one place.' Brogan smiled broadly. 'Such teamwork.'

'And that's when Rose shot him with the arrow and made him really angry.' Ned winced as he recalled what happened. 'He attacked Willow first by destroying all the vegetation nearby causing her to crumple to the floor. He took Jenni out with a nasty spell. She fell and cracked her head on a rock, stopped moving. He was yelling and advancing on Rose, so I just... released my magic at him. It had been building up the whole time.'

'And you banished him,' added Fred, his eyes shining in admiration.

'Yeah, that's what happened.' Ned shifted under the scrutiny of everyone. 'But you know, these things always happen so fast. It's hard to remember exactly who did what. Like Brogan said, teamwork gets the job done.'

Nobody spoke, and the silence began stretching uncomfortably.

'We all thought you were dead,' said Brogan,

nodding at Griff, who opened his arms wide and gave a seated bow. 'Killed in Fidelia.'

'That, my friend, is a story for another day, eh?'

'I will hold you to that. It is good to see you alive – can I add you as a preferred supplier?' Brogan had his BSS and pen out again and was scribbling before Griff even had the chance to agree. The barbarian was multi-tasking with great efficiency and began to pass out several forks topped with the sizzling sausages he had been cooking. 'No plates means no washing up, plus forks are lighter to carry. Top tip that. Never miss an opportunity to eat, especially when you're on a job.'

'How did you make the fire so quickly, Mr Brogan, Sir?' asked Fred.

'Barbarian approved firestarters.' Brogan showed them all a metal clicker that sparked. 'Comes in handy when you don't have a fixed hour contract. Everyone needs to eat.'

The others nodded their agreement and began doing just that, except for Flake, who had excused himself and was sitting outside in the snow. Ned grabbed a fork and joined him at the cave entrance.

'You sure you don't want anything to eat?' he asked.

'No, I don't eat meat. We are vegetarians. My wife does, did a lovely salad.'

Flake's voice wobbled on the word wife and Ned put a hesitant hand on the Meh-Teh's shoulder.

'We will do everything in our power to avenge her and get your boy to safety. You know that, right?'

The Meh-Teh nodded but couldn't stop a tear from escaping and a beautiful opal fell onto the snow. He picked it up and handed it to Ned.

'It's best if you keep hold of that. It wouldn't do for a passer-by to see such things out in the open. It encourages Meh-Teh hunting.' Flake's voice was laced with such sadness that it made Ned's heart hurt. 'We should start moving. We can make it to my home in a couple of hours.'

'Are we ready to move?' asked Ned over his shoulder to the rest of the team.

'Almost. I recommend adding these to your shoes.' Brogan handed out slip-on ice grips that went over the bottom of a shoe. 'We have no idea how icy it's going to get. These will help some.'

Everyone bent to slide the grips onto their feet and began hoisting bags back on. Brogan kicked the fire out and a shared look of determination shone on faces. Ned tried to take comfort in that. If they all believed, he could too.

The same spine-chilling howl filled the air. This time, it was a lot closer. Too close.

'Flake?' Ned called out, wanting the Meh-Teh to tell him everything was fine and not to worry.

'Prepare to fight!' yelled Flake, crouching into a defensive posture, the temperature dropping and an icy sleet beginning to fall in stinging waves.

There was no time to get ready. Suddenly, two giant wolves had leapt out in front of them. Magnificent animals who radiated menace from the tip of their snarling muzzles to their wicked sharp claws to their bushy tails that were whipping back and forth in delight at the prey before them.

'Shall I throw the bang bang Mr Spinks, Sir?' yelled Fred in a much higher-pitched voice than normal.

'No! Save that for the giants. We need fire here. Mia?'

'I'm on it!'

Brogan wasted no time in leaping forward, yelling

wildly and waving his wicked looking axe towards the wolves.

'Make yourselves big and noisy!' he yelled, screaming barbaric obscenities at the creatures.

Ned whipped out his baton with a loud crack and bellowed noise. His fear threatened to take over, but he forced sound out his mouth. It was senseless and primal, but it was having an effect. Griff was shouting something in another language and even Fred was screeching something or other. It sounded like he was telling the wolves off and that they should be ashamed of themselves, but whatever it was, the collective din was working. The dire wolves weren't used to prey standing their ground and being noisy. They joined in the fray and growled back, spittle flying from their mouths crowded with sharp teeth. As muscles coiled, ready to leap, Mia let loose with a couple of fireballs. They landed on fur with a sizzle. Pained yelps filled the air, followed by even more frenzied snarling and snapping of jaws.

Brogan leapt forward with a snarl of his own, swinging his axe in wild abandonment, catching a glancing blow on a dire wolf paw that swiped out in retaliation. His success encouraged the others to surge forwards, waving their weapons. The dire wolves snarled louder but grudgingly gave a little ground.

'Again, Mia!' yelled Brogan as Flake intensified his storm, causing hail stones the size of marbles to rain down on the wolves.

Another series of fireballs peppered them, singing fur and turning snarls into yelps before the two dire wolves turned tail and slunk away, back into the snow and ice.

Everyone stood panting for a moment. Senses on high alert in case the wolves returned. But they didn't.

'All okay?' asked Ned, adrenaline coursing through his body, making his hands shake and his words wobble a little.

A trickle of yes's were called out by equally shaky voices as triumphant grins were shared.

'Did we just beat two giant wolves?' asked Fred, in awe. 'With the power of our voices?'

'And a handy fireball or two,' replied Brogan, with a chuckle. 'Definitely one for the BSS.'

'Are you okay, Flake?' asked Ned, relieved that the fierce storm had died down.

'I am, but it is unusual for dire wolves to be this far south. I fear they are attracted by the same evil magic in the snow your sprite felt. Where there is one, there will be more. We must be vigilant. And hurry. We must hurry.'

Chapter 44

Whilst the climb towards Flake's home didn't require specialist equipment, it did require concentration, plus the tension of potentially being attacked by dire wolves again made everyone's nerves raw. There was no convenient pass from Mount Firn to the rest of the mountain range it belonged to. It was passable but not without high levels of difficulty and danger, so it was no good for peddlers and trade caravans but the perfect place for a Meh-Teh to call home. The inhospitable weather that usually shrouded Mount Firn put off keen day walkers and the villagers of Blyz actively sold hikes to the mountain next door. The group had to focus to make sure their feet were placed safely. There was no actual path, but there was plenty of ice. In fact, the ice slides grew the higher they got. A clear calling card from the Ice Giants.

'Good call with the grips,' Ned said, puffing slightly. He wasn't used to inclines. In Roshaven, it was more likely to be a sharp dash around a corner.

They continued in silence, punctuated by small grunts and the odd rasping breath. The air was beginning to thin. Flake held up a hand.

'We are as close as I would like to get in our current formation. If we are going to pursue this ruse, then we should prepare ourselves.' He pointed a shaggy hand to the left. 'There is a rocky outcrop that way, which would make a good hiding place for the spellcaster. If the talkative one follows in my wake, he will not be seen and can throw his distraction. The rest of you will have to wait here until that time, then you can rush forth. My home is just around the bend.' He cast his gaze over the group. 'I thank you for your bravery.' And he gave each of them a small bow.

There were a few quick nervous grins as they got themselves organised. Brogan suggested leaving their packs tucked in safely by a large rock. No need to carry extra weight into the fight. Griff rolled his knives, checking they were easy to access, and Fred made a few practice throwing motions.

'You ready?' Ned asked Mia, who was holding the glittery vial in her fist tightly.

'Yeah. I've got my words of intention to chant. You ready?'

Ned puffed out his cheeks.

'As I'll ever be. Let's do this.'

He made sure he spoke a few words or shook hands with everyone in the party and was surprised to be almost thrown off his feet when Flake enveloped him in a furry hug.

'Hey, it's okay,' Ned patted the Meh-Teh's shoulder and wriggled himself free. 'We have a good plan. Do you want to do the honours?' And he held his wrists up to the Meh-Teh.

'I do not understand.'

Ned chuckled softly to himself and pulled a set of shackles out of his pocket, placing them onto his wrists but leaving them unfastened. He would be able to flick out of them with a single wrist motion.

It was so quiet you could hear a snowflake fall.

Ned's footsteps crunched loudly. The snow was falling heavier. Nervous energy on Flake's part? Possibly. Ned heard his own heart thumping in his ears and tried to take some comfort from the imposing bulk behind him. They rounded the corner and saw huge, jagged, savage, impossible behemoths.

The Ice Giants were man-shaped but massive. Three times the size of Ned, at least. Blue in skin colour, yet not made of ice, so their original attack idea was out the window. Their giant eyes glinted sharp and cold, and their hair looked like frosted blankets of matted fur. Ned had to crane his neck to look all the way up at them. He fleetingly wondered if they'd all just walked into their death when one of them spoke.

'This him?'

Clearly not keen conversationalists.

'Yes. I bring you Ned the Sorcerer Slayer in exchange for my son.' Flake's voice was timid.

A second ice giant pulled a short version of Flake out from behind him, holding him by the scruff of his neck and dangling him off the ground.

'Unlock Nowhere or we throw the kid off the mountain.'

'Nix!' Flake moved half a step forward, but Ned frowned. Despite the words, the tone of the threat was utterly unthreatening but before he could say anything, Fred darted out from behind the Meh-Teh, flung his bottle of bang-bang at the feet of the Ice Giants where it exploded in a loud flash of sparks and noise.

The giant holding Nix dropped him in surprise, but Flake had anticipated that, shooting a pile of soft snow to catch his son. Ned flung the cuffs off and dashed to the left where he'd seen Mia dash, leaving Brogan and Griff to join Fred, yelling thunderous war cries and making as much noise as possible in order to distract the giants from Mia and Ned.

'The Sea Witch sends her regards,' yelled one of the Ice Giants over the melee.

'I knew it!' Ned yelled back. 'I knew she wasn't really dead.'

'Ha! That's what you say, puny human. You understand nothing. She exists in her vessel, bending him to her will. He will not survive long but 'tis no matter. You will open Nowhere and… ARGH!'

Brogan cut him off by literally cutting off his arm with a wicked chop from his deadly axe. The giant fell backwards over a rock. Flake had a tight hold of Nix and was crouched in a defensive fighting position on the opposite side to where Mia was chanting. Brogan was now parrying jets of ice the other giants were frantically firing at him. Griff slipped past it all and managed to hamstring the fallen giant, preventing him from getting up and joining the fight. Fred was less lucky and received a staggering blow to the chest from a wildly swinging fist. But from what Ned could discern, they had caught the Ice Giants mostly by surprise.

Mia's chanting reached a crescendo and a black swirl appeared in the sky, pulling in the swirling snowflakes and loose shale, spinning tighter and tighter as it began to collapse on itself. This was the crucial moment, the point at which Mia was completely vulnerable to attack. Ned stood ready to defend her, but it seemed their plan had worked to near perfection. The Ice Giants were so surprised by the attack, they weren't fighting back.

A niggle wormed at Ned. Why weren't the Ice Giants fighting back?

'So predictable.' A voice spoke on the wind.

Ned's stomach clenched. He knew that voice. It was the Sorcerer. Mia's father. He risked a glance at Mia, whose face had drained of colour.

'Don't listen to it!' shouted Ned above the wind,

which was starting to scream now.

The immobilised Ice Giant on the floor surrendered itself to the sucking vortex that was building and shot through, presumably back to Nowhere. The other two giants cackled maniacally as they too flung themselves into the portal.

A shadow grew, gradually revealing itself to be a man. A tall, thin man who stalked towards the bewildered people standing on the mountaintop.

'No,' whispered Mia, but it was too late. Her spell had opened the portal, three had gone in, which meant the balance was in the Sorcerer's favour and he stepped through triumphantly. 'How are you here?' she gasped.

The Sorcerer smirked.

'If you hadn't of come, I could never have left.'

Tears streamed down Mia's face, but she didn't move.

'The Ice Giants were all part of the plan to draw you here. I honestly didn't think you would fall for it, but She was sure you would answer his call. Stupid child.' The Sorcerer began gathering energy into a giant fireball and shot it at them. Ned barely had time to think about reacting. He magically flexed and created a temporary shield around the group, causing the fireball to bounce off and hit a snow drift where it sizzled.

'Woah!' breathed Fred in awe.

The Sorcerer pinched his lips.

'You. Again. I think not.' He twisted his hands and once more, Ned found he couldn't move. He cast his eyes around desperately and saw that the others were immobile too. But the act of stopping them in their tracks seemed to have done the same to the Sorcerer. Ned watched as the man sagged, his face greying at the exertion. He may have escaped Nowhere, but he didn't have all his powers back, yet. Ned tried to flex his magical muscles again and there was a slight give in the stasis keeping him in one place. He looked again at Mia, who remained rooted in place, and he remembered how dismissively the Sorcerer had taken out his team last time they'd met.

'Not today,' muttered Ned and he clawed together every magical scrap he could reach, not even really knowing how he was doing it but trying to remember Jenni's lessons about being open to receiving. There was a deafening POP that made everyone flinch. Everyone flinched. Brains caught up with motion as people realised they could all move.

Brogan let out a roar and leapt for the Sorcerer, who disappeared in a vast cloud of smoke and a loud bang, disappearing from the mountain. One moment he had been there, the next gone. Brogan landed heavily and looked about wildly, but he had been too late.

Ned barely registered what had just happened when he started to hear voices coming from the portal. Maddened voices chuntering about escaping and wreaking havoc on the world once more.

'You've got to close it. Mia! Close the portal,' he shouted.

There was no response. He looked at Mia's face, frozen in shock and horror. Hopelessness and fear gripped him. He was magically wrung out – it had been a miracle that he'd managed what he had. His power well had run dry, all his reserves tapped out.

His thoughts flew to Rose and his need to protect her.

He flashed backed to the fight on a different hilltop, where she lay in danger, unprotected and alone. He couldn't let that happen again.

Thick ropes of magic glinted on the snow. Ned blinked. They hadn't been there a minute ago. He reached down and picked up one of them. At his touch, power flooded through him, making him gasp. He felt the aspects they'd all given in order to fuel the spell. He sensed Mia beside him, her magic frozen in the horror that gripped the rest of her. And he saw the convoluted shape that pulsed at the opening of the portal.

Ned narrowed his gaze. If he pulled on this bit here... the portal wobbled, and the shape began to unravel slightly. The magical rope he held got slick and threatened to escape, but Ned knew if he allowed that to happen, it would be catastrophic.

He focused on the pattern and found another bit he could pull on. Slowly, piece by slippery piece, he managed to unravel the structure, and the portal wobbled. But what should he do with all the magic in the ropes?

'You need to earth it,' croaked Mia. 'Pour the magic back into the land.'

Ned nodded and pushed the power with all his might towards the ground. It resisted, massively at first, but then suddenly changed its mind and flooded into the earth in a giant whoosh. Ned staggered as the power surged past him.

The portal began spinning faster and faster as it grew smaller and smaller. There was a massive spray of snowflakes as the vortex snapped shut with a bang and Ned fell to the floor, abruptly bereft of the huge amounts of magic he had been wielding. He panted, trying to catch his breath as he gave a shaky thumbs up to Mia.

She returned a small smile, exhaustion mirrored on her face.

A loud bellow made them both jump and turn to see

what was going on now.

Flake was lunging across the snow towards a pile of shaggy looking snowflakes that began to move. Ned grinned.

'What? What is it?' asked Mia, peering past him to try to get a better look.

'I think Flake's wife might still be alive.' Ned had a sudden coughing fit as he tried to talk, smile and breathe at the same time whilst accidentally inhaling a snowflake.

Griff came over and slammed him on the back hard, three times.

'Cough it up, eh?' he said. 'What just happened? Did we win or did we unleash something on Efrana?'

Ned shook his head. He didn't have the breath to answer.

Chapter 45

It was like looking at a new man. Flake was transformed. His perma-sadness aura had disappeared. He now teetered on jolly. All his fur was springy and those beetle-like eyebrows had morphed to happy caterpillars. He sat with his wife and son in a snowy heap on the ground, grinning broadly at the team who had performed the impossible. Snowflakes danced joyfully around them and despite the cold of the environment, Ned felt all warm inside.

'Ned! How can I ever thank you? Truly, you are a mighty hero,' bellowed Flake, causing the backs of Ned's ears to flush.

'A team effort, couldn't have done it without everyone else. Well done.' Ned nodded his thanks to the others, who were all finding semi-comfortable places to sit down. 'But I have some questions for your wife, if that's alright?'

'You want more information about the Sorcerer?' asked Eira softly.

Ned gave a nod. He also wanted to know about the Ice Giants. And how she had come back through the portal. But he was content to let her start speaking before he bombarded her with questions.

'Okay. I shall begin at the beginning. It was an ordinary day, like any other. Nix and I were going to go for a walk and enjoy the sunshine when a small man appeared. Smaller than you.' She looked at Ned. 'But not, I think, human?'

'Probably fae,' answered Ned, thinking she had to be

talking about Norm.

'Hmm. I felt power, but I do not believe it was his alone. The politeness of his tone belied the death in his eyes. They were pools of deep, dark green, almost black. I knew something was wrong. The man paid no attention to us, which in itself is highly unusual. We are, after all, mythical creatures.' Eira smiled at her husband and son. 'I urged Nix to run for his father, who was tending our small vegetable patch. We grow ice peppers and other hardy legumes. It was just me on my own when the man began muttering under his breath. A language I had never heard before.'

Flake took up the story.

'By this point, I had returned. I yelled for the intruder to state his purpose, but it was too late. Whatever devious dark magic he had been casting was complete, and the portal spun open. Eira was gone.' Flake sniffed loudly as opals clattered to the floor around him. He turned his attention away from the rapt audience and spoke directly to Eira. 'I thought I had lost you forever. I was torn asunder. A mere shell of a Meh-Teh. I am nothing without you.' The two Meh-Teh's rubbed noses affectionately while Nix rolled his eyes at his parents.

'That's when it got crazy.' The youngest Meh-Teh took up the tale. 'I was screaming snow murder at mum having just vanished when the first Ice Giant stepped through. It immediately grabbed Dad and held him easily, stopping him from retaliating at the spellcaster. Dad shouted at me to run, but I couldn't leave him. I was frozen to the spot. It was so scary. The man kept chanting his spell, but you could see it was a struggle. He turned a deep ruddy colour as if he were straining hard and the portal was vibrating, like it was fighting to stay open. A second Ice Giant stepped through and the man shouted.'

'Yes, yes. I remember. He said *I can't hold on much longer*. I do not know who he was talking to but as I struggled to free myself, a third Ice Giant stepped through the portal and it snapped shut, nearly taking the giant's leg with it.' Flake reached out to touch his wife, as if making sure she was still there. 'I thought I had lost you.'

'What happened after that? Did Norm say anything else?' asked Ned.

'Norm?' Flake looked confused.

'The little man who opened the portal. His name is Norm,' replied Ned, convinced it was Jenni's father.

'You know this person?' There was a dangerous edge to Flake's question and his severe beetles were back.

'I am familiar with him. Not really acquainted.' Ned felt the sweat rolling down the back of his neck. Now would not be a good time to admit that he knew who Norm was. He hoped Fred stayed quiet, but he dare not look at the lad. 'He is a wanted fugitive.'

That seemed to mollify Flake somewhat.

'Yes. I can see that he would be. And you will apprehend him.' It was very definitely a statement, not a question.

Ned nodded.

'Mr Spinks always gets his man. Always.' Fred piped up but for once kept it brief.

'He spoke,' said Nix, pulling them all back to the tale. 'But he was not talking to anyone we could see. It was like he was having an argument with himself. Going back and forth on whether or not he had the power to reopen the portal. Then he stopped talking mid-sentence

298

and addressed the Ice Giants.'

'And the giants, lad, they were just standing there?' asked Griff, leaning forward.

'They certainly seemed to wait for something. And when the little man spoke to them, it was not his voice at all.'

Griff and Ned exchanged a worried glance as Flake picked up the story.

'He asked the Ice Giants if the sorcerer had sent them and when they confirmed he had, he asked what the plan was now. They had a lengthy discussion, so I will paraphrase as best as I can. They accused the man, Norm, of being inadequate in keeping a portal open. He countered he had expected one person, not three giants, and that they were lucky they made it through at all. Norm then asked why the sorcerer hadn't come through and a giant replied that the strength of magic creating the portal was not strong enough. It needed to be familial or greater in power.'

'Familial... so that means...' Mia sounded horrified and leaned into Brogan as he wrapped his arms around her reassuringly.

'It wasn't your fault,' Ned said. 'We didn't have all the facts.' He turned his attention back to Flake. 'You know, you could've told us all this before.'

Flake nodded.

'Yes, you are correct. I should have, but... my mind was full of grief, and I was not thinking straight. I did not think it was of such great import, but I fear I have kept valuable information from you. Ned, I am sorry if it cost you today. I deeply apologise.' He bowed his shaggy head at Ned and waited.

Ned realised he was expected to say or do something.

'Well, it's done now. No point crying over spilt milk.'

Flake raised his head with a quizzical look.

'It's a saying. It means what's done is done,' said Ned. 'What did Norm say next?'

'There was a lot of muttering and pacing. I was struggling to break free, crying out to find out where my wife was, begging Nix to run and hide.'

'Is that when the Ice Giants took Nix, Mr Flake?' Fred refocused the discussion.

'Indeed. One of them grabbed him and said they would crush him like a bug if I didn't stop struggling. And that is when the little man came up with the plan to get you here.' Flake pointed at Ned.

'So it was pure luck that you bumped into Brogan in Blyz.'

'Yes, and no. As the little man was leaving the mountains, he underwent a severe convulsion and his eyes returned to what I imagine was their usual hue. He told me to look for Brogan, urged me to speak to him in my quest to find you.' Flake looked from Ned to Brogan. 'As I said, I was half mad with grief. I do not even remember coming down the mountain, but I remembered the urgency in the man's voice. And so I found the barbarian and spoke with him, although I think he was somewhat inebriated.'

Brogan barked a laugh and slapped his thigh.

'Good times, my friend! Good times.'

'Odd thing to say, though, eh?' mused Griff. 'It's almost as if Norm was fighting to get a message out. He must have known Brogan was with Mia and of Mia's connection to the Sorcerer and that you would come looking for them.'

Ned scoffed.

'I doubt it. That sprite thinks of nothing but himself. He put Jenni's life in serious danger the last time we met.'

'True, true, but… maybe this was his attempt at putting things right, eh? Maybe he knew she wouldn't be able to handle the snow magic.' Griff shrugged, but Ned wasn't buying it.

'Going back to what you just told us,' said Ned, pulling the conversation back. 'It explains why the Ice Giants so freely returned through the portal and knew about the Sea Witch. They worked for the Sorcerer. He must have told them about her and sent them through as his muscle to facilitate his own escape and probably promised that he would return and release them.'

'He did,' said Eira. 'But I do not think he is the sort of man who keeps his promises.'

'You heard him?' asked Ned.

'When you're in Nowhere, sound carries and the people, things in there tend to gravitate towards each other. Nobody wants to be on their own in Nowhere.' Eira looked down at her feet. 'I heard him talking to the rest of the Ice Giants he had marshalled with the help of this Sea Witch. They were exiled to Nowhere centuries ago, spread out across the black sands. It has taken decades for them to find each other and come together. They were fuelled by their desire to return to this realm and seek their revenge. The Sea Witch promised it to them, she could enter Nowhere for a short while but never as anything corporeal, always ghostly. She rallied them, he promised them. Both of them said the Ice Giants would be rewarded if they helped him to escape. He promised he would return once he had resurrected her and that together they would breach Nowhere and free all of them.'

Ned felt like he'd been dealt a body blow with this dreaded confirmation. The Sorcerer was free to resurrect the Sea Witch and together... they'd be unstoppable.

Chapter 46

Ned stood off to one side as the others said their goodbyes to the Meh-Teh's. His mind was whirling with everything they had learnt. Norm was clearly possessed by the Sea Witch and she was bent on being resurrected, using the Sorcerer to help her. Why exactly the Sorcerer would agree to such a thing wasn't entirely clear, but Ned felt sure it had something to do with becoming the most powerful magical being in Efrana. And they'd been instrumental in letting him escape Nowhere.

Griff clapped a hand on his shoulder.

'Cheer up, lad. Things always seem bleakest just before the sun shines again. We will increase our efforts to arrest Norm and, through him, stop the Sea Witch before she can resurrect, eh?'

'And what of the Sorcerer? We barely beat him before and look at how easily he escaped – it feels like we already lost.'

Griff pulled out his pipe and began preparing a smoke. Ned followed suit. It was a calming process, and he could certainly do with some calm right now. Once they were both puffing, Griff spoke again.

'There is much in Efrana that you haven't seen. Wondrous places, people and magics. Perhaps it is time you spread your wings a little and journeyed beyond your city borders? Take the fight to Norm, gathering some support along the way. I know a few people. I am owed a few favours, eh?'

Ned managed a small smile. There was no doubt in his mind that his dad knew more than a few people and was owed more than a few favours.

'What about the portal?' he asked as Mia came over to join them.

'Now that the Meh-Teh's are aware this is a nexus point, a place where a portal to Nowhere can be opened, they will guard it fiercely and ensure that no-one gains access to this part of the mountain again.' She glanced back at the happily reunited family. 'They are planning some avalanches. They seem really excited about the whole thing.'

'It's nice to have a family project,' agreed Ned.

'I just wish... I should've known. I should have listened to that tickle at the back of my mind. I should have known the dreams weren't just dreams.' Mia piggled at a small hole in the sleeve of her jumper.

'You can't blame yourself. You didn't know. None of us did. We all thought he was gone for good. What's important now is that we stop him before he can cause any more damage.' Ned held her gaze for a moment. 'We good?'

'Ready when you are, Boss,' replied Mia with a cheeky smile, the glint of a tear in her eyes.

'Boss?'

'You didn't think you would be alone in this fight, did you? The Barbaric Duo at your service.' Mia gave a little bow. 'The name needs work.'

'No, it's good. It's good.' Ned was glad to have them on board. He was going to need all the help he could get.

He was, Ned reflected as he walked back down the mountain, going to miss Flake. There had been something comforting in his furry bulk and having met a myth in real life, had made Ned feel like anything was possible. He had a lot to tell Rose, Jenni and the others in the travel journal when they got back to Blyz, he hadn't felt like writing in it sat on the side of the mountain, but he knew they were waiting to hear how the mission had gone. The idea was to spend the night at the inn and then return to Roshaven as quickly as possible, ready to plan their next steps. Ned did not know how he was going to explain to Rose that he had to go away again, go on the hunt to stop Norm, the Sea Witch and the Sorcerer, and leave her behind. She would take it stoically, committed as she was to her duty, but she wasn't going to be very happy about it.

Coming down the mountain seemed to be much quicker than clambering up it, possibly a lot to do with the fact that everyone was preoccupied with their own thoughts. There wasn't a dire wolf howl in earshot. Even Fred was quiet. Thunderous looking clouds had been gathering above their heads and as they traversed the last stretch of the mountain descent, distant vibrations could be felt. The Meh-Teh's were clearly beginning their avalanche remodelling.

It was with relief and semi-frozen toes that the party made it back to the inn in Blyz. Brogan called loudly for hot pies and ale to wash it down with, the others too tired and too cold to argue. Their collective silence remained until everyone had thawed slightly and filled their bellies with sustenance.

'Right. I'd better let Rose know how we got on,' said Ned, reaching into his pack to retrieve the travel journal.

He flipped the pages, saw the goodbye and good luck messages, then discovered a message from Fingers.

'Huh, this is odd. I thought Rose and Jenni had the book. There's a message from Fingers,' he said to the others. 'He says… he says…'

'What Boss? What does he say? Is everything alright? Did the snow lift or are they left with the great melt? Because I know the Highs had a grand plan to deal with everything and they were very excited to implement things and follow a new procedure. It's been a long time since a new procedure has been written for Roshaven on account of the Empire being steeped in so much tradition for so long.'

'Alright lad, give the man a chance to answer. What does he say, eh?' asked Griff.

Ned looked up at the others.

'Jenni's gone after Norm. She's vanished from Roshaven.'

~THE END~

Sign up for my author newsletter on my website and get a free copy of Rohaven novella, *The Interspecies Poker Tournament.*

Fae are being murdered in Roshaven and the only clue is a shifty moustache.

Jenni the sprite knows more than she's telling and when an interspecies poker tournament is set up to catch the murderer, she does everything in her power to get a seat for her boss Ned Spinks, Chief Thief-Catcher. The cards have been dealt. The stakes are high. Is this the end of the game for Ned or will he come up aces?

www.clairebuss.co.uk

Leave A Review

If you enjoyed reading *Myth in the Mountain*, please consider writing a review. Thank you so much, I really appreciate it.

My Thanks

My thanks go, as always, to my husband Kevin and my two monsters Leo and Belle as they put up with me going through the rollercoaster of writer emotions when penning something new.

Thank you to my brilliant crit group EM Swift-Hook, Darrell Nelson and Scott Tarbet for their valuable input into the first draft and to my wonderful team of beta readers – Donna Tyrrell, Ian Bristow and Martin Frowd. Your fantastic attention to detail is a life saver, as always.

Shout out to my Patreon Super Stars: Andrew Clements and Kitty Bellamy – you guys are the best!

Finally, thank you to Ian Bristow, who created the brilliant cover for *Myth in the Mountain*. You can find out more about his artwork at www.iancbristow.com

Other works by Claire Buss:

The Roshaven Books

The Interspecies Poker Tournament
Fae are being murdered in Roshaven and the only clue is a shifty moustache.

Jenni the sprite knows more than she's telling and when an interspecies poker tournament is set up to catch the murderer, she does everything in her power to get a seat for her boss Ned Spinks, Chief Thief-Catcher. The cards have been dealt. The stakes are high. Is this the end of the game for Ned or will he come up aces?

Available here: books2read.com/u/m2Vk0R

The Rose Thief
Someone is stealing the Emperor's roses and if they take the magical red rose then love will be lost, to everyone, forever.

It's up to Ned Spinks, Chief Thief Catcher, and his band of motely catchers to apprehend the thief and save the day. But the thief isn't exactly who they seem to be. Neither is the Emperor. Ned and his team will have to go on a quest; defeating vampire mermaids, illusionists, estranged family members and an evil sorcerer in order to win the day. What could possibly go wrong?

Buy your copy of *The Rose Thief* today and enjoy this humorous novel: books2read.com/u/bQaxw6

The Silk Thief

Fourteen, heir to the Empire of Roshaven, must find a new name before Theo, Lord of neighbouring Fidelia, brings his schemes to fruition.

Not only has he stolen Roshaven's trade, but he plans to make Fourteen his own and take her empire in the bargain. Her protector, Ned Spinks, is plagued with supernatural nightmares whilst his assistant, Jenni the sprite, has lost her magic. Can they figure out how to thwart Theo's dastardly plan before it's too late for his city and her empire?

Get your copy here: books2read.com/u/49NJMM

The Bone Thief

The Spice Ghosts have descended on Roshaven accusing Jenni of stealing their sacred bones and are threatening to destroy the city if they are not returned but Jenni the sprite has no idea what they're talking about.

With the help of her boss, Chief Thief-Catcher Ned Spinks, Jenni promises to find and return them however the skeletal trail leads them into the dark and dangerous waters of the dread Sea Witch. Ned is out of his depth and frantically treading water while Jenni must fight to avoid becoming catch of the day.

Buy your book here: books2read.com/u/3LRkgD

The Gaia Collection – hopeful dystopian trilogy

The Gaia Effect

A pre-determined future. A ruthless Corporation. One woman determined to fight for her freedom.

When Kira wins the right to a child, she thinks all her dreams have come true. But then the impossible happens, her friends become pregnant naturally and the truth of society under Corporation begins to unravel.

Confused, Kira looks to Gaia – a myth she barely believes in – for comfort and guidance, only to discover more lies. And when a terrorist attack undermines Corporation government and plunges City 42 into chaos and rebellion, she vows to protect her friends and family at all cost. Desperate, they flee City 42, racing into the unknown world outside the walls. There they find Corporation's subterfuge goes deeper than anyone realised.

Can Kira and her friends survive Corporation's lies and expose the truth? Or will Kira become another Corporation casualty?

If you like inspirational heroines and unique, thought-provoking stories then you'll love the first book in this exhilarating dystopian trilogy.

Buy *The Gaia Effect* today and uncover a unique vision of the future, with a twist of hope in its tale: books2read.com/u/3npA98

The Gaia Project

Nobody is ready for what they discover beyond City 42. While Martha Hamble gets to grips with being Governor of City 42, Kira and Jed Jenkins travel to City 15 but they are not prepared for what they find.

Corporation are tightening their grip on those who don't conform, threatening to split families and reassign the natural born children. With Gaia weakened, the group of friends must try to find a safe place to live and help the spirit of the Earth recover but everything stands against them.

Will Corporation succeed in their tougher regime or can Kira and her friends find a new home?

Buy *The Gaia Project* here: books2read.com/u/3RJEWx

The Gaia Solution

The human race is about to be wiped out.

Kira, Jed and their friends have fled New Corporation and joined the Resistance, but their relief is short-lived as they discover how decimated the human race has become and learn of an environmental crisis that threatens to destroy their existence.

Kira and Jed must travel up the mountain to the New Corporation stronghold, City 50, to bargain for sanctuary while Martha and Dina risk everything to return to City 42 and save those who are left. With the last of her reserves Gaia, the fading spirit of the Earth uses her remaining influence to guide Kira and her friends but ultimately, it's up to humanity to make the right choice.

Complete your Gaia series today:
books2read.com/u/mdGR21

Poetry

Little Book of Verse, Book 1 of the Little Book Series
Little Book of Spring, Book 2 of the Little Book Series
Little Book of Summer, Book 3 of the Little Book Series
Spooky Little Book, Book 4 of the Little Book Series
Little Book of Love, Book 5 of the Little Book Series
Little Book of Winter, Book 6 of the Little Book Series
Little Book of Autumn, Book 7 of the Little Book Series
Little Book of Christmas, Book 8 of the Little Book Series

Short Story Collections

Tales from Suburbia
Tales from the Seaside
The Blue Serpent & other tales
Flashing Here and There

Anthologies

Underground Scratchings, Tales from the Underground anthology
Patient Data, The Quantum Soul anthology
A Badger Christmas Carol, The Sparkly Badgers' Christmas Anthology
Dress Like An Animal and *Afraid of the Dark*, Haunted, the Sparkly Badgers' Anthology
The Last Pirate, Tales from the Pirate's Cove anthology

About the Author

Claire Buss is a multi-genre author and poet based in the UK. She wanted to be Lois Lane when she grew up but work experience at her local paper was eye-opening. Instead, Claire went on to work in a variety of admin roles for over a decade but never felt quite at home. An avid reader, baker and Pinterest addict Claire won second place in the Barking and Dagenham Pen to Print writing competition in 2015 with her debut novel, *The Gaia Effect*, setting her writing career in motion. She continues to write passionately and is hopelessly addicted to cake.

Sign up to Claire's author newsletter for regular updates.

This is Claire's LinkTree where you will find direct links to her website, social media accounts, books and writing magazine Write On!

linktr.ee/clairebuss

Printed in Great Britain
by Amazon